KINGDOM above the CLOUD

tales from adia
BOOK ONE

KINGDOM above the CLOUD

MAGGIE PLATT

Kingdom Above The Cloud

Tales from Adia, Book One

ISBN: 978-1-62020-588-4
eISBN: 978-1-62020-718-5
Library of Congress Control Number: 2020934283

Cover Design & Typesetting by Hannah Nichols
Ebook Conversion by Anna Riebe Raats
Author Photo by Hannah Lockhart Photography
Edited by Daphne Self

AMBASSADOR INTERNATIONAL
Emerald House
411 University Ridge, Suite B14
Greenville, SC 29601, USA
www.ambassador-international.com

AMBASSADOR BOOKS
The Mount
2 Woodstock Link
Belfast, BT6 8DD, Northern Ireland, UK
www.ambassadormedia.co.uk

The colophon is a trademark of Ambassador, a Christian publishing company.

For my irreverent, wise, comforting Mama who would have loved to hold this book in her hands.

Proverbs 22:6

CHAPTER 1

Murky black eyes shining with reflected fire searched the mural for anything he could have missed. In the half-light of bracketed torches, the ruby on King Damien's finger looked as black as his hair.

As he studied the images all around him, a dozen stealthy and agile guards stood at attention in the glittering throne room on the other side of the stone wall. Each guard wore a simple black bodysuit with attached gloves and held two long swords, one in each hand. There were sheathes crisscrossing their backs, but they would only stow the swords when the king was no longer in their presence.

Warm light from the domed glass ceiling made everything in the enormous outer chamber appear golden. The chains of chandeliers reached up into the heights, and a brightly painted mural covered every inch of the walls. It was this same mural that the king pondered, but his eyes fell on the darker portions, the hidden stories on the other side of the wall that were kept in deepest secret.

There were terrible mysteries waiting here, prophecies recorded with paint and brushes on upright stone slabs. King Damien had tortured and killed his own people in efforts to understand, and he felt growing frustration that he still had no answers. He could not let this forecasted future come to pass.

The king was alone, hidden within a protected corridor in the center of his vast palace. He wore the customary clothing for the mountain kingdom's royal men: black trousers, shiny black shoes, black leather gloves, and a crisp white shirt. The back of his shirt had a large circle cut out of the fabric, exposing intricate black designs that covered his skin. Most of the markings were the size of a fist, and there were seven of them forming a large ring from his shoulders to his waist. Hissing snake. Pointed crown. Unbalanced scales. Heavy chains. Thorny rose. Sharp diamond. Twisted flames. Taking up the center of this wreath was a much larger image—a highly-detailed heart, strangled by ragged veins.

His palatial estate sat on top of a low, squat mountain in the very center of the known world. Mount Damien—named for him—was encircled by a thick layer of cloud separating the civilized peak from the wild frontiers on the slopes below. When looking out from the palace's highest tower, the city looked as if it floated in a sea of white cotton with brief glimpses of greener lands beneath. Most of the mountain's inhabitants had never ventured below the clouds.

King Damien looked closely at a troubling span of the mural. It was the same spot he had obsessed over a million times before. It portrayed four warriors atop his mountain with victory in their expressions and armies coming behind them. The next scene was a barren landscape, with nothing but a small mound of rocks where Mount Damien used to be. Then, the mural stopped.

With each year of his reign, more of the painted prophecies came to pass. All that was left was this last corridor behind the curtain. Would these final scenes come to be, too? Had he done enough to stop these conquerors? What if he had been wrong about their identities? How exact were these paintings, and did he have the power to change them?

He had a nagging suspicion that he had missed something. He daily paced along this wall looking for any hint that would lead him to answers. His middle-aged son and heir, Prince Ajax, sometimes joined him, but he didn't share his father's enthusiasm for deciphering the future.

The future. Damien hated the thought of the future. He hated how little he could control without knowing for certain the identities of those four conquerors and if he had really put an end to them. But how could he ever learn these things when the artist who painted the scenes left the mountain nearly fifty years ago? It was enough to drive him mad.

It was in this madness that he had created a bit of a game. Six months had passed since he gathered seven of his most powerful up-and-coming leaders, named them the Council of Masters, and sent them below the cloud to the land of Adia, where the painting prophet had fled. The rules were simple. They must brand an Adian with the symbol of their specific expertise and bring the victim back to the mountain. The first to do so would earn a large chest filled with gold, a fortune that could fund the most lavish lifestyle for several years.

They didn't need to know that there were many deeper reasons for bringing an Adian above the clouds. He longed to interrogate one and find out if there were more prophecies, to find out if there were more murals, to find out if Adwin was still in Adia. Even more so, he salivated over the thought of Adwin himself coming to the mountain to retrieve the victim. Could he finally have Adwin in his grasp after all these years?

The click of heels against tile made his ears perk, and the king quickly passed through the thick red curtain that separated the dark corridor from the glittering throne room. He squinted at the sudden onslaught of light. The guards let him pass before reclaiming their positions.

He moved toward the center of the room and pondered the seven young people as they entered. They were his kingdom's finest weapons. Formidable. Hardened. Lethally clever.

The three men wore the same white shirt as the king, but their trousers and gloves were gray instead of black. The four women wore loosely-draped gowns of varying gray hues with gloves to match. All seven looked beautiful, uneasy, and dangerous.

Damien addressed them quietly, each syllable articulated and precise. "I must admit I'm disappointed. Six months and you bring me nothing from Adia. Is the task too difficult?"

They remained silent, staring back.

"I asked you a question," he declared, his vision going dark for a split second as the veins in his eyes pulsed. "Do you think the task is too difficult? Too much for you?"

"No, Your Majesty," they responded in unison.

"Maybe the reward has been too small?"

"No, Your Majesty."

"Well, I am a gracious king. You do not ask for more incentive, yet I am prepared to offer it. If mere gold does not entice you, would an entire kingdom suffice?" He allowed the words to sink in before going on, enjoying the play of emotions as these young weapons tried to understand. He ascended three marble steps and sat on his emerald-encrusted golden throne. His son, Prince Ajax, sat just below him to the left. Ajax's son was not present, so the seat on the king's right remained empty.

"If you are the first to mark an Adian and bring the fool to this mountain," Damien continued, shifting forward for a better view of their faces, "You will be the rightful king or queen of Adia. I will send my armies to defeat that rebellious land, and I will place you as the crowned ruler. It would all be yours."

That would get their attention. None of their demeanors had changed a bit, but he had always been good at reading stony faces. Hunger and greed glowed in many of their eyes, terrified panic in a few. Some of them were growing soft.

He stood from his throne and approached them once more, starting with the far end of the line. Xanthe had long lemon-yellow hair with one thick aqua stripe that reached from scalp to tip. She was tall and slender, with excellent posture that betrayed the hours and hours her mother spent turning her into a perfect young woman. Xanthe's eyes were intensely purple, and they were dull and cold as they stared at the far wall. She was betrothed to the king's grandson, Prince Jairus, who was not in the room. As Damien drew near, Xanthe took a sharp breath and lifted her chin, but her gaze remained unfocused and distant.

"What's wrong, Xanthe?" the king asked with over-exaggerated concern, stroking her smooth cheek with his wrinkled finger. "Don't you want to rule your own kingdom one day?"

"Of course, Your Majesty," she replied with no sign of emotion. "But not Adia."

"Not Adia?" Damien prodded, poison creeping into his voice. "Why not Adia?"

"I will be this mountain's queen one day when Jairus is king. I have no need for another kingdom."

"If you were truly invested you would want both. So, you will not continue in this quest. You may leave."

"Your Majesty, I didn't say—"

"You will not go back," he ordered forcefully. "Leave us."

Xanthe's eyes locked on the king and flashed with hatred as she turned to leave.

"Is there anyone else who would like to leave these ranks? This Council of Masters?"

No one moved.

"That's what I thought." Damien sauntered along the line, eyeing each weapon and looking for signs of cowardice. He took an especially long time examining Eryx. He was huge—an excellent athlete and fighter. He had recently shaved his head, which added to his menacing aura. He towered at least six inches over the next tallest Master, and his highly-defined and powerful body was crisscrossed with white scars, trophies of his time in the fighting ring. "What about you, Eryx? Enjoying this game?"

With great articulation but no fervor, he answered, "It's not a game, Your Majesty."

"Oh? Isn't it?" Damien asked with feigned innocence.

"'Game' is too trivial for this assignment, Your Majesty. Your orders are law."

Damien loved the words, but he hated the monotonous delivery. "Hmm. Thank you for this passionate speech, Eryx. You will do well to use this spirit and zeal in the next fight."

"You haven't put me in a fight for years!" Eryx bellowed, a sudden fire lit in his tone. "It is below my status as Master."

"You argue with me?" Damien asked softly and dangerously, standing toe to toe and looking up into Eryx's face. "You will fight when I tell you to. You will prove you are still able to harness your power. Now, off with all of you. You have much work to do."

His eyes bounced to each of them in turn as they filed through the door. Without looking at his son, he asked, "Ajax, what are your thoughts? Who is leading this race?"

"You already know I don't care for your stunts, Father. You should just send the armies now if defeating Adia is what you're after."

"That's just it," he said softly, dreamily, as he imagined a better world. "Defeating Adia is only a small part of what I'm after. Yes, I want their land. Yes, I want its rich resources and fertile soil and clean waters. But I want so much more. I want Adwin to quake in fear at the mere mention of my name. I want him to hurt. I want him to *break.*"

"Adwin? This is about Adwin? Wouldn't defeating Adia make him 'quake' as you call it?"

This snapped the king back to attention. Sternly he asked, "How old are you, Ajax?"

"Forty-nine."

"In forty-nine years, you still have not learned. We could burn every tree and building in his village to the ground, and it would not shake him nearly as much as marking one of his beloved Adians with my symbols."

"I doubt that very much. But you didn't answer my question. Why have you never mentioned to me that this silly game is about Adwin?"

"My son, when will you discover that *everything* is about Adwin?"

CHAPTER 2

Meira stood in the shadows of a balcony on the seventh floor of a sad, dilapidated building. The neighborhood was called the Bottom Rung, and she thought that was appropriate since most people believed you must climb past it to achieve anything in life. But she had lived further up—much further up—and she preferred life down here.

Her face was smudged from a long day of work in the mines, and her hair was bundled on top of her head and covered by a headwrap that was so dirty no one could make out the colorful pattern it once had. Her job made her muscular, but the lack of dependable food kept her lean. She was in her mid-twenties, but she could have passed for over thirty. The mine tended to do that to its workers.

A green sign swung a few floors below where Meira stood. It advertised tailoring with a picture of a needle and thread, but this was just a front. The building was really used for much more than mending and altering clothing.

Packed inside was a group of men, women, and children from every neighborhood on the mountain who denounced Damien as king. They vowed to follow Adwin, even though it was widely believed that the old king—creator, god, prophet, whatever someone wanted to call him—had not stepped foot on Mount Damien for nearly fifty years. It seemed as though he had abandoned the mountain, but these were the people who refused to give up on him and a better way of life.

They gathered in this headquarters as often as possible without being caught. Those at risk of arrest moved there permanently. It was a safe-house that would quickly become very dangerous if discovered. Luckily for them, those closest to the king usually avoided the Bottom Rung.

They called themselves the Hidden Heart, for each of them had a strange marking on the inside of their left palm, a roughly-drawn brown heart. Everyone on the mountain was born with it, but most faded over time. Damien had made the possession of this heart illegal, an illogical move since no one was certain what it meant or how to control it. The members of the Hidden Heart had hearts that were still well-defined and visible, and they hid them beneath gloves in their daily lives.

All the grass and trees withered away decades ago under the hot mountain sun, and the only breaks from the monotony of their royally-assigned work were brief holidays celebrating Damien's reign. But there were stories—oh, there were stories! Greener, more jubilant times when children sought adventures and parents had time to worry about something other than taxes, royal guards, and food for the table.

There was movement in the street below, and Meira's eyes followed the footsteps of two people, both with fiery orange hair. Leeto and Rhaxma. Siblings. Two members of the Council of Masters. In the stillness of the night, their arguing echoed off the cobbled streets and tall buildings.

"We need to stick together," the sister demanded, putting a hand on her brother's arm.

Leeto stopped and grabbed hold of Rhaxma above the elbows. "No, we don't. I am making progress, and everything would be a waste if we were noticed down there. You must agree that it's hard to keep the both of us hidden. We don't exactly blend in with the surroundings." He gently tugged at her long orange hair. "Go on your own for all I care, but you can't come with me."

"Since when do you strike out on your own? We are a team. We are a family."

"Of course, we are. Our family is the top priority of my life. That is why I must go alone. I am going to win this for us, Rhax. It's all going to be ours. Trust me." He walked away toward the mines, leaving his sister fuming in his wake. She waited a few seconds and then took off after him, silently following his footsteps.

Meira walked inside the top floor of the Hidden Heart Headquarters and descended to the fifth floor. Several people were huddled at a table, illuminated by a single candle in the middle. She took her seat and said, "Thad, I just saw two of your dear siblings down below. It appears the game is still on."

Orange-haired, yellow-eyed Thad didn't look surprised in the least. "Of course, the game is still on. Damien won't give up on getting an Adian that quickly. I'm just impressed those valley dwellers haven't fallen for any of it yet. They are made of tougher stuff than I imagined. Is there anything we can do for them to keep them strong against the Masters? To keep them strong against my dear brother and sister?"

A man in his late thirties with green hair and a kind face answered, "I don't think we can help without being noticed. We need to focus on our mission here."

"You're right," Meira said. "Let's get started." All eyes moved to hers and several heads nodded. "Who has a newly-discovered heart to report?"

CHAPTER 3

As the early dawn haze ran away from the light and the birds began to wake, Tovi Tivka sprinted along a familiar ridge never pausing to consider the danger should she fall. Her breezy yellow dress billowed in her wake, as did the long waves of her dark blue hair. She was petite in every way, short and wiry. She had an angular nose, a stubborn chin, and dark brown eyes with one small purple star on the edge of her left iris. To her left was dense forest. To her right, a cliff that fell to boulders far below. Under her tough, bare feet was the hard-beaten path she had run every morning for the last six months.

Tovi lived in the land of Adia, a peaceful village nestled in a lush valley. Adians worked hard but didn't know it, spending their days doing what they loved—building or gathering or anything that was both pleasant and occupying. They delighted in their sweat, blisters, and long days in the sun.

They lived in a sprawling network of tree-top cottages. Instead of inviting others to their homes, they would say, "Come to my tree." Each little house had a thatched roof and open windows. Some had half doors, but the purpose was to keep small children in rather than to keep others out. Their community buildings were built in the same fashion, only much larger. "Main Street" was a cluster of trees so dense that it was hard to know which limbs belonged to which trees. Everywhere you looked there were bridges, rope ladders, and swinging vines connecting the general store, doctor's office, cafe, meeting house, and so much more.

Adians lived in plenty and had a bountiful trading system. There was always enough of everything for everyone, and they all knew and loved the satisfied feeling of being tired at the end of a full and lively day.

The people of Adia were happy. At least most of them were.

Tovi stopped running when she reached her usual place along the path, where the dense forest abruptly opened to a stunning vista of a deeper portion of the valley and the mountains beyond it. Adians called this place "the ridge," but it was more cliff than ridge. No one knew where the name started, but no one particularly cared.

Tovi caught her breath and strained her eyes for any sign of movement on the horizon. All she saw were the oranges and pinks climbing over the mountains in the distance. Deep in thought and disappointment, she sat and dangled her legs over the frightening expanse. She opened her left hand and examined her palm where an untidy and asymmetrical brown heart marred her skin. It looked as if it had been drawn by a child, but she—and everyone she knew—was born with this mark. The point reached nearly to her wrist, and the curves touched the base of her fingers.

"I hate you," she said aloud. "Do you hear me, Adwin? I hate you!" Her voice echoed below, as hollow and unheard as she felt.

A soft breeze rustled the grasses nearby, and something blue caught her attention. She reached out to trace the edges of a strange flower, the same color as forget-me-nots but much larger, with an unravelling indigo center flecked with orange pollen. She loved flowers, a striking contrast to the tough exterior she tried to project. She was fascinated by the complicated patterns that made up such a small thing. It reminded her of herself. Small and complicated.

Tovi had never fit in with the strange people of Adia who lived in whimsical tree houses. When she and her twin brother, Tali, were no more than a few hours old, they arrived in Adia, bundled in elegant blankets that were far finer than anything found in the valley. An aging and childless couple named Ganya and Avi Tivka took them in and told them that Adwin himself had instructed that they care for the little ones.

Adwin. Tovi had many doubts about the legends surrounding Adwin. Supposedly, he was some sort of god who had created their world and everything in it. All the people of the village spoke of Adwin as if he was real and lived nearby, but Tovi needed some proof. She had never seen him in the flesh, and there was plenty of evidence that it was all a bunch of wishful thinking. People were always looking for something to make life make sense, and Tovi figured the legend of Adwin was simply a way for Adians to explain the unexplainable.

Tovi and her brother Tali grew up in the Tivkas' charming tree house. The children had identical coloring, from their navy-blue hair to their brown eyes with little purple stars. They were the delight of Avi and Ganya, who embraced their new role of adoptive grandparents.

Tali had no trouble fitting in with the other youngsters in the village. He loved adventure and exploration, and he often came home from his outings covered in mud, burrs, a little bit of his own blood, and a huge smile. He sometimes coaxed Tovi to come along, and she would grudgingly agree. But she never felt like she was one of them. There was something deep and aching that was missing from her life, and she preferred to spend her time searching for answers while even the right questions remained elusive.

Where Tali was free-wheeling and fun-loving, Tovi was serious and impatient. Where Tali was outgoing and popular among his peers, Tovi was aloof and independent. Where Tali was free, Tovi was captive. Captive to what or to whom, she did not know.

Tovi pinched the base of the blue flower's stem, snapping the emerald column under her fingertips. Lifting it to her nose, she breathed in a mixture of blueberries and honey and something magical. She examined the flower, turning it this way and that, running her finger over its velvety exterior.

"I hate him," she said aloud, divulging her frustration to her little discovery. "If I ever find Adwin, I'm going to tell him just what I think of him."

The sound of moving branches broke her reverie and made her turn toward the trees. A young man about her age emerged from the woods. His messy brown hair with golden streaks almost reached his sparkling blue eyes. His faded green tunic, tan linen pants, and bare feet were splattered with orange and blue paint.

Silas sat down beside her. "The dream again?"

Tovi nodded, blinking back sudden unwanted tears and ripping petals from the flower. Realizing she had destroyed it, she threw the blossom over the edge of the cliff. They both watched it fall.

Six months ago, before the dreams began, Tovi had woken to find her brother's bed empty. This was not particularly strange, but something didn't feel quite right. She looked for him all day, but he never came home.

No note. No goodbye. He was just gone.

In front of others, she kept a stoic face. In private, she wept until her sides ached. There was no relief and no comfort to be had. Her brother had been her everything.

Ever since, Tovi woke each morning from a terrible dream. In this nightmare, she found a letter from Tali telling her that he was leaving forever, but if she ran fast enough, she could catch up to him at the ridge. Her dream-self sprinted there at once. From the very edge, she could see Tali in the distance, and she was able to call out to him, begging for him to come back. When he turned toward her, she would wake covered in sweat.

Each time Tovi woke from her dream, having seen Tali's face in the hazy distance, she couldn't help running to the ridge as quickly as she could. She would run to the point of desperate exhaustion only to be disappointed when she saw no one out there in the wilderness. She knew it was foolish and irrational, but it had become a daily routine. It seemed to be her method for dealing with her deep, shattered grief.

Silas almost always came to the ridge with Tovi. Sometimes he ran with her, and sometimes he appeared when she was finished. They would sit and look at the mountains while Tovi calmed her fortified but broken heart, and often they would talk about the questions that were always on her mind.

Silas was the same age as Tovi and Tali and lived in the tree next to the Tivkas. His home was perched just above and to the side of theirs, and throughout their childhood he often swung on a vine from his porch to theirs.

Silas and Tali were as close as brothers, and he was the closest thing Tovi had to a friend. She didn't spend as much time with Silas as Tali did, but Silas knew her better than anyone else in the village.

"I miss him, Silas," she said, picking another flower from the nearby grass and frowning in concentration.

Silas sighed. "I know you do."

"And then there's the whole Adwin thing," she said, rolling her eyes at the mention of the mythical man she suspected was purely fiction. "If he was really out there, he could snap his fingers and bring Tali back. How convenient that I can't find Adwin. Why won't anyone tell me where to look for him?"

Smiling apologetically and looking out toward the morning sun, he answered, "You know the answer to that."

"Hmmph," was her irritated reply. Tovi knew the old legends. They were repeated incessantly, especially among the oldest and youngest of the village. Not so long ago—a little less than fifty years ago—everyone lived above the clouds on the squat Mount Lemuel to the northeast of their valley. Adwin made that mountain and oversaw everything and everyone on it. He was kind and peaceful and taught the people to be kind and peaceful as well. However, his benevolence did not stop a young man named Damien from seeking power for himself. Rather than be forced off his mountain by Damien's growing army, Adwin left the mountain of his own accord. He climbed down the mountain to a beautiful valley, trailed by a small band of followers, and thus Adia was formed.

The newly-crowned King Damien renamed the mountain Mount Damien. From that day on, the people of Mount Damien and the villagers of Adia had little contact, and the chasm between them widened. Adians became afraid of their higher-altitude relatives and never ventured up the slopes.

Not long after the split, Adwin went into some sort of hiding, the part of the story that Tovi found the hardest to understand. He was supposed to be there with the people of Adia, but at the same time he kept himself hidden. It was frustrating. How could she ever get her questions answered when the only person who could answer them was shrouded in secrecy?

Tovi had never once seen the evasive Adwin. Everyone she knew —except her brother—claimed to have met him at least once. It was all so unfair. If Adwin really existed, why couldn't they find him? Why hadn't he made himself known to them? Most infuriating, why would no one tell them where to look? She knew there was something magical and odd about him. The stories all spoke of his powers and how he had the ability to gift them to others. Had he used his magic to become invisible? Was he hiding from them?

Tali's disappearance only made matters worse. The twins had shared everything, including their quest to find Adwin and answers about their family. However, Tali's attitude had always been vastly different. While Tovi sought answers and retribution, Tali never let go of his hope that Adwin really was as good as people said. He looked for Adwin with a far more open heart and mind, fully believing there would be a good explanation for their circumstances.

"It's just so maddening," Tovi said to Silas, trying to sound tough even though she was dangerously close to crying. "It's not fair. I was taken from my parents, and now my brother was taken from me. It's not fair, Silas! Adwin, if he's really out there, owes me some answers."

"Give it some more time."

To distract herself from the tears brimming just below the surface and to keep her feelings at bay, Tovi jumped to her feet and started the trek back toward Adia with Silas in tow. She let her hand glide along the tops of the tall grasses as light filtered through the leaves, speckling the ground and casting a cheerful yellow-green glow. The earth was soft but not muddy. Their bare feet left slight impressions in the path.

While the two were walking along the edge of a stream, something caught Tovi's eye. Etched deep into the rich soil of the shoreline was a strange pattern unfamiliar to her. Always curious, she knelt to get a better look.

"It's a shoe print," Silas said.

Tovi's forehead creased and her eyebrows drew together. "What's a shoe print?"

"You know the stories about Mount Damien? On the mountain, people wear coverings on their feet. They're called shoes. Someone wearing shoes has been in our forest."

Spine prickling, Tovi wondered what it could mean.

"Don't be afraid," Silas said, his expression relaxed.

"I'm not!" she countered defiantly.

Silas rolled his eyes, and they continued through the woods. They were crossing a shallow pond, jumping stone to stone, when Silas stopped and looked over his shoulder. "There is something I need to do. You go ahead," he said.

She followed the line of his vision, but she saw nothing in the thick forest. Shrugging, she walked on through the trees, turning just once to check on Silas. He still stood in the same spot on the last stone in the pond, staring into the woods. He seemed tense and alert, as if he was waiting for something.

When she arrived in the village, she climbed a long rope ladder to Ganya and Avi Tivka's cottage nestled in the crux of five willow boughs. To some, it would seem imperfect and rustic with missing knotholes and nothing uniform about the length and width of the boards. Gnarled vines created a diamond pattern in the windows, and the inside of the upper branches made a perfect dome high above the thatched roof.

The interior was wide open, their dining room, kitchen, and sitting area all flowing together in one large round space. Brightly-colored rugs, richly-painted canvases, and vases full of fresh flowers were the room's only adornments. Everything else was as rough and natural as the exterior. Avi had made big, comfy chairs out of branches and woven grass, and Ganya had crafted plates and cups from the soft clay of the earth. Everything had its rightful place and perfect nook, with nothing out of order.

Two doors opened off opposite sides of the room. One led to Avi and Ganya's bedroom, with its light green curtains and shelves carved into the trunk of the tree that were filled with knickknacks and family mementos.

On the other side of the house was Tali and Tovi's room. Their beds were made from sturdy but imperfect oak and were covered in soft quilts Ganya made from scraps of yellow and green fabric. Tali's bed was against the far wall, but Tovi liked to keep hers right next to the window. Sometimes at night she would sit on the puffy mattress and look out into the sky, getting brief glimpses of sparkling stars through the softly waving willow leaves.

"Good morning, Ganya," Tovi called.

A short, chubby, radiant old woman put down her rolling pin. Her white hair with its orange swirl was bundled on top of her head, and flour nearly covered her pink apron. "Good morning, my sweet Tovi," Ganya greeted warmly, placing her soft hands on

Tovi's cheeks and leaving streaks of white powder. "Did you have the dream again?"

Tovi nodded, and for the first time that morning she let the tears flow. She allowed herself to be wrapped in Ganya's plump arms, wishing beyond anything else that they were her mother's.

CHAPTER 4

Leeto perched high in the trees of Adia observing the valley dwellers and itching for the prize. An entire kingdom. His very own kingdom to rule and control.

Leeto had smooth, pale skin, blinding orange hair and acid yellow eyes. He was very slender with a shorter-than-average frame and narrow face. Each of his features was pointed and sharp—his nose, his chin, even the corners of his mouth. He had a way of looking like a fox and snake at the same time.

He came from the Pyralis family, a clan with a long history on Mount Damien. Leeto's grandfather—Evander Pyralis—had always been an especially close friend of King Damien. One of Damien's first projects, after building his own palace, was creating a mansion along his large cobblestone courtyard for the Pyralis family. His Majesty ensured that they never wanted for anything. None of Evander's descendants had ever labored a day in their luxurious lives.

As a child, Leeto never knew to appreciate the fine things that surrounded him and took his wealth for granted. In the Pyralis family, money wasn't what mattered most. Family was. They did everything together, and it was not uncommon to see all the living Pyralis generations together in one place, special occasion or not. They abided by the deeply-held belief that there was no one else they could completely trust, no one else who would look out for them in such a dangerous world. So, while his fortune and fancy belongings did not impress Leeto, he cherished his family and their bonds above all else.

Leeto had shown his aptitude for persuasion and politics early on. Whether he was born with natural talent or had learned it from observing his father, no one was quite sure. He could convince the cooks to make him his favorite foods, his tutors to grant him an afternoon off, and his sister to give him everything she owned.

King Damien often humored himself by placing young Leeto near his seat during banquets and festivals. He seemed to enjoy talking with Leeto, especially when he had the audacity to try to control him—the King of Mount Damien. Rather than making Damien angry, the king was always deeply amused by him.

"Your Majesty," Leeto had once said at the tender age of eight, his eyes large and innocent. "I haven't been feeling at all well recently. I think a break from my lessons and a slice of chocolate cake would be just what I need."

Damien roared with deep belly laughter and motioned for a servant to go to the kitchens. "You may have anything you like. As for your lessons, it doesn't appear you need many more."

Now Leeto was twenty-five years old, and he knew he was ready for his own kingdom. All of Adia would be his. No, he would rename it. All of Leeto Valley would be his, and he would be King Leeto. His mind had been buzzing all morning with his plans for armories, towers, and fortresses. The land was so vast and untouched, and there were endless resources to manipulate. He couldn't wait to begin. There would be armies and servants and beautiful, wealthy people. He would need to find a queen, but that would be no problem once he obtained all his power. Every woman would want to be his wife.

His palace must be big enough for his entire family. That would mean room for his siblings, plus children. He and his queen would produce plenty of royal offspring. And he couldn't forget large suites for his doting parents, grandparents, and aunts and uncles. And of course, the guest rooms, ballrooms, banquet halls, and gardens. He wouldn't be outdone by the palace on the mountain.

As he daydreamed of his castle's floor plan, he sat perched in the canopy of the giant trees doing his best to stay hidden from the foolish Adians. He had a strategy, and everything was falling perfectly into place. He just had to be sure he was not seen, especially by the other weapons.

The only hiccup so far had been his run in with Silas, the arrogant Adian with the keen senses. Leeto thought he had been silent as he stalked Silas and Tovi in the woods, but somehow Silas knew he was there.

"Come here, Leeto," Silas had called as soon as the girl was out of earshot.

How did Silas know his name? Leeto was more annoyed than anything, and he slunk further into the shadows.

"There is no sense hiding from me," Silas continued. "I can help you."

Help me? Leeto laughed at the idea. He wouldn't need someone like Silas when King Damien's armies invaded. He wouldn't need someone like Silas ever.

A twig cracked somewhere below him, snapping him back to reality and out of his memories of his earlier encounter with Silas. Leeto moved his eyes without disturbing any other muscles, not wanting unnecessary movements to give away his presence. His mouth curved up and his eyes narrowed when Calix came into view. Another Master. His competition. The key to his strategy.

Calix—tall and handsome with very pale skin and black hair—crept along a branch several feet below. He approached the side of a cottage built in the center of a large willow tree and flattened himself against the wall. Leeto watched as Calix silently inched closer to the front porch where an old woman sat in a rocking chair next to the very same girl Leeto always saw with Silas—Tovi Tivka.

This troubled Leeto, whose sneering smile vanished. Six months ago, King Damien challenged the weapons to mark an Adian and bring the victim to the mountain. Leeto, a masterful schemer, found abundant joy in this task. He immediately came up with a plan: shadow the other weapons as they made their targets vulnerable, and then swoop in to take advantage of his competitors' hard work and the Adians' weaknesses. It would be efficient and painless, at least for him.

One of the other weapons—huge and powerful Eryx—set his sights on Tovi's brother as soon as the challenge was given. Eryx followed Tali at a distance, never revealing himself, never speaking. It was strange. Then, a few days into the challenge, Tali disappeared. No one had seen him since, but that didn't stop Eryx from hanging around the sister. He seemed to have switched his attention to Tovi, but still he did not speak. How did he expect to win if he never spoke to his Adian target?

With no progress between Eryx and Tovi, Leeto had turned his focus to the other weapons. Plenty of Adians were being groomed in secret, but Leeto hadn't felt the time was right quite yet.

Now, high in the trees, Leeto peered at Calix. Was Calix playing the same game? Had he been watching Eryx stalk Tovi? Or, was he completely unaware that this girl was already a target? Had Leeto missed something important?

There was an itch across his back, and he concentrated on not moving a muscle, despite his longing to scratch. He wasn't used to clothing covering his marks. On the mountain, he wore a shirt with a hole in the back. Here in Adia, it seemed best to dress like the locals. The soft fabric felt funny as it covered the seven symbols and the heart etched on his skin. These designs stood for lessons he had learned on the mountain. Power. Perfection. Adoration. Prosperity. Pleasure. Wisdom. Control.

Each of the seven weapons was particularly trained and talented in one area, and each had earned the title of Master. Leeto became a Master of Control when he was only fifteen years old, skipping over the traditional beginners' assignments. As with any Master, Leeto was entrusted with specialized tasks from King Damien, most of which centered around training others in the art of skillful manipulation. If only he could teach one of these Adians about the beauty of control . . .

Tovi and the old woman rose from their seats and went inside the house. Calix, still unaware of Leeto's watchful eyes and ears, disappeared around the other side of the tree. Alone again, Leeto finally gave in and mercifully attacked the skin of his back with his fingernails. He closed his eyes in sweet relief, but only for a moment.

He climbed toward the other side of the village and mulled over all that he had seen. So intent on his plans and schemes, he hardly paid attention to his surroundings.

If he had more presence of mind, he wouldn't have been so surprised to find himself jerked from his feet and pinned to a tree trunk, one enormous hand grasping his throat and cutting off his air supply.

"Leave her alone. She's mine," growled Eryx, his glowering brown eyes with one little purple star only inches away. His face and shaved head were covered in old scars, and one of them just below his eye had reopened in his fury. Something black and tar-like slowly seeped out.

Leeto spluttered and gasped.

"Do you hear me? Leave her alone," Eryx demanded, releasing his grip and letting his prisoner fall to his feet, narrowly escaping a long plunge to the earth far below.

Leeto rubbed his neck and took deep gulps of air. "Yes, yes. I hear you. No need to get violent, Eryx. You know I'm not the only one with my eyes on her, don't you?"

"I'm aware."

"Are you going to try to murder Calix, too?" Leeto asked snidely.

Eryx grabbed the front of Leeto's tunic and lifted him to eye level. "What makes you think I would hesitate from destroying your family? Leave Tovi alone, or they will be the ones I punish. Understand?"

A cold chill ran through Leeto. "I understand," he gasped, having trouble breathing with his shirt pulled tightly against his throat.

Eryx swung him over open space and let him dangle there. Leeto clung to Eryx's wrists, his fingers sinking into the taut flesh of the larger man's arms, desperate to keep hold. Panic took over as he writhed and spasmed, looking for some sort of escape. He panted, struggling to take in air.

"How do you think your mother would feel if I let go right now?" Eryx asked menacingly.

Suddenly Leeto was free falling. Eryx had let go, and Leeto's mind went terribly blank.

Before he could regain himself, he tumbled onto a thatched roof just a few feet below. Leeto looked up into the hateful eyes of Eryx who still stood on the branch above. Without a word, the large man turned and stomped further into the forest.

Of all the things he despised, a spiral out of control was what Leeto hated the most. This interaction was not in his plan. How had everything gone so wrong in so little time? If it weren't for this roof, he'd be dead. Or had Eryx dropped him here on purpose? Was Eryx weakening?

He had so many more questions now than he had just that morning. The biggest question of all: What did he need to do to regain the upper hand?

CHAPTER 5

Tovi sat on her puffy little bed next to her window, holding two soft blankets in her hands. She and Tali were wrapped in them as newborns when they were delivered to the Tivkas in the middle of the night, nameless and crying. She often returned to them when she was looking for comfort.

She closed her eyes and tried to remember all that Tali had been up to right before he disappeared. He had suddenly been spending a lot of time without her. She thought he was with Silas, but was she wrong? Had he discovered Adwin in those hours away?

Tali. Even his name made her heart ache. There was so much about Tali that Tovi envied, but not so much that she despised him. She wished she could be more like him—somehow adventurous and grounded at the same time. He could be bold and tender, outlandish and careful, reckless and wise. She missed him more than she could bear.

Ganya and Avi began taking the children out into the wilderness as soon as they could walk and fend for themselves a bit. They would explore caves and marshes and dells, often playing games invented by Avi to keep them entertained. Who could pick the largest flower? Who could spot the strangest bird? Who could climb the highest in the tree? Who could swim the furthest in one breath? As the sun sank and the moon rose, they would lie on their backs and listen to Ganya tell the stories of the stars. They would sleep in one big bundle on the ground, warmed by a colorful fire.

As they grew older, Tovi and Tali went on these adventures without Avi and Ganya. They were often accompanied by Silas, but sometimes they wanted to go just the two of them. They were both lean and strong and had identical coloring, but there were some differences. Tali's dark blue hair was short and thick with several cowlicks sending patches in odd directions, and Tovi's was long and wavy. While Tovi was petite, Tali had grown very tall, and his features were far softer, possibly because he scowled so much less than his sister. Many of the girls in the village blushed or giggled when Tali was around, but he took little notice. With so much adventure on his mind, there was no room for romance.

Tovi and Tali were convinced that there were more villages out there, that it wasn't just little Adia and the big city on Mount Damien. They would spend several days traveling in different directions, seeking any sign of habitation, convinced that Adwin and their parents were out there somewhere. Once, when circling Mount Damien so they could explore the foothills to the north, they startled a man with green hair holding a bow and arrow. They found themselves staring past the black arrowhead that was just inches from their noses, into the eyes of the strong hunter.

A few seconds passed, and the stranger did something unexpected. He lowered the bow, propped it against a tree, and removed one of his tattered gray gloves. He opened his palm, holding it in the air and showing Tali and Tovi the brown heart outline, just like those marking the Adians' hands. Without a word, Tali raised his own hand, showing the matching heart. Just then another hunter crashed through the trees, and the mysterious man quickly re-gloved his hand and signaled that the twins should hide.

They left, but Tovi always regretted not staying and learning more about this strange sequence of events. They returned to that spot several times, but they never saw the green-haired man again.

Growing up, Tovi and Tali shared a bedroom. Once they were both in bed and the lanterns blown out, Tali always wanted to talk deep into the night. He would whisper across the room, prodding her for her feelings and thoughts. Sometimes the talks were deep and meaningful. More often, there were light-hearted arguments and Tovi's constant commands, "Be quiet!" "Let me sleep!" "Leave me alone!"

"But, Tovi, did you see that hill beyond the one that we've explored before? How do you think Adwin's magic works? What do you think he looks like? Where should we go tomorrow?"

She would throw a pillow at him, but it rarely stopped the barrage of questions or his attempts to get her to communicate. While she pretended to be annoyed, she adored her brother too much to really be mad.

Tovi folded the baby blankets and put them back in the trunk at the foot of her bed, closing the lid and securing the latch. She sat on her puffy mattress, leaning on her wooden windowsill and looking out into the forest.

Tali. She missed him so much that it physically hurt. Where had he gone? What happened to him? Was he ever coming home? Was he even alive? She felt so off-kilter without him. He had been the light that balanced her dark. What was she going to do?

"Hey, Tovi! What are you doing?" came a voice from above her.

Tovi looked up through the window toward Silas' cottage and saw his downturned face.

"Want to head down to the river? I heard a lot of noise coming from there a little bit ago."

Tovi hesitated. She had little interest in the fun and games of her fellow Adians, but Silas was already swinging on a vine and landing on the porch.

"Seriously, come on," he prodded.

Reluctantly, Tovi left the safety of her little house and joined him. It took only five minutes for the water to come into view, and it appeared that all the young people of Adia had come out to enjoy the sunshine and warmth. There was much shrieking, laughing, and whooshing as water sprayed everywhere.

One by one, more Adians arrived as if the joy of the morning had called them closer. Some dove in from overhanging branches or leapt from boulders. Some ran straight in toward the center of the commotion. There was dancing, splashing, and water moving in every direction. Total, complete, wonderful chaos.

"Silas! Join us!" someone called from the center of the pandemonium. Silas swung into a nearby tree, ran along the lowest branch, and flung himself into the air, curling into a tight cannonball. He landed in the middle of the river, a huge wave engulfing his friends.

Tovi watched. She had known them her whole life, but she never felt as if she was one of them. Silas belonged. Tali belonged. But she did not. They would never understand the fears and painful questions that lurked in her heart and that Tali had somehow escaped.

Without a goodbye to Silas, Tovi returned home. She went back to her room and opened her trunk with the intention of holding the blankets a little longer. They were the only link she had to her family. She liked to imagine a lovely mother wrapping her babies in the blankets, gently and sweetly. Maybe their father, strong but tender, held one baby in each arm and kissed their foreheads. Maybe they sang a lullaby over them before they were taken away.

Goosebumps rose along her arms and neck. There was only one blanket in the trunk.

"Ganya, have you been in my room?" she yelled.

The older woman came to the door, wiping a bowl with a colorful towel. "No, dear. What's wrong?"

Tovi stayed silent as she picked up the remaining blanket. She knew without a doubt that she had left the other folded inside, too.

CHAPTER 6

Calix watched the young Adians splash in the river below. There was something feline about his striking features, long and muscular body, and the way he moved, like a panther stalking his prey in the treetops. His jet-black hair was just long enough to ripple slightly in the breeze, and his black eyes were framed with almost-feminine, thick lashes.

"There is no way those blankets are from this valley," Calix said to himself, stuffing the stolen one into the satchel slung around his chest. He had been watching her stroke them repeatedly throughout the last few weeks, and finally he had the chance to snoop inside that trunk. It was clear the blankets were far too elegant for the looms and thick home-made yarns of Adia. They were velvety and rich, much more like something you would find in the wealthy areas of the mountain. How did they end up here in Adia? He would take the blanket back to the mountain and see if he could investigate its origin.

He eyed the exuberance of the Adians playing in the water. There was very little he found as distasteful as wasting time. Didn't they know they could be using these hours for something greater? Something worthwhile? Wealth and success and stability?

Unlike many of the young Masters on Mount Damien, Calix had not been born into prosperity. His father was a low-ranking soldier, and his mother worked as a nanny in the palace. When his father was killed in an accident during practice drills, his mother did not know what to do. She could no longer afford to pay someone to watch young Calix and his infant sister BiBi while she worked, yet she had to work in order for them to eat.

At the time, King Damien's son, Ajax, was married to Princess Thomae. Despite her horrid husband, Thomae was kind and understanding. When Calix's mother begged Princess Thomae to allow her children to come with her to work, Thomae was delighted. The nanny's children were nearly the same age as the royal children. She prepared an apartment for Calix's small family, and they moved to the palace. It was more than Calix's mother could have ever dreamed.

Calix and his sister grew up in the palace learning to love elegant things. Their mother constantly pounded them with the belief that it all came from King Damien, and they owed everything to the monarch. They would be nothing and have nothing without him and his kind daughter-in-law who gave them work, money, a place to live, clothing, food, and much more.

When Calix was summoned to an audience with the king at ten years old, he visibly trembled.

"No need to be afraid, my boy," the king said kindly, a pleased smile on his face.

"Oh, n-no, Your Majesty," Calix said with reverence. "I am not afraid. I . . . I . . . I just hope I can please you."

Clearly delighted, King Damien watched him. His eyes traveled to Calix's hair and eyes—hair and eyes of the deepest black that matched the king's. King Damien asked to see his hand, and he nodded in acknowledgement when he saw that there was no heart outline hidden beneath the glove.

"What is it you would like to do with your future?" he asked.

"Anything that would make you happy, Your Majesty. Anything to repay you."

Damien nodded. "That is wise of you, my boy. Tell me about yourself. What are you best at?"

"Me, Your Majesty?"

"Yes, you. What are your skills? Your talents?"

Calix didn't know how to answer.

Damien seemed interested in Calix's hesitance. "Young man, you need confidence. You are handsome and have the potential to be very charming. If you just learned a little more about yourself and all you have to offer, I think you will make a fine Master of Adoration someday."

"A M . . . Master?" Calix confirmed in awe.

"Yes," Damien said with a warm smile and kind eyes. "A Master. You could be great. Not as great as me, but great all the same because you see the importance in revering me above all else. You are very wise beyond your years. You will begin with simple tasks. If you complete them as well as I suspect you will, you will be a Master before you turn twenty."

Calix was a Master by the time he was eighteen. Through the intense tutoring of some slightly older Masters of Adoration and Perfection, Calix became a star pupil. He relished every task and assignment, deriving unspeakable joy from the many "well done" compliments he received from King Damien and other important officials.

He learned very quickly that he had much more command over women than men. Men weren't so easily drawn under his influence. He would try and try to convince them that they should worship the crown, and eventually it might work. But one smile, one word in the direction of a woman, and he had her hooked.

Women tended to fall in love with him. There was no other way to say it. His dashing smile, his smooth words, and his talent for flattery were all weapons in his arsenal. When a woman fell under his spell, she tended to put her trust in the things he trusted. She would enjoy the things he enjoyed, seek out the things he sought. Or at least she would pretend to, becoming the image of the woman she believed he would want. Once she was sufficiently pathetic, it was time to abruptly cut off his attentions. She would wildly cling to anything that might win him back, including fully worshipping his idol, King Damien. Little did these women know that each move was calculated and how closely they always followed his script.

Ever since this discovery, he had spent a great deal of time honing his skills in both Control and Pleasure. He saw them as closely linked to his mastery of Adoration. Control them. Teach them to desire him. And soon they would be loyal to him, which was, in reality, one step away from adoration of the king.

He watched the Adians playing in the water and thought about Tovi. She was undeniably beautiful. He smirked as he thought about his task. Not only would it be easy to ensnare her with a few of his smiles, but it could also be enjoyable. It had been a long time since he had been attracted to a woman. The girls on the mountain were just his playthings. Since discovering Tovi, he couldn't help wondering what it would be like to kiss her and see the look of adoration swell in her eyes.

The bough on which he stood suddenly dipped. Calix tensed like a startled animal, and his eyes locked on Eryx coming toward him. The sounds from the water below had masked his competition's approach. Calix bolted, making his way to the forest floor as quickly as possible. He could run much faster on solid ground. Eryx chased him through the woods, his thundering footfalls booming ever closer behind him. They tromped on ferns and whipped through tall grasses for what seemed like ages before finally coming out near the ridge. Eryx threw himself forward and tackled Calix to the ground. They grappled for a few seconds before Eryx's fist connected with Calix's nose. Black blood poured out, and Calix's concern over his appearance distracted him from his fight and flight.

As he pinched his nose and checked for broken places, his adversary stood and crossed his arms over his chest. "Leave her alone. She's mine."

"And why would I do that?" Calix responded nonchalantly, not bothering to look up.

"Like I already said: She's mine."

"I serve His Majesty, King Damien," Calix said with reverence. "I obey *his* orders, not yours."

"Find someone else to serve your purposes. She's mine. She's my target. She has been the whole time."

"Oh really?" Calix finally glanced up. He had stopped the flow of blood, but there were dark stains down the front of his shirt and the places on his sleeve that he had used to mop his face. "So why haven't you spoken to her yet? I've watched you, Eryx. You've never once attempted to attract her attention. You've never even shown yourself to her. How do you plan on marking the girl if you just sit in the trees all day? Don't forget that I'm a Master of Adoration. I can see it in your eyes, Eryx. I recognized it weeks ago, as soon as you shaved your head. You are perfectly content pretending to scout her, while in reality you are trying to protect her."

Eryx's chest heaved, and his hands clenched into fists.

Calix looked at them and laughed. "Are you going to hit me again?"

Eryx glared at him for a moment. Whatever thoughts were swirling in his mind remained masked. Without warning, Eryx slammed his fist into Calix's stomach. Calix fell to his knees and retched. Black sludge spewed from his mouth and pooled on the ground between his hands. By the time he was done vomiting, Eryx was gone.

Calix rolled onto his back, the warm grass soothing and fragrant. *All of this will be worth it one day,* he thought while looking at the blue sky. When he won the challenge and pleased His Majesty, all of this would be worth it.

He gritted his teeth and rose to his feet. Looking at the position of the sun, he knew there was still plenty of day left. No need to head back toward the mountain yet. He moved swiftly through the woods, back the way he had been chased. Nearing the river, he climbed into the trees, mindful of his sore stomach and throbbing nose. He made a mental note that Eryx deserved retribution.

He crept from tree to tree until he was close enough to see the antics still going strong in the water. He spotted Silas, still enjoying the afternoon with the others. Good. His way was clear to collect a bit more information.

Still splattered with black sludge from his run-in with Eryx, he climbed higher and travelled deeper into the canopy. He skulked outside of Silas' cottage, and when he was sure no one was near, he sneaked inside.

The house was a mess. Brushes, palettes, and jars of paint covered the counters, chairs, and floor. But what really caught his attention was the floor-to-ceiling mural that covered every inch of the walls—fascinating. It reminded him of another mural—the mural in the palace.

Calix began searching through the images, careful not to disturb anything as he walked along the edge of the room. All he wanted was information on what this man was up to. In all his time scouting the Adians, Silas had proven the most interesting. No family and no stories of where he had come from. He was always out visiting other Adians or holed up in this house, working on his painting. Calix was particularly curious about him because he spent so much time with Tovi. What, exactly, was the nature of their relationship?

He stopped in front of one scene in the mural. It looked finished, and he peered closely at the details. It was a painting of an enormously fat tree almost entirely covered in vines and large yellow flowers. There were little orange, purple, and pink dots surrounding it, and he couldn't quite decipher what they were meant to be.

He had seen a tree just like this in the forest that morning. He ticked through some facts he knew about the village and its inhabitants. His eyes darted from the tree scene to others along the wall. He thought about the mural in the palace.

Some pieces began to click in his mind, forming a picture he hadn't expected.

CHAPTER 7

With the first golden rays of sunset glimmering through the willow leaves, Tovi and Ganya took their usual seats in the rocking chairs on the front porch. They rocked in tandem, both deep in thought.

Tovi glanced at Ganya—mother, grandmother, and guardian all wrapped into this one wonderful woman. She wished she could go back in time and see Ganya and Avi in their prime. They did not have a sweet, romantic love story. Instead, their relationship blossomed in a time of great danger and violence. It was hard to see these kind, elderly grandparents as the fierce rebels who had to brave such horrors.

Both Avi and Ganya were born on Mount Damien, then known as Mount Lemuel, but they never met as children. They were the last generation to know the mountain as peaceful, green, and jubilant. The brown heart outlines appeared in everyone's palm when Avi was about twenty years old and Ganya closing in on twenty-one. It was one of Damien's first creations as an apprentice to the king, a symbol that showed you belonged to Adwin. Avi once told Tovi that this was the first sign of things to come. What seemed innocent on the outside was really a dark clue to Damien's obsession with detecting each person's loyalty.

When Damien began his campaigns and recruitment, preaching his ideas of prosperity and efficiency, Avi and Ganya were part of the few who were not swayed. They remained loyal to Adwin, even as it became perilous to be so. Damien outlawed the very heart in the palm that he had created, teaching the masses that the heart would disappear only when one acknowledged that he was the true king of the mountain. He imprisoned anyone who showed the symbol. Gloves became a necessity. There was an unspoken understanding on the mountain: anyone who valued his life pretended that gloves were in fashion. No one spoke of the heart beneath.

The number of Adwin's followers continued to shrink, and soon they were meeting in secret for support and to discuss strategy. Avi and Ganya met at one of these meetings and were first attracted to each other's minds. Just a few months later, Adwin left the mountain. Avi followed him, as did Ganya. Neither knew that the other had done so. They came face to face in the brand new land of Adia, thrilled but not surprised to discover that the other had the same courage and loyalty to Adwin.

They spent most of their adult lives helping refugees settle into the valley. It was difficult but rewarding work, especially as time went on and the people they helped had less and less knowledge of Adwin. Then, as their generation aged, the refugees stopped coming. The ones who knew Adwin but had become loyal to Damien would never leave the mountain. The rest of the people were too young to know any difference, so they stayed above the cloud, working in Damien's kingdom. It was around this time that tiny Tali and Tovi arrived in the night.

Ganya broke the silence after several minutes of rocking. "You seem to be thinking rather hard, Tovi. What is on your mind?"

Ganya already had so much to worry about—Tali's disappearance and Avi's declining health. Would it really do any good to tell her the blanket had been stolen?

Tovi didn't answer and stared at her own hands. She traced the heart in her palm with distracted fingers. Finally looking up, she asked, "Why can't I find him, Ganya? Where is Adwin? Why won't any of you tell me where to look?"

"What have I always told you?"

"That I will know where to look when I'm ready," she answered dully.

"That's right," Ganya replied, turning her head to look at the perplexed young woman. "But I'm sure that doesn't satisfy you."

Tovi shook her head.

"You aren't the only one with this struggle, although I fear you often feel alone. There are others. I had a cousin who was convinced that Adwin didn't exist at all, that he couldn't find him because he was nothing more than a fable."

Tovi shifted guiltily in her seat and wondered how much Ganya suspected. "What changed his mind?"

"It wasn't about changing his mind. It was about changing his heart. He had closed himself from many of the things that brought him joy and peace, like his love for exploring the woods or sitting quietly by the river in the early morning, which are gifts straight from Adwin's heart. Once my cousin allowed himself to experience those things again, it wasn't long before he encountered Adwin. But I'm afraid that's where it becomes a little different with you."

"What do you mean?"

Ganya considered her words carefully, pursing her lips and not bothering to hide her hesitation. After a deep sigh, she said, "I am afraid, my dear, that you might want to find Adwin for all the wrong reasons."

Tovi narrowed her eyes. "And what reasons are those?"

Ganya was unfazed by Tovi's flared temper. "Sweetheart, you want to find Adwin so you can point your finger in his face and tell him you hate him."

Tovi opened her mouth to argue but closed it when she realized Ganya was right. She exhaled forcefully.

Ganya smiled. "I'm sure he is rather looking forward to that confrontation. Nonetheless, he doesn't make a business of appearing to people on their preferred timetable. He has one of his own." Ganya reached over and held Tovi's hands between her own. "Tovi, if you want to find him, talk to him. Even if you feel silly for talking to the air around you. Yell at him. Say nasty words if you need to. He will hear you, and he will understand. And when you are ready, you will find him. Well, really he will find you."

Oh, how she would love to yell at him. To tell him how she hated him so! To declare that he was evil for letting her brother disappear, terrible for making her grow up without her parents. She heard a weak cough through the window. Ganya looked toward the house, her eyes growing sad. "Tovi, dear, I'm afraid we're nearing the end."

"Don't say that!" Tovi cried, standing and facing Ganya with terror in her eyes.

Tovi could only remember the death of one person, Ganya's brother, who died three years before. The family gathered around to say their goodbyes, and when the time came, he had grown faint and then disappeared completely. To Tovi, this seemed horribly sad, mysteriously uncertain, and at least a little bit scary.

Now that it was Avi who faced this fate, there were so many things she wanted to know. "What will happen to him?" she asked.

"That is something that none of us understand. All we know is that when we fade, there is a great adventure waiting for us wherever it is that we reappear."

"You've told me that you can ask Adwin anything, and he will tell you the truth. Ask him what will happen to Avi."

"I have."

"Well, what did he say?" Tovi asked impatiently.

"That I have to wait and trust him. He always answers honestly, even if it's not the kind of answer we want."

Another cough rattled from the bedroom. Tovi moved toward it, but Ganya reached out to grip Tovi's arm. "I have been trying to prepare you over the last several weeks, but I must put it very bluntly now. Avi does not have much longer with us. I don't mean years. Maybe not even months or weeks. Go in there and have a nice chat with him. Savor these moments and the words that you share. There might not be many more."

Tovi had not taken the time to ready herself for life without Avi. Her mind flashed to scenes of sitting by his side as he whittled, of splashing through creeks as they chased fish, of long walks when they seemed to talk of nothing and everything at the same time. She swallowed to dislodge the lump in her throat.

He was the closest thing she had ever had to a father or grandfather. She adored this man far more than she had ever been able to admit. She had been a surly child, but Avi's love was stubborn. He refused to be shut out of her life, and this meant more to Tovi than she could ever say.

Tovi knocked softly on the door as she entered the dimly lit bedroom. The curtains were pulled over the windows, with just enough light coming through for Tovi to see Avi's shrinking outline.

"Is that my baby girl?" the weak and crackly voice asked, somehow managing to sound cheerful.

She carefully sat on the edge of the bed near his feet. "Yes, Avi, it's me." She reached out to hold his hands and could almost feel the strength draining out. She rubbed his hands softly, trying to memorize every line and knuckle and nuance. He struggled to keep his eyes open.

He lightly squeezed Tovi's fingers. When he gathered enough strength to speak again, he slowly lifted his eyelids. "I love you very much, Tovi. I know we're not blood, but I wouldn't have wanted anyone else for a daughter. Not anyone."

Her emotions churned, and a tear splashed onto her hand. She knew that opening her mouth would mean surrender to the tide of misery that was building inside, so she quietly leaned down to kiss his sunken cheek.

"Sweet pea, why do you look so sad?"

Her voice cracking every few syllables, she hesitantly responded, "It sounds like you are saying goodbye."

He sighed and tried to smile. "That's exactly what I'm doing. It's not time for me to go quite yet, but it will be soon. There is something I want you to do for me."

"Anything. What is it?"

"Please don't give up on Adwin. He's out there. He is above and beside and within. You will find him. I love you, Tovi."

She patted his hand again and composed herself long enough to say, "I love you, too, Avi."

Tovi stood and walked out, barely holding in her emotions and closing the door softly behind her. She turned to Ganya, and when their eyes met, the weeping began. Grief erupted out of Tovi like a boiling overflow. Ganya reached out, but Tovi pushed her away.

Her desire to escape her despair was overwhelming. It was as though there was an enraged animal locked inside her chest, desperate to be free of its bindings. She couldn't explain it. She just had to run.

She sprinted out the door and tore along thick branches and down rope ladders. She sped past neighbors who called out to her, ignoring their worried questions. The muscles in her legs pumped faster and faster as she reached the hard ground. She kept going.

She ran, the air whistling in her ears and her breath stinging her overworked lungs. Her eyes stared straight ahead into the graying evening, not focused on any one thing. She wasn't aware of anything around her, except the oppressive need to run. To get away.

She was almost to the ridge before her mind registered anything except the sound of the wind. Then, another set of thumping footfalls was the first sensation to occur to her since leaving the house.

She slowed her pace and turned, gasping sharply when she realized she wasn't alone. She came to an abrupt halt.

"How long have you . . . ?" she asked, searching for breath.

"I've been with you the whole time," Silas answered, hardly winded. He combed his fingers through his light brown hair, as the setting sun reflected off the golden streaks.

"I didn't hear you or see you."

"I know. You were pretty intent on shutting me out."

"Why did you come after me?"

Silas sat down on a fallen tree trunk that made a perfect bench. "I thought you might need someone to talk to."

She sat down and began to cry again, leaning her face into her upturned hands. The tears were severe. Violent. She shook with the ugliness of them.

Silas scooted closer. "I know it hurts."

"You don't understand."

"You'd be surprised how much I understand."

Tovi raised her red-streaked face that was scrunched with anger.

Silas ignored the scathing look and continued. "You were saying goodbye to Avi, and this agony seemed to spring to life inside of you, threatening to rip you to shreds from the inside out." Her puffy eyes widened. "It reminded you of how you felt when you lost your brother, which always leads to thinking about how badly you wish you knew your parents. All you could think about was getting as far away as possible, to outrun all of the pain you have experienced. Your instinct was to run, to press on until everything was gone. But then you got here, and the hurt followed you. You can't get away from it, just like when you realized Tali was gone."

Tovi sobbed loudly and turned away from Silas, collapsing onto her knees.

He followed her down, sitting on the ground and pulling her close to his chest, ignoring her attempts to push him away. After a few moments of struggle, she gave in, burying her face in the hollow between his chin and shoulder. He stroked her hair and let her cry. "This kind of running won't get you anywhere."

Her shoulders heaved with each ragged inhale.

Silas rested his chin on top of her head. She could hear his heartbeat beneath her ear. "You can't make it go away on your own. You did the right thing earlier, except you went the wrong way."

"What—what do you mean?" she asked.

"You were right to run. When you feel pain like that, run. Run as fast and as hard as you can. But next time, don't do it alone. Next time, run toward me."

Tovi continued to weep until the sun was well below the earth. Silas whispered tender encouragement and comfort as her spirit calmed and readied itself to return home.

CHAPTER 8

As the city darkened around him one light at a time, Leeto sat on the stone balcony of his family's mansion, sipping red wine and organizing his thoughts. He had changed into his usual clothing for the mountain, discarding the homespun tunic and donning the stiff, white button up with the large circle cut out of the back. He enjoyed the feel of the red velvet cushion directly against his skin.

His eyes did not blink as he observed with distrust and disdain the magnificent home across the courtyard where Calix lived. Calix and his sister, BiBi, were inside the extravagant, brightly-lit dining room, finishing up what looked like a massive meal. They never drew the curtains. BiBi especially loved for all who passed to see their fine things.

Images of Calix lurking around the Tivkas' home still played in Leeto's mind. What was he up to? As a masterful schemer, Leeto hated when he could not deduce the plans and wiles of a lesser man.

And Calix was most definitely a lesser man, attempting to cover his childhood poverty and shaky upbringing with his pretentious tone and smooth words. It didn't work. It was easy for the Pyralis family—along with the rest of the old, rich families—to see Calix didn't really belong in Damien's inner circle. It was annoying enough to see his comings and goings to his house on the courtyard, an area meant for only the very best. But it was worse when they were in the palace and Calix acted like royalty, like he was one of the royal grandchildren.

Yes, Calix had grown up inside those walls, but as a child of a penniless, widowed nanny. He was no prince.

Leeto turned his eyes to the palace, ablaze in lights. He could see the silhouettes of the guards posted on balconies and in windows. After the events of the last week, Leeto was no longer content with winning Adia. He now had a plan and the means to not only rule the valley, but to reign over the mountain as well.

The ebb and flow of his confidence throughout the week had been extreme. He started one day feeling victory in King Damien's competition was close at hand, had survived a series of crises, and then lucked into the most incredible information. It was unfathomable. Now, he knew he was ahead of his adversaries. There was no way anyone else could possibly know what he had learned.

He rubbed the front of his neck where it was still tender and bruised from the stranglehold inflicted by Eryx. What a strange week it had been. What a strange and wonderful week.

"Tell me, what has you up here thinking so deeply?" his sister, Rhaxma, demanded too sweetly as she sashayed onto the porch. She had thick orange hair tied back from her face, and her bright yellow eyes stood out against the dark makeup lining her lids. She was beautiful but severe. Most people were terrified of her until they realized how friendly she was.

While Leeto was short and skinny, the rest of the siblings came from a more robust stock. His brothers were tall and broad-shouldered, and they ranged from strong and solid to down-right fat. Rhaxma was not skinny like Leeto or fat like some of her other brothers. She also wasn't muscular like her brother Thad. She could only be described as elegant and voluptuous—curvy and soft. Somehow her waist was still tiny, making her upper and lower body look bigger than they really were.

Rhaxma and Leeto's minds were both calculating and strategic. The subtle difference was that Leeto used his calculations to control his actual circumstances while Rhaxma preferred to control other people's opinions of her circumstances. She learned from an early age that as long as others thought you were the best, you were. It was that simple. Her image could give her access to people and fortune that others with lesser reputations could only dream.

Rhaxma and Leeto were the youngest in a family with five children. Their elder siblings had no ambition and lived off their family's wealth, wasting their days with others who had the same lack of drive. One of them had even been seen frequenting a home of disrepute in the Bottom Rung, the poorest, most deplorable neighborhood of the city. It disgusted many of the Masters, but Leeto and Rhaxma loved their brothers too much to abandon them. Instead, they resolved to always protect their family reputation and their lofty way of life.

It hadn't been until their teenage years when they discovered their identical drives and complementary ambitions. They could use one another and be spurred on by the other's successes. After all, one's success always bolstered the reputation and wealth of the other.

Leeto was the first to recognize it. During a festival honoring King Damien in the year that Leeto was eighteen and Rhaxma was sixteen, the other Pyralis siblings lounged on their family's balcony, drinking dark wine and shouting insults at commoners as they passed below. Rhaxma was not there. Leeto was curious, so he stood at the railing to see if he could spot his sister's bright orange hair in the crowd. He could. She was working her way through the people, conversing with everyone on their same social level or just below. It didn't matter if they were old or young—she made time to chat and ask questions of anyone who could possibly be beneficial to her at some point in the future.

She was playing his own game. Instead of frightening him, it made him nearly burst with pride. As soon as she was back home, he pulled her into the parlor. "Where did you learn that?" he asked urgently.

"Learn what?" was her impatient reply.

"You worked the crowd brilliantly. I was watching. Where did you learn that?"

Her eyes began to smile before the corners of her mouth slowly turned up. "You've already recognized it, haven't you? I was only following your example. I've seen you do it countless times."

They had been allies ever since.

In the crisp night air on the balcony, Rhaxma wrapped an arm around Leeto's chest, leaning over his shoulder from behind and kissing him on the cheek. Leeto clasped Rhaxma's hand and pulled her around so she could sit opposite him on the darkened porch.

"I have something to tell you, but you have to swear not to tell a soul," he said, trying his best to make his tone convey the seriousness of the matter. He knew he could trust his sister, but only if she understood the gravity of what he was about to tell her.

"Of course," she said, her brow wrinkling.

"This trip to Adia was different than the others. I planned for it to be nothing but the usual observations and preparation for when I finally make my move. But then things got completely out of hand. Silas confronted me, and then Eryx did as well. I also saw Calix moving in on the same target as Eryx. It was mayhem. Nothing stayed true to our plans. I came home in the darkest of thoughts and feeling defeated. But then the most incredible thing happened."

"Don't tease me!" Rhaxma cried. "Tell me!"

"His Majesty summoned me to the palace to discuss one of my students here on the mountain. But when I arrived, he was in a deep conversation with Prince Ajax. I listened at the door. He was talking about Tali Tivka."

"The blue-haired one? The twin?" Rhaxma seemed confused and unsure as to why this could be so important.

"Precisely. He has been away from Adia for six months, since right after this contest began, and nobody knows where he went. But there has been an informant. I don't know who reported it, but King Damien was telling Prince Ajax that Tali has been spotted. He was nowhere near Adia. They think he is completing some sort of mission for Adwin.

"Then, they started talking about something totally different, and I am trying to figure out how they are connected. We were only children when it happened, but do you remember the stories we've been told about His Majesty's heirs?"

"How he killed them off because of something in the mural in the palace?"

"Exactly. There's more to that mural than what we see in the light. It continues behind the curtain. I've never seen it myself, but I was told ages ago that the portion of the mural behind the curtain shows four people, two women and two men, joining Adwin and defeating King Damien. Nearly thirty years ago, Prince Ajax married Princess Thomae. First, they had a little girl, Princess Helena. No one thought anything of it. Next came a little boy, our friend Prince Jairus. That was when King Damien took notice. The two children had the exact same coloring—hair and eyes—as two of the conquerors in the prophecy. Princess Thomae conceived again. Terrified of what this could mean, King Damien knew he must watch this third child closely. If the baby's coloring matched one of the images in the prophecy, he knew Princess Thomae must be put to death before she could bear a fourth.

"The night of the third birth was chaotic, and no one knows exactly what happened. The next day, Princess Thomae, the new baby, and Princess Helena had disappeared. Some say that Damien panicked when he saw the baby's colors, and he immediately executed the mother and children, leaving only Jairus as an heir. But no one knows for sure what came of them. Princess Helena, the eldest child and rightful heir to the throne after Ajax, could still be alive. All of us have assumed she was killed that night, but we don't really know. What if she ran away? What if she took the baby with her?"

He took another dramatic pause, then continued in a hushed voice. "Rhaxma, I can think of only one scenario that makes sense, why Damien was talking about both Tali and the children in one conversation. Adwin knows that the children survived, and he has sent Tali to find them and bring them back."

Rhaxma's eyes grew to twice their usual size, and a few beads of black sweat rose from her forehead. She dabbed at them with a stained handkerchief. "But what about the fourth conqueror in the prophecy? That child was never born."

"Who says all four must be heirs to the throne? It could be someone else. The fourth could be you or me for all we know. If we could gather the three and get behind the curtain to determine the identity of the fourth, what is stopping us from defeating King Damien and taking control of this mountain?"

"Leeto, that sounds extremely dangerous. And it would mean joining forces with Adwin."

"Only until the mountain is ours. Then we could get rid of the old man."

Rhaxma sat back against her overstuffed cushions. "What will you do with this information?"

"Nothing, at this point. I'm going to continue my quest to mark an Adian and bring her to the mountain. I want His Majesty to send his armies to conquer Adia and set me up as king. In the meantime, I'm going to search the same area where Tali was seen. Damien said something about caves in the foothills north of here. If I can find Tali, there are ways of forcing information from him. I will find out what he is up to."

"What will you do to him?"

"Leave that up to me."

CHAPTER 9

Tovi's hands rested on her knees as she caught her breath. Another dream about Tali, another run to the ridge, another morning filled with anger and disappointment. She sat down, smoothed her hair away from her face and made her daily examination of the distant horizon. No movement. No sign of Tali.

An image from when they were young popped into her mind. They were about thirteen years old, and Silas had excitedly told them to come see something he had discovered in the woods. It took them an hour, but the hike was worth it. A wide, shallow creek meandered lazily through the forest, and four enormous trees grew on the banks, two on each side. Their branches reached across the water, tangled and woven together. By swimming in the creek and diving below the lowest limbs, the trio emerged inside the tangle of branches. Sunlight escaped between the leaves and sparkled on the water below, reflections dancing all around them. Tovi remembered being so in awe that she had trouble catching her breath.

Tali threw his arm over her soggy shoulders and sighed happily. "Things like this couldn't come from nothing. Someone thought this up. Someone made this. I'm going to spend the rest of my life looking for places like this. Then I'll find Adwin. I just know it."

In that moment, she could almost believe like him. She could almost feel the way Tali did, hope in something that she had been taught but had never seen. Almost.

A throat cleared behind Tovi, interrupting her thoughts, and she turned away from the ridge expecting Silas. A dark-haired stranger stood close behind her, and her heart thudded in sudden fear. She scrambled to her feet, sending loose rocks plummeting toward the boulders below.

"I'm so sorry to startle you," he apologized, holding his hands out as if to prove he meant no harm. Even in her terrified state, the first thing she noticed was there was no heart on his palm. "I was walking by, and you looked upset. Are you all right?"

Tovi was nervous and on high alert, but one eyebrow rose in curiosity. He looked to be about her age, maybe a few years older. Her eyes darted to each feature, trying to get used to his unfamiliar face. She took a step backwards. One of her heels was now over empty space. A few inches further and she would teeter over the edge.

He had black hair just long enough to ripple in the breeze and eyes that looked like they were wells of thick ink. His soft lips shouldn't belong to such a masculine face. His jawline was distinct, leading her eyes to the small cleft in his chin.

Silent for too long, Tovi shook herself. "Who are you?"

"Calix," he said, his smile revealing straight, white teeth.

He sat down and made himself comfortable, and Tovi's heart skipped a beat. "You're wearing shoes," she accused, circling around him toward the safety of solid ground.

"Yes. And why do you look so afraid of them?" He chuckled. "I promise they are perfectly harmless."

"I'm not afraid!" she said with more bravado than she felt. "You're from Mount Damien."

For a moment his eyes hardened, and his displeasure was evident, but he quickly smiled with delight. "You've heard of it? That's wonderful!" Calix held out his palm in a gesture of openness. Where the heart should have been, his skin was criss-crossed by dark veins just below the surface. "I know there's been some bad blood between our kingdoms, but surely you're not one of those people who blindly believes the old tales."

Tovi crossed her arms and pursed her lips. "I don't blindly believe anything."

"Hey, now, I'm not accusing you of anything. I think we started off all wrong. My name is Calix," he said slowly, as if he was introducing himself to a child. "I'm from Mount Damien. I decided to spend a few days exploring a little more of the world below the cloud to see what adventures I could find."

"And have you found any?"

He paused for a brief second, twirling a piece of grass between his fingers. "No," he drawled, looking at the blade, then smoothly glancing up to catch her eye, "But I think that's about to change." He gave Tovi a half smile full of intention.

Her pulse quickened. The implied danger of this man from the mountain intrigued her. Thrilled her. Made her feel alive. Hiding this sudden excitement, she sat beside him and picked flowers from the grass, stealing furtive glances every few seconds. "So, tell me about Mount Damien," she commanded, nodding toward the distant granite walls.

He looked toward the wide, low mountain silhouetted against much larger ones behind it. "We live at the very top. You can't see it from here, but the city is beautiful."

"More beautiful than Adia?"

Calix cocked a condescending eyebrow. "This place isn't even close."

"Amazing that the great Adwin would want to leave the mountain then," she said with disdain.

Calix tilted his head to one side. "So you *do* believe all that Adwin nonsense."

"Of course," Tovi said. "Well, kind of. A little."

"Why?"

"Someone has to be in charge of it all, right?"

"Have you ever met him?"

"No. I haven't found him yet."

"Let me make sure I'm understanding. You believe in an invisible god who's going to pop out of nowhere when he thinks you're good enough to deserve it? Has it ever crossed your mind that it could all be made up? Or that there once was a man named Adwin, but he is long gone now?"

Tovi's eyes narrowed. "I believe there might be a defeated king who has hidden himself so that he doesn't have to take responsibility for what he has done. If he exists, I will find him."

Calix whistled and sat back against his elbows. "King Damien doesn't hide, and he's incredibly powerful," he gushed. Tovi's eyes were drawn to a dark vein in his neck that began to visibly pulse.

He suddenly changed the subject again, giving her a soft, melting look. "You know, Tovi, I bet you don't even know how pretty you are. It was no accident that I was here today. I've seen you many times, and something about you kept drawing me back. Today was the first time I had the courage to come out and speak to you."

Between the warmth of his words and the closeness of his face, Tovi found herself lost and befuddled.

"If it was just that I thought you were pretty, there is a chance that I could have forced myself to move on without approaching you . . . but there was something more. You always look so deeply sad. Why is that?"

"I'm not sad."

"Are you sure?" he prodded.

"*Sad* isn't the word I would use for it."

"How would you describe it then?"

She was silent, not ready to share her secrets with this stranger.

"If I took a stab at it, I would say you feel lonely, not because there is a lack of love in your life, but because there is a lack of *true* love. You are looking for something deeper than they can give you. Your family can't give it to you. Your friends can't. This hidden Adwin definitely can't give it to you. But it's out there, and when you came here this morning, you felt that this love was getting so close that you could feel it."

By the end of this speech, Calix's face was so close to hers that she felt she should back away. Instead, she sat very still, entranced by the danger of their proximity and the way his voice caressed the words.

Tovi had never thought any of those things about romantic love before. In fact, Calix's words weren't true in any way. Yet, they were hypnotic and found a way to connect with her yearning spirit. She whispered, "How did you know?"

"I have felt the same for a very long time," he whispered back. "I'd really like to see you again, but we might have to keep it a secret for a while."

"Why?"

He scratched his head, looking frustrated, and then dropped his hand into his lap. "Your people are afraid of anybody from the mountain. They won't understand our . . . friendship . . . at first, so we will have to be careful."

He jumped to his feet, startling her again. He held out his hand, and she instinctively reached out with her own, allowing him to help her up.

"Well, Tovi, I'd better get going. I'll make sure we see each other again soon." He squeezed her hand and shot her one last brilliant smile before striding along the ridge. Tovi stood speechless.

Before he was out of eyesight, the bushes behind her rustled and Silas stepped out into the clearing. In the distance, Calix turned around. The two men made eye contact, and Tovi's gaze bounced back and forth between them. There seemed to be a spark of recognition, or at least there was something that held their attention. Calix was smiling, but in a dangerous way. Silas had neither a smile nor a scowl. He was just very, very serious.

When Calix turned and disappeared into the forest, Silas looked at Tovi with the same intensity and hard-to-interpret expression that he had given Calix.

Tovi crossed her arms and pursed her lips. She was under no obligation to tell Silas about her new acquaintance. He had no right to tell her who to befriend or how to live her life.

"Are you all right?" he asked.

It wasn't at all what she expected. "That's really what you're going to ask right now?"

"What else would I say?"

"I don't know. Something about him," she said, jerking her head and shoulder toward the place where Calix had made his exit. "Or a lecture about my decisions."

"We have been friends all of our lives. When have I ever lectured you? When have I ever been concerned with anything but your wellbeing?" he asked, undertones of anger slipping through. "If you're feeling guilty over who you spend time with, that's a totally different discussion. All I asked is if you're all right."

"Guilt?" she spat, and walked away from the edge, closer to him, looking him square in the eye. "Guilt? I don't feel any guilt. Why do you feel like you can say things like that to me? I've done nothing wrong."

Silas held her gaze. "You're right, you haven't done anything wrong. And I ask you again: Are you all right?"

"Stop accusing me!"

"I *just* said you haven't done anything wrong," he said, nearly yelling.

"But you, but your tone, but . . . " She let out an aggressive, frustrated growl and stomped her foot. "You just don't understand."

"You cried into my shoulder in this very spot, just yesterday. And today you act as though I have some agenda, some motive, behind my concern for you. What changed between last night and this morning?"

Tovi wanted to cry out, "I don't know! Help me!" Instead, as she always did, she buried her desperation beneath the rubble of her anger and independence. She marched around him, skirting the edge of the cliff, and left him there. She heard him following, but her stubbornness kept her from turning. If he really wanted to continue the conversation, she knew he was more than capable of catching up to her.

When she reached home, she went inside and slammed the half door.

"Well, good morning to you, you bundle of sunshine and rainbows," Ganya greeted. "What happened? Are you all right?"

Tovi had already made her way back to her bedroom and was throwing a few of her belongings into a small satchel. "Why does everyone keep asking me that? I'm fine!"

"Yes, clearly."

Tovi paused long enough to frown at Ganya, who now stood in her doorway, and then continued packing.

"Where are you going?"

Tovi sighed. "I need to get out of here for a few days. I'm going to go search some of those caves that Tali and I found a year or so ago."

"Have you forgotten you promised to help Granny Leora with her berry picking and pie baking for the festival?"

Tovi threw down her bundle and said several nasty words. Ganya bit her lip, but a few chuckles escaped. Tovi was not amused.

"I guess I'll just be gone for the day. I'll be back tonight or tomorrow morning at the latest." Tovi picked up the satchel and left the house, irritated to see Silas waiting on the porch. Before he could say a word, she said, "I'm going to look for Adwin. Don't follow me. I want to be alone."

He seemed like he wanted to say something, but he nodded and remained quiet, a shadow of sadness and exhaustion shrouding his usually-twinkling eyes.

As Tovi ventured into the forest, the vision of the woven trees over the water came back into her mind. She turned completely around, heading southwest, away from the mountains. She, Tali, and Silas had been back to their magical little hideaway many times as youngsters. Even though it had been several years since she last visited, it was easy to find.

The stream that used to meander between the trees had run completely dry, its bed now a dusty, rocky path. She ducked under the lowest branches.

She stood motionless, taking in the beauty that she found. The entire floor of the enclosure—once just water, roots, and mossy banks—was completely covered in the dark blue flowers she had seen at the ridge. There were hundreds clustered together so tightly that she couldn't see the ground. The brief sparkles of sun that used to reflect on the water now danced across the blooms.

She climbed onto one of the branches. She was high enough that she could not reach the flowers, but low enough that she could smell their sweetness and see the details of their orange pollen and green ruffled leaves.

Tovi allowed her mind to roam from question to painful question. Most of it was the same as always, a constant cycle of Tali, parents, Avi, Tali, parents, Avi. This time, however, there was a new part of the mix. Just as she began to despair, she would see Calix's face, and for a moment she would be distracted from it all.

Calix. She thought about his words and his smile. Her heart raced with the excitement and danger of it. What would the other Adians think of it? What about Ganya and Avi? What would Tali think? Her heart constricted, and the cycle began again: Tali, parents, Avi. Tali, parents, Avi.

CHAPTER 10

"You finally talked to her?" Rhaxma asked, her tone a bit too casual, her yellow eyes a bit too severe.

Sitting in one of the chambers in the palace, Calix reclined on the sofa opposite her, his arms behind his head, staring into the distance. He was always the first to arrive for these Council of Masters meetings with His Majesty, so he always had to wait. His punctuality was well known, and he suspected that this was why Rhaxma frequently appeared just a few moments after him. She knew she would have a few minutes of Calix's time to herself.

"Answer me," Rhaxma pouted. "Did you talk to her today?"

Calix turned his head and looked at her. He had done too good of a job with this one. He could see the hunger in her eyes and the carefully-disguised desperation in her actions. He hadn't worked on her in years, yet she still pathetically clung to him and their past. It was he who had made sure the mark of Adoration—a crown—was etched into her back. She had also earned her rose—the mark of Pleasure—in their time together. It was when he took his attention away from her that the heavy chains appeared on her skin, showing she had learned the lesson of Wisdom.

"Yes, I talked to her," he answered, keeping eye contact and monitoring the emotions on Rhaxma's face. Her feelings amused him.

"Did you kiss her?"

"Not yet."

Rhaxma swallowed hard. "Do you love her?"

Calix snorted. "Love? Of course not. It's just part of the game. I intend to win, and I'm getting close."

This seemed to mollify Rhaxma, and a coquettish smile raised the corners of her mouth. She rose and slowly crossed the space between them, and he noticed the way she let her hips sway. What was she after?

She sat on the edge of the sofa next to his outstretched legs and leaned in toward him. "When you are King of Adia, you will need a queen," she said, her face so close that Calix could see the tiny black veins in her eyes. He pushed her away.

Feigning nonchalance, she sat back and crossed her arms. "I suppose I won't tell you what Leeto discovered yesterday."

"Fine, don't tell me."

She narrowed her eyes, letting go of any pretenses. "I have information that will help you win. You need me."

Calix sat up so quickly that Rhaxma didn't have time to react before he grabbed her chin between his thumb and finger, squeezing hard. "I do not need you. If you want to help me, so be it. Tell me your secrets. But don't make the mistake *again* of thinking you can control me with your information. Or your body."

"The heirs are alive. The conquerors in the prophecy," Rhaxma hissed, smiling smugly when Calix's face registered his shock. "And Leeto knows how to find them."

Calix dropped his hand, which had left red imprints on her skin, and thought through the implications of this news. If it was true, Leeto could use this information to gain tremendous leverage. This could not be.

The door swung open, and Eryx, Leeto, BiBi, and Megara entered, stealing Calix's opportunity to ask more questions. That would have to come later.

Rhaxma rose from the sofa and spoke with the other ladies in a corner, occasionally glancing in Calix's direction. Leeto plopped down on the sofa recently vacated by his sister.

"Any news?" Calix asked.

"No, nothing out of the ordinary yet," Leeto said cheerfully, although his eyes had been darting between Calix and the finger marks on his sister's face. "How are you doing with your Adians? Any headway?"

"Just some slow progress, nothing substantial," Calix answered. So this is how they would play it. Neither willing to tell the other how close they were to gaining power and control.

A butler came to usher the group into the throne room. Calix always tried to be first, and he slipped his way to the front of the line. He wanted His Majesty to see his face first, a sign that he was the most loyal of them all.

"What news do you bring from Adia?" King Damien asked from his golden throne, eyeing each as they entered. This time he was flanked by Ajax and Jairus.

The meeting was short. No one gave a report worth noting, and Calix wondered how many of them were hiding something as important as Leeto's secret. The king did not seem at all pleased with the lack of progress, and he informed them that his patience was growing thin.

Calix's mind whirled with thoughts of Princess Helena, whom he grew up calling Lena, and the unnamed baby. If he could collect them for himself, there would be no end to the favor he would receive from His Majesty. He resolved that he must get behind the curtain and learn more about the conquerors.

King Damien rose and led the weapons toward his formal dining room. Calix's brain worked quickly to create a plan. "Jairus," he called, not even bothering with the prince's formal title. They had been boyhood friends—practically brothers. "Could I please speak with you for a moment?"

Blond-haired, violet-eyed Jairus gave a curt nod and stayed in the room rather than following his grandfather. When they were alone, he asked, "What is it?"

"I received some information that I want to share with His Majesty, but I don't want to bother him if it is not true."

Jairus' handsome face looked bored and annoyed. "How am I supposed to help you?"

"If I could take a look at the prophecy behind the curtain, I could check to see if my information is accurate."

"Fine. Guards, let Calix through the curtain." Jairus turned back to Calix. "Anything else?"

"N-no," Calix stuttered, unable to believe how apparently easy this was going to be. Jairus left the room without saying farewell, and the guards parted to allow Calix behind the curtain. He stepped through with disbelief and trepidation. Only royal eyes had ever seen what was behind the throne room wall. But he would be royalty soon enough.

It took a moment for his eyes to adjust to the darkness. He had always believed the curtain hid just a small portion of the throne room's wall, that once the curtain was parted, he would be facing a small expanse, approximately ten feet across. Instead, he was overwhelmed by the long passageway that stretched before him. He glanced along the wall, hoping it would be obvious what he was looking for. He passed many different scenes painted on the stone, but few made sense.

He recognized several portions of the mural as places he had seen on the mountain, including the palace and the courtyard. Various events and activities were taking place in the pictures; some he understood, some he didn't.

He was shocked to see so many of the scenes set in the dirty streets of the Bottom Rung. How could that trashy, dishonorable, and disgusting neighborhood be worthy of space on these sacred walls? There must be something he was missing, for he knew His Majesty would not waste so much of his precious time worrying about the happenings there. Surely there was a different part of the mural that concerned the king.

Throughout it all, in almost every picture, there was a man with sky blue hair and matching eyes. Calix took several minutes to examine this man who seemed like a very important character in the drama. He had seen these odd color traits just twice before—on a man that lived in Adia, and in the mirror when he was a small boy. Before Calix's hair and eyes had turned black, he had light blue hair and perfectly matching eyes. No one knew for sure why colors changed over the course of their lives, but Calix was proud that he had changed to match His Majesty.

Just as there were thousands of people with black hair and eyes, he was sure that these light blue colors could belong to many people as well. But it still gave him the shivers. Each time he looked at this man's painted face, he was sure that it was the Adian that he had seen on several occasions before, and this confirmed for him some theories that had been stewing in his mind. He continued down the wall, growing more and more uncomfortable with each sighting of that man.

There it was. Four warriors atop the mountain, leading a large band of followers. He stepped closer and his brow wrinkled in concentration. This had to be the bit of prophecy that so many spoke of. This had to be the part that concerned His Majesty.

Jairus was one of the four, although his colors were all wrong. Jairus had been born with hair that was half brown and half maroon, with light brown eyes. These were the colors in the mural, and it seemed to be Jairus' face. But, Jairus' colors had changed long ago to match his sister's. When he was only a child, he had taken on Lena's colors, and later his girlfriend, Xanthe, took them on as well. Lena, Jairus, and Xanthe all had lemon-yellow hair with an aqua stripe. Their eyes were purple. However, the mural showed Jairus with his original colors.

Next to Jairus was a woman with yellow hair and violet eyes. Surely this was grown-up Lena. The face did not seem to match Xanthe.

The next form was not someone Calix recognized. She had long wavy brown hair with thick golden streaks and baby blue eyes. The face looked familiar, but he couldn't place it.

His heart jolted and his head spun for a moment when he took a closer look at the final member of the conquering party. No longer did Leeto have the upper hand. Calix had just made a discovery that made Leeto's information seem trivial. There was no denying it—the fourth conqueror was alive. Calix had seen this man before.

A man with navy blue hair and brown eyes.

Tali Tivka.

It was his colors, and it was his face. Adrenaline poured through Calix's body.

What was his connection to the mountain? Why was he there in the painting with Jairus and Lena? Calix looked again at the young woman standing between Tali and Lena. He wiped black sweat from his forehead. He must discover her identity.

Jairus was in the palace. It was believed that Lena was alive, somewhere nearby. Tali was wandering somewhere north of the mountain. But that final girl. Who could she be? Where might she be? If only he could find her, he would be infinitely closer to his ultimate goal—ruling side by side with His Majesty King Damien, sovereign over their neighboring kingdoms.

His mind turned to the current assignment. Mark an Adian, bring her to the mountain, and become king over all Adia. It wouldn't be long. But to achieve this dream, he couldn't be content with merely earning the Adian crown for himself. He had to save the mountain from these rebels, proving himself useful and worthy of His Majesty's utmost trust and confidence.

But first, the assignment from His Majesty. Tovi Tivka was spirited and stubborn, but she wasn't all that different from the women on the mountain. He saw the same softness come over her face as he used his smooth words and smiles. Some of his lines had not gone over well, but it seemed to enhance the challenge. He grinned at the thought of what it would be like to present her to His Majesty, his mark, a pointed crown, clearly emblazoned on her shoulder. His Majesty would be proud. His Majesty would applaud him. His Majesty would want him as an ally for the rest of his life once he proved he could succeed in such a lofty task.

He took a deep breath and began to plan. He must get Tovi to the mountain.

CHAPTER 11

Morning dawned brightly through Tovi's fluttering curtains, but the sunlight did not take away the terrible dream or her need to run to the ridge. As soon as she was out the door, Silas joined her, keeping pace but not getting in her way. They ran in silence as the beautiful landscape whizzed past them.

In the back of Tovi's mind, she hoped Calix would come today. It had been nearly two weeks since his first appearance, and he had found ways to surprise her almost every day. But would he approach her if Silas was with her? She was irritated by her friend's presence and wished he would go away.

When they arrived at the ridge, she made her usual futile search of the panorama. No Tali. Also, no Calix. Instead of sitting down, Tovi turned to Silas. "I want some time by myself."

"You can talk to me about whatever is on your mind."

"Don't patronize me. I want to be alone."

Silas sighed. "Come find me later if you want to talk. You know where I'll be."

As soon as he left, Calix appeared in the clearing. Her heart leapt, but she tried not to show it. Over the last twelve days, she had experienced something completely new and exhilarating. Her cynical nature warred with the simple pleasure of attention. She wanted to stay aloof, but most days spent with him made her turn into something very silly and giddy. It was his eyes, she told herself. Definitely his eyes. Was this what happiness felt like?

He greeted her with a wink. "I have a surprise for you."

"What kind of surprise?" she asked.

"You'll have to come with me to see it." He turned and walked briskly toward the forest, away from Adia. Tovi tried to keep up, her yellow dress and blue hair flying in waves behind her.

"Where are we going?" she called out. Her bare feet pushed into the damp earth of the forest floor, making a strange pattern between Calix's shoe prints.

"That is the surprise! You will know soon enough."

They finally stopped in an area of woods that didn't seem anything but ordinary to Tovi. "We're almost there, but now you have to trust me." He walked behind her and put his hands over her eyes. He led her forward, whispering instructions into her ear. His breath on her cheek tingled. She felt herself moving through tall grasses and noticed the sudden warmth of sun on her skin.

"Are you ready for your surprise?" Calix asked, his mouth still close to her ear. She nodded in response, opening her eyes at the same moment that he lifted his hands.

It was a scene of lavish beauty. Yellow lilies grew on a vine that wound around the fattest tree she had ever seen. More of the blossoms hung from the huge sloping boughs. Purple, pink, and orange butterflies swooped between the blooms. The tree was vibrant, shimmering with energy.

"Do you like it?"

"It's incredible," Tovi whispered.

They walked the rest of the distance toward the trunk of the tree. Large limbs drooped nearly to the ground, and Calix began to climb.

Perched on a branch, sitting side by side with their feet suspended in the air below, they picked up their conversation where it left off two days earlier. They talked and laughed well into the afternoon. He told her stories about his life on the mountain, and his attentive charm brought down her walls and kept her usual coldness disarmed. She shared how much she missed her brother, desperately wanted to know her parents, and feared losing Avi. He listened to every word, offering just the right comments when she would pause. He seemed particularly interested to learn she was not originally from Adia, and he asked several questions about Tali. The butterflies floated lazily by, sometimes landing on their shoulders or knees for a moment before moving on. It was magical.

"I've always known I am lucky to have him," Tovi said, as they discussed what it was like to have a twin brother. "He has always been so good to me, listening to my constant questions, pushing me to get out of my own head. Now, with him gone, I don't know how to feel or what to do."

"That must be terrible," Calix said with concern, brushing a flyaway strand of hair out of Tovi's face. "How has it been for Ganya? Is it hard on her, too?"

"It is hard, but not like it is for me. She trusts Adwin. She thinks we have no need to fear, because Adwin will take care of Tali. She misses him, but it is not the same. Besides, she has other things on her mind."

"Like what?" He cocked his head, intent and interested.

"Avi doesn't have much time left. He's very sick, and I don't think any of us are prepared for life without him. I can't imagine what it's like for her. I have loved him my whole life, but that is only twenty years. Avi and Ganya have spent nearly every day together since they were my age. That's over fifty years. I don't know how she'll go on."

"It sounds like they truly love one another."

"They do. It's beautiful, really."

Calix smiled sweetly. "And it sounds like you really love him, too."

Tovi bit the inside of her cheek and breathed deeply. "I do. No matter how difficult I was or how much I resisted, he always loved me." She smiled despite the tears that were welling, and when she continued, her voice cracked. "When I was a little girl, he did everything a good grandfather would do. He showed me how to fish, read books to me, and taught me how to make a kite. I never agreed to spend time with him at first, but he would ask and prod until I had little choice. And he was so sweet that I always gave in eventually. But my favorite memory is one day after a rainstorm. There was a leak in our roof, and Ganya had put a big clay pot underneath it to collect the drips. Tali was off with Silas somewhere, and I was in my room.

"I saw Avi put a ladder against the house, and I was so curious that I stuck my head out the window to get a better look. He offered to let me help, and I said no, even though I really wanted to. He pretended to get mad. Standing halfway up the ladder, he put his hands on his hips and said, 'Young lady, climb out that window and get your britches over here to help me.' I was shocked. Climb out the window? To be difficult I just walked through the front door. But maybe that was his goal all along."

"Sounds like a smart man."

Tovi nodded. "I loved that day. I helped him patch the roof, and all the while he asked me questions about all that I was learning, my adventures with Tali and Silas, and whatnot. It was one of those days when I knew deep down that someone really loved me and wanted me to be around."

Calix put his arm around her shoulders and hugged her to his side. "I hope this is one of those days, too."

Tovi tried to hide a smile. "I wish we could stay here all day."

"What's stopping us?" Calix asked.

She twisted just enough so she could face him, unintentionally bringing their noses a mere inch from each other. Her breath caught in her throat as she explained, "My cousin, Ganya and Avi's nephew, is getting married." It had never been so hard to form a sentence, or so uncomfortable to maintain eye contact. She moved her gaze down, not realizing at first that she was now staring at his lips, which curved up into a knowing smile.

She watched as his tempting mouth formed the question, "When will it be your turn, Tovi?"

"My turn?"

"Your turn to be happy. When will it be your turn to find the love that Ganya and Avi found with each other?" he murmured, the small space between them heavy with expectation.

Suddenly feeling awkward in this new romantic territory, she summoned the power to break away, turning violently to look out into the sharp patterns of sunlight and blue skies that danced between the branches.

Calix tore a flower from the tree and threw it out into the open. "It just seems so ridiculous that no one in your village thinks you are beautiful."

At first, she thought it was a compliment, but her delight vanished behind a storm of rage. "Excuse me?"

"Don't be stupid," he said, scooting down so that his back was against the trunk and his legs extended out along the limb. "I was trying to tell you that I like you, that I think you're beautiful."

She crossed her arms and looked away. His new position blocked her easiest exit.

"No, really, Tovi. You are beautiful, funny, smart. You deserve to be loved. It's not fair that you are lonely. I think this Adwin of yours is holding out on you."

Her head whipped back toward him. "What is that supposed to mean?"

"If he exists the way you think he might, he could make someone for you. He could send you a partner, someone to love you. He would protect you and provide for you. Instead, Adwin stole your parents, then your brother, and left you to fend for yourself."

"You're not telling me anything new. Get out of my way."

His words circled in her mind throughout her cousin's wedding. She hardly noticed the beautiful decorations or the rows of perfectly aligned chairs. She didn't hear the angelic music. She didn't take in the smiles and general excitement. Instead, she saw visions of yellow lilies and hypnotizing lips that made her angry and lonely at the same time.

When it was over, the bride and groom made their way down the center aisle, waving to the cheering crowd. The sun had completely disappeared, and lanterns full of lightning bugs cast a cheerful, twinkling glow under the trees as everyone stacked chairs and prepared for an evening of celebration. The bride's family filled the buffet tables while several friends tuned their fiddles.

During the first song, Tovi sat and watched the couples swing around the dance floor. As a young girl, this had always been her favorite part. Avi would scoop her up and make a ridiculous scene, whirling and jumping, running into the rest of the couples and pretending it was an accident. Her heart ached with her fear. He wasn't strong enough to come down from the tree to attend the wedding. How much longer did he have left?

The music slowed, and her musings were interrupted by a familiar voice.

"Want to dance?"

Silas took Tovi by the hand and led her into the crowd, placing one palm at the small of her back. Every nerve came to life under its warmth. His other hand lifted hers, her delicate fingers resting perfectly inside his strong ones.

Silas was a good leader. She felt her body move at all the right times, responding to the barely perceptible guidance from the pressure of his hold. Somehow, under the direction of Silas' movements, it seemed natural to turn this way and that, moving her feet in time with the music.

He looked different tonight. Gone were the paint splattered tunics and wrinkled linen pants. He was dressed instead in dark brown trousers with a soft baby blue tunic that matched his eyes. But there was something else—something about the urgency in his expression—that made him seem changed.

They continued to sway slowly around the dance floor. "How are you, Tovi?" he asked softly.

This was so unlike the Silas she knew. Had he seen her with Calix again today? Was he angry that she asked him to leave the ridge? Was he jealous that someone else had spent time with her there, in their special place?

She struggled to find words and awkwardly shifted her eyes to the collar of his shirt, studying it as she responded, "I've been better. There's a lot on my mind."

"Anything you want to talk about?"

Her heart began to race.

"You know you can tell me anything, don't you?" he prodded.

Just as she opened her mouth to respond, the music ended. Silas continued to hold her, giving her the chance to answer his questions. But when she took her hand from his shoulder and looked away, he relinquished his hold. He kissed her other hand and went to mingle with the crowd. Tovi watched him sadly, feeling like she had just barely missed out on something important.

Interrupting her thoughts, she heard someone whisper her name. She turned, looking for whomever was beckoning. All she could see was the tall, dense hedge that formed the natural boundary of the wedding festivities. "Tovi!" she heard again, this time slightly louder than before. She walked toward the bushes, confident that the sound was coming from them.

"Hello? Who's there?" she asked.

"Come around here and see for yourself." Her heart beat out of her chest as she recognized Calix's voice. She ran along the line of the hedge until she came to an opening. She was far enough away from the dancing and celebrating that no one seemed to be watching, and she slipped behind the foliage.

They stood several feet apart, smiling at one another for several breathless moments. Their morning spent together ran through Tovi's mind, and she felt transported back to that beautiful tree bathed in sunlight and the way she felt when she was so close to him. Yes, they had fought. Yes, he infuriated her. But there was something about him that woke a passion inside her. Something about him that was dangerous and wonderful and exciting.

He walked forward and took her in his arms. The music was floating all the way to where they stood. Taking hold of both her wrists, he lifted them so she could clasp her hands behind his neck. He held her close, his feet leading them in slow circles. She had never danced like this before.

"I'm sorry for the way our morning ended," he said.

Tovi stared into his black eyes but didn't say anything. As the last bars of the song sang out into the night, Calix brushed his lips across her cheek, letting them linger there. She had no idea what to do next, but she willed herself not to look away. Before she knew what was happening, Calix stopped dancing, pulled her into a crushing embrace, and leaned down to press his lips against hers.

It wasn't nearly as nice as she thought it would be. She had a hard time breathing as he kissed her, and she wondered if she was doing something wrong.

After a while he eased up, smiling down at Tovi as if they had both just experienced something amazing and wondrous. Tovi grinned back, pleased that Calix had wanted to kiss her, and even more pleased that he was happy. She knew that something was different between them now, and that knowledge gave her more tingles in the pit of her stomach than the kisses had.

Calix held Tovi's hand as they walked to the base of her tree, leaving the wedding festivities behind. He squeezed her fingers, kissed her more gently, and said, "Goodnight. There's a surprise on your window ledge." He winked and backed away with a smile on his face. "See you tomorrow."

Tovi watched him leave and climbed up to the top of the willow. Saying a quick goodnight to Avi, she entered her room and looked for her surprise. It was a glass jar with three butterflies—purple, orange, and pink—resting inside. She knew at once that they had come from their tree.

Sitting on the edge of her bed, she held the cool glass in her hands, noticing how the winged creatures sat on the bottom. Their prison was too small to allow much flying. She crawled over to her window. Setting the jar on the sill, she carefully opened the lid and tilted it to the side, allowing the butterflies to escape into freedom.

They floated up and out on graceful wings, one landing on the top of her hand before taking off into the wide-open night so full of possibilities. She imagined their journey back to their tree and wondered what it looked like in the starlight. She couldn't help smiling.

CHAPTER 12

Just far enough into the darkness to where Tovi could not see, a quick, silent fist slammed the delicate pink butterfly into the side of a tree, crushing it with a fury that was reflected in his deep brown eyes with a little purple star.

CHAPTER 13

"Tovi!" Silas called through the morning mist, his tone strong and serious. She didn't stop. She had to run. She had to see if Tali was out there. She had woken from the dream again and had just reached the ridge.

"Tovi," Silas repeated, getting closer. "You need to come with me. It's Avi."

Numbness fanned out through her body, starting with her heart. Somehow, she failed to instruct her lungs to keep breathing.

"He's still holding on, but just barely."

She couldn't speak, but she nodded just enough to acknowledge she had heard him. They rushed back toward the village while she stared ahead through water-filled eyes, hardly taking in anything around her.

When they arrived at the porch outside of her willow tree, Silas reached for Tovi, putting his hands on both of her shoulders. "You are going to see and hear things that you won't understand. I want you to think about them after this is over. Promise me you will pay attention."

After the numbness that had taken over Tovi on their hurried journey home, the rush of white-hot anger hit her with force. She glared at her old friend, loathing his presence. First her parents. Then her brother. Now Avi would be stolen from her. How dare he demand anything of her?

Shaking his head, Silas said, "Come on. It's time to go in."

"Why are you going in?" she asked, but he was already through the door.

When they entered, there was a general sigh of relief from the Tivka extended family. "I'm so glad you're back," Ganya said to him. "I really don't think he will be with us much longer."

Avi lay in his bed, eyes closed and struggling for air. Ganya sat close by his side, stroking his thin hair and holding his limp hand. There were frail smiles and an unexpected peace on both of their faces.

The rest of the Tivka family crowded the room, packed into every nook they could find. Some of the smaller cousins sat atop the roughly-hewn dressers. Everyone had sad eyes, but they weren't crying. They looked crushed, but no one was wailing.

"Don't worry," Silas said. "He's not going anywhere without me."

Tovi saw the hint of a grin turning the corner of Avi's mouth. Silas smiled, too. What on earth was happening? Where was he going with Silas? Why was Silas there with the family in the first place? Tovi wanted to scream, but she was too confused to know what words to yell.

Silas moved to the head of the bed, placing himself close behind Ganya. He wrapped one arm around her and used his free hand to grasp Avi's shoulder. "Avi, can you hear me?" he asked.

The old man's paper-thin eyelids fluttered open, and he nodded. Silas looked up and addressed the entire group, but his eyes locked on Tovi. "Now listen to me, all of you," he said kindly. Tovi couldn't look away, and Silas' calm presence strangely soothed her, even as her anger and confusion mounted. He continued, "Don't be afraid. I know this is really hard. Keep remembering that everything you have learned is true. There is no reason to fear this next phase of Avi's life."

The emotion in the room thickened. Tovi wanted to close her eyes so she wouldn't have to see what was about to happen, but something in her needed to watch the end.

After an interval that felt like ages but was mere seconds, Silas said, "Avi, it's time."

For a brief moment Tovi caught a glimpse of a much younger and stronger man. Then Avi faded—not just in consciousness, but in actual substance. He shimmered and became nothing but translucent colors before disappearing completely.

Ganya's hand, still cupped as if she was holding Avi's, fell to the bed, and silent streams trickled down her cheeks. Silas wrapped his arms around her, and she turned into his embrace.

Ganya and Avi's siblings joined them and wrapped a protective layer around her. Then came the nieces and nephews, adding another circle of arms and love. They all wept together, including Silas.

Overwhelmed, Tovi began to back slowly out of the room. It seemed as though the walls were closing in, and she felt dangerously close to being crushed by the weight and enormity of death. Just as she picked up her pace, she locked eyes with Silas.

"Tovi!" he called over the sounds of the mourning family. "Tovi!" Every face lifted, some understanding, some questioning.

Her parents. Her brother. Avi. Her parents. Her brother. Avi. Round and round their faces—even those of her parents which she invented in her daydreams—danced through her mind, tormenting her with reminders of her pain. She felt the oppressive need to run, to get away. Then, Silas' urgent blue eyes came to the forefront of her mind, and she remembered what he had said.

Next time, don't do it alone. Next time, run toward me.

"No," she spat aloud, as if the voice had been more than a memory. "No! I won't run toward you, Silas. I don't even know why you are here!" She sprinted from the room, ignoring the shocked looks coming from the Tivkas. She didn't stop until she had wound her way down the stairs and vines and bridges, finally reaching the grass.

She wouldn't have stopped, but she had no choice when she slammed into Silas' chest and was instantly bound by his arms. She struggled against his strength for a moment, then sagged into him, her whole body sobbing and grief-stricken.

"Tovi, talk to me," Silas said quietly.

She felt tired and so breakable. "Why were you in that room?" she asked, begging for understanding.

"Think, Tovi. You know, deep down."

"It doesn't make sense. None of it fits. Why did everyone else think it was right for you to be there? You're just his neighbor." She continued to sob, completely falling apart.

"Come on, Tovi," he coaxed tenderly, loosening his grip. "You're so close."

She wrenched herself from his embrace, leaning back and glaring into his face. Her anger overtook her sadness once more, and she snarled, "For once, just stay out of my life and leave me alone."

She walked away, waves of intense nausea and heartbroken sobs coming and going as memories surfaced of her beloved Avi.

When she reached the ridge for the second time that morning, she walked straight to the edge and let her toes curl over. A small piece of rock crumbled away and fell to the boulders far below. "I hate you, Adwin!" she screamed into the wild, as the wind whipped her navy-blue hair across her face. "First my parents! Then Tali! Now Avi! Where are you? You have to show yourself. You owe me an explanation! I hate you! I hate you! I hate—"

"There you are!" Calix called, coming out of the forest. "I was beginning to think you weren't—" He stopped short. "What's wrong?" He ran toward her, grabbing hold as she nearly lost footing and swayed over the edge. He pulled her in tight against his body.

"Avi," she said, her voice hitching on the second syllable, her throat dry from yelling.

"What happened?"

"He's gone." Her sobbing continued, deep and broken. They stood this way for a long time, his hands skillfully rubbing the tension from her shoulders as her fingers clutched at the back of his shirt.

"I hate him," she declared.

"Who?"

"Adwin. I hate him! He took me from my family. He stole my brother. He's taken Avi from me. Who's next? Ganya?" Her voice broke again. "What's the point of life, if all there is, is one painful goodbye after another? I can't take any more of this."

Calix took hold of Tovi's arms and moved her away from his body, just far enough so she could see his face. There was a strange look in his eyes, and his neck veins pulsed, dark and foreboding. "Come with me," he said.

"What? Where?"

"Back to the mountain. We can leave all this behind and start over. No one should have to go through all that you have endured. Don't you see this place is wicked? Come with me. I can take care of you. I can protect you and won't ever let anyone hurt you. Come with me, Tovi."

She hesitated. "I—I don't know. I guess I need to think about it."

Disappointment clouded Calix's usually handsome features. He untangled himself and walked a few feet away, his back to her as he sulked.

"Calix, I'm sorry," she called after him. "Just give me a day or two to think. I just can't . . . I just . . . There's just been too much today." She angrily swiped at the streams still flowing down her cheeks.

Calix turned to her, a cold light flaring in his black eyes as he spat something dark on the ground. After a few tense moments, he trudged into the woods.

Tovi sank to the ground and rested her forehead on her knees as she balanced precariously on the edge of the ridge. Her weeping returned, convulsing her whole body in overwhelming despair.

Just a few minutes later she heard footsteps approaching through the grass, and she lifted her head hoping that Calix was coming back. Instead, a stranger with orange hair stood before her, and she was terrified and mesmerized by his bright yellow eyes.

CHAPTER 14

A set of soft black eyes belonging to a kind, dimpled face watched through the leaves and vines as the family mourned. It was an accident—she hadn't intended to intrude on such an intimate, sacred rite. Now she couldn't look away, and she struggled to interpret all that she had seen.

Strands of deepest black hair fell into her eyes as she shifted on the branch. She swept it away without thinking and continued to gaze at these strange, wonderful people.

Recently, she had often taken to finding a comfortable branch, high in the trees, where she could watch from a distance. She hadn't yet built up the courage to speak to any of them. She knew her brother had worked on the blue-haired girl, Tovi, and she fully expected him to win the contest. He would do anything for His Majesty, and BiBi loved him so much that she had no desire to work against him and seek her own victory.

BiBi was the newest and least experienced Master on the Council, and she held a dark secret. From the first moment she had spied the Adian people, the treehouses, and the peaceful river, she had been captivated. She returned to these trees over and over again, watching them work and play and fish and laugh.

She couldn't understand the way her heart seemed to explode and contract at the same time when she spied on this totally foreign life. She was curious to be sure, but hungry was probably a better word for it.

That morning she watched as Silas left the treehouse in a rush, followed by a parade of Adians entering the house. Eventually Silas returned with Tovi. BiBi had quietly crawled closer to the bedroom window. She could see a little bit, and she could hear everything. When the sweet old man disappeared, BiBi had to cover her mouth so that she wouldn't gasp aloud and draw attention to herself.

When Tovi burst through the door, BiBi froze in panic. She was so close to the house and easily visible. But, Tovi didn't seem to notice. Silas came out next, and the strangest thing happened.

He made the briefest eye contact with BiBi, and then his head swiveled to his right. His voice rang out, but somehow not from him. His voice, as clear as day, came from below. BiBi looked down, and she could see Silas trying to speak sense into Tovi. "Think, Tovi. You know deep down," she heard him say.

She shook her head violently. Was she dreaming? Silas stood just a few yards from her, and at the same time he was on the ground down below. She heard his voice, but the Silas before her hadn't opened his mouth. Yet.

Then, the Silas in front of her spoke into the woods. He was stern and demanding. "Come face me, Megara. Now."

The foliage shuffled and another weapon emerged. Just like BiBi, Megara had pitch black hair and eyes. But that is where the similarities ended. Megara was so skinny that she looked frail and sickly. The bones of her face protruded at severe angles, and her broad, evil smile looked like a horrible slash across her face.

Silas squared his shoulders toward her, and Megara's smile faltered just a fraction as her eyes narrowed. "What do you want with me?"

"You are not permitted any closer to this home today."

She cackled. "Not permitted? Like you could stop me. This family is ripe and ready for the lessons I could teach them. Death and misery lend themselves quite well to the finer points of Wisdom, don't you think?"

"Go back to the mountain. You are not to come any closer," he said again, his voice staying even.

She laughed again as she took a stride toward the tree house, but she sprang back and howled in pain just a moment later. Her spiteful glee vanished, and her normally dead-white skin reddened just a bit. She pushed her hand forward, and once again she cried out, pulling her hand back in close and cradling it as if it hurt very badly.

She pursed her lips, shot an angry glance toward Silas, and disappeared into the trees.

BiBi's mouth hung slightly open as she watched the exchange. Very little of it made sense to her. But one thing was clear: there was much more to Silas than she realized.

"Sir, do you want me to leave, too?" she asked shyly. Down below, Tovi had run away toward the ridge, and the other Silas was speaking to several Tivka family members and villagers.

The Silas in the trees approached her, putting his hands in his pockets and smiling kindly. "No, BiBi. You can stay. Stay as long as you like." His attention felt like the purest of gold. His voice brought her peace that she didn't understand. "There will come a day in the not-too-distant future when you will not feel safe on the mountain. When that time comes, I want you to remember today and everything you saw here. And I want you to come back. For now, stay and watch, and store these things deep in your memory." And suddenly he was gone.

CHAPTER 15

"Oh my, it looks like something has upset you. I hope you're all right," Leeto gushed. He pulled a handkerchief with a few faded black stains out of his pocket and handed it to Tovi, who wiped the moisture from below her eyes.

"You must be Tovi. I'm Leeto," he said, putting out his heartless hand.

"How do you know my name?"

"How do I know your name?" he spluttered. "Calix is my dearest friend. He's practically my brother. He's told me everything about you. Are you saying that he's *never* mentioned me before?"

"No, I'm sorry."

"Hmmm. Well, I was supposed to meet both of you here today. I've been dying to see this perfect woman he keeps telling me about. And I must say, you are even more beautiful than he described."

She didn't say anything. Rather, she turned back toward the mountains, looking out over the ridge. She didn't feel it was necessary to be hospitable toward a stranger after all that had happened that day.

"Anyway, since he's not here," Leeto continued, his voice implying he wouldn't give up on conversation so easily. "I'll ask the question that's been on my mind the last few days. Do you really love him?"

Her face whipped back toward him. "Of course, I do! What are you implying?"

Leeto looked surprised. "That's wonderful. He was worried that you didn't—that it was more of a curiosity thing, like you were using him just to learn about the mountain. You know, to find out if your brother is there, or maybe even your parents."

Her heart thudded in her ears. "How do you know about my family?"

Leeto ignored her question. "I know Calix, and I know that he has many insecurities," he said. "He was afraid you were using him to get information on your brother. So, what happened to make you so upset?"

"None of your business."

"He asked you to come to the mountain, didn't he?"

"How did you know?"

"It just makes sense."

"How so?"

"He adores you, and you claim to care for him. So the natural thing would be to move to our city. Then the two of you could be together, and you could search for your family. What did you say to him?"

"Again, that's none of your business."

Leeto shook his head slowly and whistled. "Oh, Tovi. This is a mess. I can see both sides. He loves you and wants you to move to the mountain, naturally. You have been through so much since your brother left, and you can't wrap your head around more change. What to do? What to do?" He paused. "You know, Tovi, it's not such a bad idea for you to come to the mountain, even if it's not really about Calix. You will never be happy until you know what happened to your family. This is an excellent opportunity for you. But at the same time, you need to be careful. You'll hurt Calix if he thinks that is your only reason for coming to the mountain, and his feelings are already tender."

Tovi eyed Leeto, trying to discern his trustworthiness. "How would I make this right? I mean, if I were to decide to go with him."

"Well," he said thoughtfully, "you should go back to your village and spend one last night there. Don't make any rash decisions. It would be wise for you to wait for the morning, when you have had plenty of time to think it through. But, in case you decide to leave, you should make all your preparations tonight. Write a nice note to your friends. Tell them that you need a few days to think about all that has happened. Tell them you've gone into the woods to search for Adwin."

"That's a lie."

"You say that like it's a bad thing. Lying is not so terrible, when used wisely. Wouldn't it hurt them if they knew you were leaving?"

That sounded reasonable, but she had an unsettled feeling in the pit of her stomach.

Leeto continued, "Then, once you are well rested, you can wake up and decide if this is really a move you want to make. If you do, come back to this spot. I'll make sure Calix comes back tomorrow, and you can tell him you are ready to leave with him. Tell him how much you love him and that you can't wait to spend forever with him. Whatever you do, do not tell him you spoke to me."

"Why not?"

"It's best if he believes you made this decision on your own. You don't want him to think that you are going only because I said you could look for your family. He needs to think you really are going for his sake. You don't want to hurt him, right?"

After Leeto left, Tovi sat in silence staring across the empty expanse, her mind and heart so confused. She alternated between anxiety over her decision, unsettled discomfort regarding her new orange-haired acquaintance, and broken-hearted sorrow at the memory of Avi. She replayed all the old scenes, tormenting herself with reminders that she would never see him again. Soon enough she wasn't just mourning Avi. She was grieving her brother and parents all over again too. She didn't move all day, allowing the sun to beat down on her as her tears came and went in rhythm with her thoughts.

As the day faded and purple seeped into the sky, Silas came down the path and sat beside her. He didn't say a word for a long time and rested with his hands in his pockets, looking out into the distance, just like her. Birds called to one another from the treetops, and a bee buzzed nearby. The slight wind washed over them every now and then, causing his hair and her hem to flutter. Still, they were quiet.

Finally, Silas spoke. "I know you asked me to leave you alone, but I figured you could use a friend."

She nodded and bit her lip, trying to control the new round of tears that threatened to fall.

"You can talk to me about it. All of it," Silas said.

"That wouldn't do any good. You would just get angry with me."

"No, I won't get mad."

"How could you promise that? It's not just Avi. You don't know the secrets I've been keeping."

"I can help you, Tovi."

Still looking away from him, her eyes glassy and unseeing, she said softly, "I don't think you can."

They didn't exchange any more words but stayed at the ridge until the sun had fallen down the other side of the sky. So many thoughts careened through her mind. Could she really leave her home? Worse than that, did she have the strength to lie to Ganya, to be dishonest?

Would Calix believe that she came to her decision on her own, without the help of Leeto? Would he still offer to take care of her? More than anything else, her pulse quickened at the thought of finding Tali or clues about her parents.

Eventually Tovi and Silas got up to leave, and their slow pace made the silent journey home last more than an hour. Silas stayed silent by her side the entire way. When they finally glimpsed the village of tree houses, the pain of the morning crashed over her again.

There was a tradition in Adia, started long ago, to honor loved ones who had faded into their great adventure. The mourning family would put a large candle on the front porch of their home. Any Adians who wished to honor the dead would light their own smaller candles from the flame and leave them to burn in jars all night.

The sky was dark around the cluster of trees, but the whole village was lit with the soft glow from the many lives impacted by Avi Tivka. The individual flames seemed to tell stories as Tovi climbed past them, stories of wisdom and courage and love held inside those glowing jars.

She approached the big candle on her porch, which was dripping wax down its cylindrical sides. She picked up a small candle from a nearby pile and held the wick to the flame, slowly turning it and allowing it to light as she stared at the flickering brightness. Silas lit his own candle and held it in one hand while putting his other arm around Tovi. They stood like this for a while, watching the wicks lengthen and curl.

Then, he leaned down and kissed her forehead. "I love you, Tovi. I'm here for you. Always."

She nodded, pulled away from his embrace, and walked into the cottage.

She could tell Ganya was already asleep when she entered the house. Everything was quiet, and the only light was from the candles streaming through the windows. A note lay on the kitchen table in Ganya's curvy writing:

Goodnight, Tovi dear.

I love you very much and hope you had

a meaningful time at the ridge.

Tell me all about it in the morning.

Love, Ganya

The morning! For the few minutes since lighting her candle, she had forgotten what might happen in the morning. She could be leaving Adia and all that she knew. On top of everything else she experienced that day she didn't think she could take any more pain.

She took a deep breath and tried to think logically.

Her deepest desire: to find Tali.

Her only chance of searching the mountain for him: Be led through the mysterious cloud and into the infamous city by Calix.

How to make that happen: Pretend to go with Calix for Calix's sake. That way she would have a place to stay and something to eat during her search. She had no other means of providing for herself once she was on the mountain.

It was decided. All that was left was to find a way to keep Ganya and Silas from worrying about her during the journey. She pulled out a piece of scrap paper and wrote:

Gone to spend a few weeks in the forest to look for Adwin.

I love you with all my heart, Tovi

She felt a stabbing sensation slice into the back of her shoulder. She yelped in surprise. Rubbing at the tender spot, she wondered if the stress of the day was enough to cause such a physical reaction. Too tired to do anything else, she tumbled into the warm pile of fluffy blankets without undressing. Despite all that was on her mind and the pain in her shoulder, she quickly fell into a deep sleep.

CHAPTER 16

Eryx had to work doubly hard to stay hidden in the trees with so much light coming from the candles on each porch. He had watched over Tovi all day, from her morning run to Avi's death to her interactions with Calix, Leeto, and Silas. Now he sat just above the Tivka cottage waiting for any stirrings of his enemies. No one else would harm her tonight.

It was very late, but the Tivka porch was not empty. Silas sat in a rocking chair next to Ganya.

"You could have let yourself in and made yourself at home," Ganya told her guest.

"I didn't want to disturb you while you were finding some rest." Silas rocked back and forth, looking at the old woman. "How are you doing? The first night of widowhood is surely one of the hardest."

She nodded slowly, her eyes unfocused and full of sorrow. She closed them for a moment. "Is he all right? Does he like it there?" she asked.

"You know I won't tell you much," he said, his voice more tender and kinder than anything Eryx had heard in years. "But yes, he does. He has acclimated quickly to his old legs."

Ganya stared at her candle for a while, watching the glittering flame as it held its vigil. Silas' hand patted hers in rhythm with the rocking of his chair. Somewhere in the distance cicadas sang, leaves rustled, and a family of owls fluttered into flight.

"I'm worried about Tovi," Ganya said. "She has not been herself, and the way she reacted today makes me fear that there is something terribly wrong."

"You have always been very perceptive, Ganya. Something is very wrong. Tovi has been speaking with two men from Mount Damien, and there has been a third watching her for some time."

Eryx's eyes grew large and he leaned forward to listen more closely.

"Men from Mount Damien?" Ganya gasped. "How could that be?"

"One of them in particular has been meeting her at the ridge. His name is Calix. He hasn't completely succeeded, thanks to her stubbornness. But he *has* strengthened her doubt and introduced some dangerous thoughts."

"What about the other two? Have they had a hand in this?"

"One of them spoke to her for the first time today. Leeto said very little, but those few minutes were horribly potent. While Calix set the groundwork, Leeto seems to have dealt the biggest blow." Silas paused for a moment. "That's not all."

"What more could there be?" Ganya's voice was tinged with pain.

"We might lose her."

"Lose her? Surely, she is not going to die," Ganya gasped.

"No, at least not yet. But she plans on leaving Adia in the morning. Once she is on Mount Damien, there is no end to the danger she will face."

"Leave Adia? Leave everything she has ever known? For what?"

"She is miserable, dreading leaving you. She is so afraid to hurt you, to cause you more heartache, but I'm afraid she has been convinced that leaving here is her best chance to find her parents and Tali. She has changed in these last few days. She stopped looking for me. I have left so many clues for her to find, and many of them have remained undiscovered," Silas said, picking at a yellow streak of paint on his hand. "Calix has even used some of them against me."

"Isn't there something you can do to stop her?"

"You know my options are limitless. But I won't do it."

"Why?" Ganya wailed.

"For the same reason I left the mountain," Silas said urgently. Eryx detected frustration, a feeling he knew well. "For the same reason I did not command any of you to follow me here."

They were silent for a long time, both deep in thought, until Ganya's brow wrinkled in concentration. "Didn't you say that there were three men here?"

"Yes, I did."

"Who is the third?"

"His name is Eryx."

Eryx's pulse thudded in his ears. Silas knew his name, and for the briefest moment, he thought he saw Silas' eyes glance in his hidden direction.

"He has been watching Tovi for the last six months, but he has never attempted to speak with her."

"Do you know his thoughts the way you know ours?"

"Yes, but it would do you no good to hear them. Go back inside and I will give you some rest. I have some work to do before morning." He rose slowly, bending over to kiss her on the cheek.

Eryx watched Silas leave Ganya's porch and silently followed him up to his cottage, spying through the open door as the painter mixed several jewel tones on a palette and used his right hand to sweep his messy dark hair out of his face.

He set to work, first using a broad brush to stroke green paint into basic stems and leaves. He did the same with large, strange shapes created out of ruby and topaz. He bent close to his work, examining every minute detail. He worked with painstaking precision, every slash of color finding purpose as the masterpiece took form.

Several times Eryx came close to barging in, or at least banging on the door frame. He knew he should get this man's attention. If there was any hope of keeping Tovi safe, this was it. But he feared that his usual violence and threats wouldn't do the trick.

With a few flourishes, Silas added golden swirls to the deep red petals and put down his brushes. He mixed new colors and turned to a different empty space on the wall. Eryx watched Silas work all night. As the hours of darkness dwindled and the first signs of dawn crept over the horizon, he put the finishing touches on other projects.

After Silas rinsed out his brushes, Eryx stepped back into the shadows. Silas climbed down his tree and started making his way across a wide limb that served as a bridge between willows. Eryx followed silently. About halfway across the expanse, Silas abruptly stopped. There was a slight smile on his face as he turned around, making pointed eye contact with Eryx through the thick foliage.

"If you have something to say, by all means, say it," he called.

Eryx parted the leaves and stepped forward. "Aren't you going to stop her?" he growled.

"No, Eryx, I'm not."

"How do you know my name?" Eryx asked fiercely.

"I know everyone's name," Silas answered, matching Eryx's combative tone. "Do you know mine?"

"Yes," Eryx said through clenched teeth.

Silas' face flashed with intensity. "Tell me who you think I am."

"You're Adwin, but now you go by Silas. You used to rule over the mountain, but you left us. You claim to love people, but that's a lie."

"Why do you say that?" Silas asked, suddenly gentle.

"You would stop her if you really loved her," he growled, pointing toward Tovi's window. "You wouldn't let her leave. You would have protected her from us." He jabbed his finger into his own chest.

"I will never cage my creatures, even at the risk of losing them. When I designed them, I gave them wings in order for them to soar and experience the rush of the wind. Chaining them to the ground would be far crueler than permitting a test of their freedom."

Eryx snarled and looked away, frustrated tension building in the muscles of his jaw. Without warning, he turned and slammed his fist into the side of a nearby tree, shattering the bark and leaving a deep hollow in the wood. "Those words are useless," he said, taking the last few steps between them. Now they were face to face. "None of that matters. She's a person! Who cares if a bird gets snatched out of the air? No one will ever know the difference. But Tovi . . . " He couldn't finish the sentence, overwhelmed by images of a different kind of predator.

"Why do you care?"

Rage ripped through the sinews of Eryx's body again, shaking him as he attempted to harness the furious power. He breathed raggedly and grabbed hold of two limbs to steady himself. Two of his older scars—one under his right eye and the other along his left shoulder—tore open, and he could feel the blood and a thick black sap ooze slowly through his shirt. "I have a better question," he said through gritted teeth. "Why *don't* you care, Adwin?"

"I do care. I love Tovi." Silas' voice remained even, his eyes fiery and firm. "And whether or not you choose to believe me, I want a better life for you."

Eryx glared and clenched his jaw, causing the skin of his cheeks and forehead to shift slightly. A better life. How could there be value in any life? There was no escaping this existence, this life of a Master. A weapon.

He stormed away, shaking the trees with his heavy footfalls and trying to undo the hope inflicted by Silas' words.

CHAPTER 17

In the soft light of early morning, Tovi crept outside. She stood for a moment, her shaking hand still on the door.

"Good morning, Tovi. Where are you headed?"

Tovi gasped, and her hand flew to her heart. Silas was sitting against the railing of her porch, his legs stretched out in front of him like he had been there for a while.

"I'm just going out to the forest for a few days. I'm going to look for Adwin . . . " Tovi faltered, grimacing and rolling her shoulder. Sorrow filled her heart as she realized this was all the goodbye she could give her best friend.

Silas stood, and she folded herself into his arms, trying to memorize how it felt. He kissed her hair and said, "I don't want you to go."

She pulled back and looked in his eyes, those sparkling blue eyes that looked so bereaved. Did he know? How could he? "I'll be back soon," she said, another stab slicing across the skin of her shoulder.

"Just remember that I love you. No matter what happens out there, I'm always here for you. You can turn around at any time."

She nodded, still unsure if he was talking about her false hike into the woods or the real journey to the mountain. Surely there was no way he could know.

She hugged him again and began to walk away.

He called after her. "Do you want me to come with you?"

She pretended not to hear.

When she came to the ridge, Calix was standing nearby holding a large bouquet. Each flower's stem seemed twisted and shredded, as if it had been torn—not picked.

The moment he spotted Tovi, he ran to meet her. He wrapped his arms tightly around her waist, hiding his face against her neck and murmuring apologies and promises. "I was so worried you wouldn't come. I was awake all night. I'm so sorry for the way I acted yesterday. I will *never* get angry again. I'm so sorry, Tovi. I never should have suggested it, especially with all you are going through."

He pulled away, showing her the flowers in his hand. "These are for you."

She ran a finger over a deep red one with golden swirls.

"They are beautiful, Calix. Thank you," she said, standing on her toes to kiss him. Then she laced her fingers through his. "I came here this morning to tell you that I changed my mind. I'm ready to go with you."

His mouth hung open for just the briefest of moments. He watched her shift her shoulder uncomfortably, and his mood changed all at once. He swooped her up in his arms again, this time lifting her off her feet and twirling her around.

It took them the rest of the morning to reach the base of Mount Damien. Tovi had been to the foot of the granite giant many times in her adventures with Tali, but they had never attempted to climb through the cloud. She had always been told it would be dangerous to do so, and her imagination had created all sorts of pictures of what that could mean. Were the legends of instant death true? What about the stories of blindness and irreversible damage?

But Calix and Leeto had both made it through the cloud, so there must be a way.

They were quiet most of the way. Calix seemed determined to reach their destination quickly, and Tovi's mind kept wandering back to Ganya, Silas, and the houses in the treetops. How long would it take them to realize she was gone? Would they ever forgive her?

Each time she caught herself asking these questions, she forced herself to refocus on the mission at hand. Go to the mountain. Search for Tali. Maybe even find her parents.

Just when they should have begun the trek up the gradual slopes, Calix reached for her hand and pulled her toward a boulder at least twenty feet tall.

That was when she spotted it: a large, unravelling indigo flower with orange pollen. Her mind travelled back to that morning not so very long ago when she had first seen another just like it. Silas' face flashed before her eyes. She had shared that moment with him.

She sighed, homesick and tired.

Behind the boulder was a path, barely distinguishable in the dusty rocks. Tovi's feet objected to the sharp gravel, but she didn't complain. After a few challenging minutes of slowly navigating this trail, they came to the mouth of a large cave. Her pulse quickened. She and Tali had never found this cave before. Her mind raced with all the possibilities before her. They weren't even above the cloud yet, and Calix had already brought her to a new, unexplored place.

But all thought of her mission faded to nothing when she stepped inside. She was overwhelmed by totally foreign sights and sounds.

She and Calix stood on a terrace. What seemed to be a large cave from the outside was really a gaping entrance into what appeared to be the hollowed inside of the entire mountain. It was dark, but there were burning torches at regular intervals, spiraling up the dirty rock walls that grew closer together as she looked up. Four massive stone columns had been left to support the mountain. Each was as wide as her entire house back in Adia, and they reached up what must have been several thousand feet. She couldn't see the top.

When she finally tore her eyes away from the heights, she looked down. The hollow stretched below her as well, the columns reaching down another fifty feet. At the bottom, hundreds of tattered and dirty workers teemed and moved like a restless ant hill. With pickaxes, they cracked the floor. Someone else would come and scoop the rock into large metal carts big enough for several people to fit inside. When a basket was full, a worker tugged on a rope. Somewhere in the endless heights, a pulley system sprang to life, lifting the basket into the unknown.

Tovi was awestruck.

Calix put his arm around her shoulder and pulled her close to his side. "Amazing, isn't it? This is all the work of His Majesty. Everything we need comes from this mountain. Many materials and our food come from the outside, but gold and granite are on the inside."

Tovi nodded, but she wasn't really paying attention. She was looking at the faces of the workers. What if Tali was down there?

She noticed that one worker seemed to be in charge. A woman with her hair wrapped in a dirty cloth and her face smudged with grime was calling out instructions and walking among the rubble. As Tovi stared, the woman turned in her direction, meeting her eyes across the distance.

"Let's find an empty basket," Calix said. "The ride is a lot of fun. You're going to love it." He noticed her rubbing her goose-bumped arms. "And it's much warmer once you're outside above the clouds. It's a completely different world up there."

He lifted her into one of the empty metal containers and told her to be careful not to touch the sides unless she wanted to get dirt all over her clothing. When both were inside, he tugged on the attached rope, and the basket flew into the air. Tovi had to grab hold of Calix to keep from falling.

He laughed. "Sorry, I should have warned you about that."

Tovi's stomach lurched as they swayed and rose past torch after torch. It was the most unpleasant sensation she had ever experienced. When they were still several hundred feet from the ceiling—a giant, flat expanse supported by the four columns—the basket stopped unceremoniously. A worker used a long metal hook to pull them onto a large stone shelf where they disembarked.

They were surrounded by full metal baskets, and she noticed for the first time that they were on wheels. Workers pulled the baskets to long tables, where more people were busy sorting the rubble into piles.

Calix took her hand and pulled her through the chaos. Bright sunlight poured through an archway, and she had to blink many times as she stepped into balmy air heavy with heat. Tovi stopped in awe once more.

CHAPTER 18

Ganya rarely slept in, and the brightness of the sun through the willow leaves seemed almost unnatural by the time she opened her eyes. She moved and stretched beneath the covers, enjoying that perfect warmth of morning blankets.

And then she remembered.

She turned on her side and looked at Avi's pillow. She didn't cry. She just stared for a very long time. While her eyes remained still, her mind replayed his disappearance over and over again. She wished she could be happy for him. But for now, her heart ached.

She heard a few clanks of pots and pans followed by the sizzle and smell of bacon. *Good. My worries for Tovi were unfounded. She is still here.*

It took great effort to pull back the blankets and put her feet in the slippers beside her bed. With one last great sigh, she forced herself to stand and shuffle into the kitchen. It was time to put her sorrow aside and go take care of Tovi.

But it wasn't Tovi in her kitchen. The last person she ever would have expected was tending to the bacon on the stove.

His dark blue hair had grown long, and he had it tied on top of his head. He had never been able to grow much of a beard, and his stubble was patchy and unkempt. As soon as he saw Ganya he dropped the spatula and closed the distance between them with just two strides.

"Tali, my boy," she cried, wrapping her arms around his waist and squeezing. Her cheek rested against his chest. "You're home."

"Not for long. I have more work to do, but Silas told me to take a break for a short visit. I am sorry I wasn't here yesterday," he said with a hitch in his voice that made him sound much younger than his twenty years. "I didn't get to say goodbye. I cannot believe I didn't get to say goodbye. I didn't get to tell him thank you or that I loved him."

"He knew you loved him," Ganya replied tenderly. "And he was so proud that you were out there, on a mission for Silas." She had never seen this much emotion from him. Part of her was distressed by his pain, but the other part of her was relieved he was letting it out. He had never been one to let on that he was hurting. In fact, sometimes Ganya worried that his insatiable desire for adventure was his heart's way of burying pain and heartache. It had always been easier for him to run off to the mountains rather than put words to the tragedies and hard times of his life.

Tali shook himself and dried the wetness from his face with a sudden swipe of the back of his arm. He went to the stove and turned the bacon.

"What did Tovi think when she saw you?" Ganya asked. "And where is she?"

Tali took his time flipping the last piece. He wiped his hands on a dish cloth and picked up a folded piece of paper from the counter.

He approached Ganya slowly, and Tali's wrinkled brow told her that something was very wrong.

"She's gone, Ganya," he said, handing her Tovi's note.

Ganya held it with trembling fingers, but she kept her composure as she read. She wasn't surprised by the lies, but they compounded her grief. How could she take any more?

“That’s the real reason why Silas sent me home for a bit. He didn’t want you to be alone when you found out,” Tali said with a tired, apologetic smile. “He would have been here himself, but he told me you’d rather be with me than him right now.”

Ganya returned his less-than-half-hearted grin. She had loved Tovi and Tali since the moment she first held them, wrapped in blankets and crying from being jostled in the night. So much had changed in the last twenty years, but her love had only grown. Now, after reading the note, she ached, but she really wasn’t all that shocked by Tovi’s decision. Ganya willed her heart and mind to turn toward this young man. She rarely had time with him these days, and she refused to let her sadness for Tovi steal the gift of her moments with Tali. She said a silent prayer that she could focus, even if just for a few minutes. Her grief for Avi and Tovi needed to wait.

“Silas is right. I can talk to him any time. It’s you I’ve been missing. Bring that bacon out on the porch. I want to hear everything.”

CHAPTER 19

Tovi tried to take in the mass of tall, angular buildings climbing up to the plateau at the top of the mountain. They were built directly on the ground and stretched several stories into the sky. How could this be safe? Were they not afraid of floods here?

She looked behind her, but the clouds blocked any view of home. It was strange to think she was standing on the squat mountain she had seen so often from the other side of the ridge.

The soles of Tovi's feet discovered the smooth stones of a cobbled street. They were warm and soothing. They came around a curve, and she was able to see far down a narrow street lined with buildings, all almost as tall as the trees back home. They were gray and had small windows climbing their facades. Dark railings seemed to hold the buildings together. Skinny children played in the streets and dug through piles of trash. There was an odd smell, too—something completely new and unpleasant.

Crowds of people rushed along the street, all wearing varying hues of gray. Vendors called out, advertising their wares. Laughter erupted from one building, followed by the crash of breaking glass. Tovi searched each face for any sign of Tali. Many stared back, and she was suddenly very aware of her bright yellow dress and how it stood out among all the gray.

"Sorry you have to see all of this," Calix said as he pulled her further into the city. "This is the Bottom Rung. There won't be any need for you to come back here. It gets better as we go further up."

They continued winding through alleyways, and Tovi noticed that the neighborhoods gradually became cleaner and less rowdy. An arched tunnel led them into an enormous stone-paved square. She realized that this flat expanse was the very peak of the mountain, as there was nowhere left to climb. The massive area was surrounded by towering buildings, and the entire side opposite the tunnel was taken up by a palace unlike anything Tovi had ever seen. The edifice appeared to be made of golden brick, and there were endless layers of towers and turrets.

"This is the courtyard. It's where people gather for important events. I live over there," Calix said, pointing to a line of huge homes squeezed together along one side of the square and leading Tovi in that direction.

Peeking inside windows as they walked, Tovi saw elegant women in long, silver dresses with strings of sparkling stones around their necks and gloved wrists. She noticed that each of the garments was nearly the same, draping fabric around the women's bodies and exposing their bare backs which were covered in dark designs. The men wore fancy gray trousers of varying hues, gray gloves, and crisp white shirts with large holes cut out of the back, revealing the same ring of black marks.

"Calix, what are those pictures on their backs?"

"They are marks of honor. You will have all of them eventually, too."

This answer did nothing to help her understand, but she was too distracted by the newness around her to bother asking more questions.

As they reached the steps to his house, he turned to her eagerly. "I know the last few days have been really difficult for you, but there's one more thing I'd like to do before we relax and get you settled in. Are you up for it?"

Her feet hurt, her back ached, and she desperately wanted to crawl into a comfortable bed for a nice long nap. "Of course," she said, as another pain stabbed her shoulder.

"We are gathering across the courtyard to watch the fight. You don't even know what that is, but you'll love it. Let's freshen up a bit, and I'll take you to meet King Damien. You can borrow something from my sister's closet."

He had a sister.

She was stunned.

What else didn't she know about this man? She had just given up everything she knew to follow him here. What had she done?

She didn't have time to think thoroughly about her discovery because they had just entered Calix's house. Her hands ran over the furniture upholstered in materials softer than anything she had ever felt. She passed floor-to-ceiling windows surrounded by thick, rich drapes tied back with golden cords. There were gilded mirrors and marble statues, ornate candle holders, and elaborate tapestries. Everything was extravagant.

Calix called someone's name, and a girl with dark hair and eyes—just like his—appeared wearing a stiff gray dress. It was knee-length and had long sleeves that buttoned over her gray gloves. "Cora, please take Tovi and find something suitable for her to wear. Please be quick."

Cora nodded politely and led Tovi up a flight of wide, curving marble steps. Her otherwise modest dress had a large circle cut neatly out of the back, revealing the same marks Tovi had seen through the windows of the other houses.

She looked at them closely as she followed the girl into a large bedroom. It was an intricate design. Or, more accurately, it was an intricate system of small designs, almost like a wreath made of separate symbols. Cora's was not complete, however. It started on her right shoulder and curved down toward the base of her spine. The one at the top was a set of unbalanced scales. Moving clockwise, there was a rose, its stem covered in menacing thorns, and then a pointy crown. The details in each of the three designs were so exquisite that Tovi didn't watch where she was going. She just wanted to examine the fine lines and perfect shading.

Cora walked straight to a tall mahogany wardrobe that opened to reveal gowns of every gray from lightest silver to darkest charcoal. She set to work, first removing Tovi's homemade clothes and making Tovi blush. Cora replaced them with soft and flowing silk. It was strange. Even though she was wrapped in more fabric than before, she felt shockingly exposed.

As Cora selected long strands of beads from a collection hanging inside the wardrobe, Tovi tried to strike up a conversation. "I didn't know Calix had a sister. It's nice to meet you."

"Oh, no, miss," she said, not looking up from her task. "I work here. I normally tend to his sister, Miss BiBi."

Working in someone else's home? What did that even mean? Tovi filed it away in her mind, telling herself she would remember to ask Calix about it later. The list of questions was growing with every passing minute.

When Cora was finished dressing Tovi, she went to fetch Calix. Tovi was left alone to wait for his arrival. She saw her reflection in a long mirror, and she wondered what Ganya would think to see her in all this splendor, with gloves up to her elbows and her hair piled and pinned on top of her head. Her heart shuddered painfully as she thought about Ganya's smile and how she would probably say, "My goodness, don't you look scrumptious!"

There was a soft tap on the door, and Calix entered. He had changed into gray pants and a white shirt like those she had seen through the windows. The shadow was cleanly shaven off his cheeks, and somehow, he looked more severe than before. Severe and dangerous and completely entrancing.

Calix stopped just inside the door, buttoning his gray gloves and looking at her, starting with her hair and traveling all the way to the floor. When their eyes met again, he smiled and declared softly, "You are stunning, Tovi."

Her confidence growing, she returned his grin and spun around for him to get a better look.

His adoration swelled for a moment, only to freeze in a look of confusion turned to horror. He took long strides toward her, grasping her shoulders and turning her to face away from him.

"No," he muttered. Then louder, "No."

Calix jerked her around to face him again. With those black eyes mere inches from hers and his fingers digging painfully into her shoulders, he bellowed, "When did you meet him?"

"You're hurting me!"

He slapped her hard across the face. "Leeto. When did you meet Leeto?"

Stunned from the blow and the sudden rusty taste of blood in her mouth, she gritted her teeth. "How dare you strike me?"

Calix grabbed her wrists and yanked her toward the massive bathroom attached to the room. All four walls, plus the floor and ceiling, were made of mirror, and he pulled her into the very center.

Exponential reflections surrounded her at every angle as she fought against his hold.

"Look at your back," he ordered, letting her go.

In defiance, she stood still, staring at him. A million thoughts raced through her mind, and she couldn't make sense of what was happening.

"Do what I say," he growled, wrenching her arm once more and backing her closer to one of the mirrored walls. With one hand acting as manacle on her wrist, he used the other to force her chin over her shoulder.

She froze, looking at the black mark branded on her shoulder, exactly where her pain had begun the previous night.

"My mark is a crown. That," he said, jabbing at the hissing snake, "is Leeto's mark." His voice had become a dangerous snarl, and the veins in his neck throbbed with darkness. He pushed her away, and she stumbled in her foolish high heels. "That snake means you are worthless to me. Worthless!"

CHAPTER 20

As soon as he witnessed Calix's moment of discovery, Leeto sank back on the balcony, ensuring that he wouldn't be seen. He climbed over a railing and dropped to the floor below, slinking down to the courtyard as quickly as possible.

It worked. It had actually worked. Seeing the snake on her shoulder was the greatest triumph of his life, at least thus far.

He hastened toward the palace intent on finding His Majesty, announcing his victory, and going into hiding until Calix had time to calm down. He would stay close enough to protect his family should Eryx make good on his threats, but otherwise he would lie low, making plans for his future schemes that centered around Tali Tivka. Phase one was complete. Time to move on to phase two.

There was a great swell of people crushing into the courtyard. Of course. Today was the fight. Eryx would be getting in the ring for the first time in years. That would buy him some time, especially if Eryx were to lose.

He entered the palace and asked the butler for an immediate audience with King Damien. After a few moments of waiting, he was led to the throne room. King Damien was alone except his guards.

"I have done it, Your Majesty. I have completed the task."

Damien stared at Leeto, not saying a word.

"She's here, an Adian. She is in Calix's house right now. The snake is on her back, clear as day."

Damien brought his gloved fingers together in front of his face in contemplation. "Explain yourself. Who is she? Why is she with Calix?"

"Her name is Tovi. Calix and I both met her in Adia, but at different times. Calix was working too slowly, and I saw a good opportunity to deliver an Adian into your hands right away. I taught her Control. She used it brilliantly, I must say. I think he thought it was Adoration, but it's my snake on her shoulder, not his crown. I completed the task. I won."

"I'm sorry to tell you, Leeto, but I have changed my mind on the parameters of this task. I am no longer content with an Adian merely being here on the mountain. To hear the new rules, come to the next meeting when I summon the Council. You are still in the running, but I am not convinced we have a winner yet."

Leeto stared at the king, wide-eyed and quiet. He had been fooled. King Damien was the ultimate master of Control, and he had wielded it against the weapons. He should have seen through the reward. King Damien would never give up land or wealth or power.

Without saying goodbye, he turned on his heel and left the palace with his head held high. He went home long enough to pack a small satchel and then rushed out of the city. The idea of finding his own way to power raised his spirits. He didn't need to win a contest for His Majesty. He could do it all by himself. He would learn what task Tali was up to for Adwin. Then he would use that information to take over the mountain. He couldn't wait to force Damien to look upon one of his former weapons sitting on his old throne.

He scurried through the Bottom Rung and went straight to the mines. He hopped into one of the large metal baskets and rode down to the bottom. If he turned to the southwest, there was an arch that would lead him out near Adia. Instead, he turned north, following the large stone terrace to another arch. This one would eventually take him out in the dense area of forest in the foothills.

Hidden in the depths of this woods was a cluster of boulders that overshadowed a cave. This cave held his biggest secret. He hadn't even told his dear sister about it. It was the exact cave where Tali Tivka was last reported to be seen.

When he reached the right place, he climbed behind a giant fallen tree and stealthily entered the mouth of a small cave. There was hay on the ground as if someone had been sleeping there regularly, and the charred remains of a fire looked as if it had been cold for only a day or so. There was a small pile of edible plants next to it, along with a small knife and black kettle. *Good, good. He didn't pack up for good. He'll be back.*

Leeto went back outside and looked all around him. He spotted a tree with a wide limb that would be perfect for a long stake out. He climbed, settled in, and waited for Tali to return.

He knew his small body and unpracticed muscles would be no match for Tali Tivka, but he had a plan.

CHAPTER 21

Tovi sat on the edge of the canopied bed unbuckling her shoes and trying to fathom this turn of events. Light streamed in through large arched windows that extended from the floor to the top of the vaulted ceiling. She had no idea where Calix went or how he would behave when he returned. What would she do if he kicked her out? The only other person she knew on the mountain was Leeto, and she had met him only once. Would he take her in? Probably not, considering he claimed to be Calix's close friend.

She wondered if it was too late to go home. Could she decipher the maze of streets and get to the mines? Would they allow her to ride down to the exit? Or, would she be better off risking a trip through the cloud, despite the legends and stories?

The door opened, and Tovi froze. She clutched her removed shoe a little tighter, wondering if it would work as a weapon.

It wasn't Calix. A girl about Tovi's age poked her head inside the room. She had a kind face with dimples and perfectly straight, shiny black hair framing round black eyes. "May I come in?" she asked gently.

Tovi nodded.

"I'm BiBi, Calix's sister. I know you've had a long day already, but we've got a lot of work to do before you are presentable. We'd better get going." She looked Tovi up and down with an expression of friendly sympathy.

"Before I'm presentable? For what?"

"To meet His Majesty. We've got less than an hour before the fight."

"The fight?"

"Just get in here," BiBi said with a laugh, pointing to the mirrored bathroom.

Tovi followed BiBi and took a closer look at her marks. BiBi's back had the same hissing snake, along with a pointed crown, thorny rose, tipped scales, sinister flames, a sharply-cut diamond, and a coil of thick chains, all surrounding a large menacing heart.

"First things first, we need to get you bathed. I can't believe Calix was going to take you out like this." She called for Cora to draw water in the large tub and instructed Tovi to sit in it while the servant used a large sponge and pungent soaps. All the while, BiBi sat on the edge of the bath, bouncing one foot and reciting facts she thought Tovi should know.

"See my back?" she asked, turning just enough for Tovi to see the now familiar symbols. "Each of these marks is very important to His Majesty. They symbolize something that he wants us to learn. They are like little badges of honor. Is this making any sense?"

"A little."

"Good." BiBi smiled, showing her dimples. "We earn each symbol as we learn from the people around us, but some people have more influence. They are better at teaching than others. See this one?" she asked, indicating a diamond resting on what looked to be a lush velvet pillow, its hard facets meticulously detailed on her skin. "I have been teaching Prosperity since I was a little girl."

Cora was now soothing Tovi's aching feet with lotion as thick as butter. "Once you have all of your marks, His Majesty will watch you closely to see what kind of influence you have on others. If you prove yourself to be good at helping others, he will name you a teacher. If you prove yourself to be *great,* he names you a Master, and you are marked with the heart in the center of the ring. I just became a Master of Prosperity earlier this year, and now it's my job to lead our city, teaching all to prosper and be happy. Don't be content with the one mark you have now. You should desire them all so that someday you might enjoy the privileges of being a Master."

The warm water and Cora's pampering hands were making Tovi sleepy. Her closed eyes and lack of response did not go unnoticed by BiBi.

"Pay attention, Tovi! You have a lot to learn before we leave for the fight."

"I still don't understand. What fight?"

BiBi groaned. "There is so much you don't know! This week, we are celebrating the anniversary of His Majesty's reign. Every year there is a huge party that lasts for several days. His Majesty loves to watch a good fight, so the big opening act of the week is a fight in the Courtyard. Two people—predetermined by His Majesty—get in the ring and compete to see who is more powerful. The winner is usually given some sort of a promotion within the kingdom."

BiBi was already moving on to the next topic even though Tovi was no closer to understanding than she was before. It was hard to keep up with the constant chatter and change of topic. As BiBi prattled on, Cora kneaded strong-smelling cream into the roots of Tovi's hair.

"I told you my diamond represents Prosperity. Now I'll tell you about the others. Calix is a Master of Adoration, and the symbol for Adoration is the pointed crown. Calix devotes his entire life to serving His Majesty. He teaches others the importance of honoring King

Damien above all else, that loyalty to the crown is the most important virtue in our society. He is *really* good at it. Ultimately, most people end up adoring Calix as well."

BiBi went on to explain each mark, but it all became very jumbled in Tovi's mind. Were the chains the symbol for Power? Or was that the flames? She was fairly certain the scales were for Perfection, but could it be Wisdom instead? She had little hope that she would ever have it all sorted out.

When Tovi was out of the tub and wrapped in a luxurious towel, BiBi called in an additional servant. The girls pulled and tugged at Tovi's hair, brushing, drying, and ironing until it shined, and her scalp felt raw. Next the servants smeared thick pastes over her skin and dusted layer after layer of silver powder onto her eyelids. They covered her lips with a bright red, shiny gloss and filed her nails into perfect points, dipping the ends in polish that matched her lips.

Pulling Tovi in front of the wardrobe, BiBi said, "I suggest you wear this one." She held up one of the many silver ensembles, one so pale that it was almost a sparkling white. She waltzed around the room grabbing items from several different chests and cabinets. Before she knew it, Tovi had several chains of alternating diamonds and silver beads draped around her neck and long silver gloves that matched her gown. "Always always always wear gloves, Tovi. Don't go anywhere without them. Forgetting your gloves is the ultimate social disaster."

When it came time to leave, a butler opened the front door for the two ladies. A tremendous roar stopped Tovi in her tracks. There was so much to look at all at once, and her head swam with inundating sensations. The tall homes surrounding the courtyard towered over her, and she could see the glint of gold on their distant rooftops. The huge cobblestone square had disappeared under the teeming feet of thousands of people, all swarming around a raised circular platform. The crowd pressed in from all sides, even filling the archways and streets beyond.

People were everywhere. The front steps of the homes seemed to rise out of the masses rather than from the ground. There was jeering and rowdy laughter. Everywhere she looked, Tovi could see bare backs engraved with combinations of the black marks.

The throng of spectators noticed the well-dressed ladies trying to pass, and they made what little room they could manage. Tovi wrinkled her nose and tried not to breathe as she was forced to brush against so many strangers, many of them foul-smelling and covered in sweat. With every step she looked desperately for any sign of Tali.

BiBi led her to the other side of the courtyard, where Tovi found herself on a set of golden steps. "Where are we?" she yelled as BiBi knocked on the door.

"What?" BiBi shouted over the deafening noise.

A butler opened the door and nodded to the ladies, bidding them to enter. When they were inside and the door shut behind them, the terrible roar ceased.

Tovi followed BiBi up an impressive spiral staircase and through a set of glass doors. A large patio overlooked the courtyard with its vast sea of people vying for position as close as possible to the platform. From this height the unbearable noise was slightly muted.

Three gorgeous creatures were already lounging on gilded chaises with crimson cushions. One of them stood and greeted, "BiBi! Who have you brought with you? What a nice surprise!" She had bright orange hair that reached all the way to her waist, and her silk gown was accented with a dazzlingly bright emerald pendant the size of an egg that hung from a delicate silver chain. Her lips were bright pink, different from the reds on most of the women. She was the most colorful person Tovi had seen since coming to the mountain. Even her eyes were a vibrant yellow, and they pierced Tovi with the look of a hundred unanswered questions.

"This is Tovi," BiBi announced to everyone on the patio. "She has come to live with Calix and me. She's from Adia." There was a sharp intake of breath, and all eyes darted to Tovi at once.

The girl's eyes grew large. She grabbed hold of Tovi's arms, spun her around, and touched a finger to Tovi's shoulder. Then, she clapped her hands and squealed in delight. "How wonderful! I should have known. Tovi, welcome, I'm Rhaxma" she said, squeezing her new guest. "But where is . . . oh, never mind. I am thrilled that you are here."

The others did not get up to greet her as Rhaxma introduced them. Xanthe had violet eyes framed by lemon yellow hair with one aqua stripe that started at her scalp and ran all the way along her loose waves. She glanced at Tovi with what looked to be acute disdain and mistrust before turning to look out over the courtyard, her face set in cold indifference.

Megara sat close by. Like Calix and BiBi, her hair and eyes were the darkest of blacks, contrasted by sickly pale skin. Although just as young as the rest, she looked tired, withered, and angry. She occasionally coughed into a stained handkerchief.

Before Tovi had time to sit down, a hand touched the small of her back. She jumped, startled to find Calix standing close behind her. Her heart thudded with a mixture of anger and fear.

He leaned down to whisper, "Just pretend that our little disagreement didn't happen. Got it? You have no idea what I could do to you. Don't say anything you might regret."

Tovi narrowed her eyes and opened her mouth to protest but thought better of it when Calix tightened his grip and dug his fingers into her side. He kissed her quickly and led her to an empty seat. Rhaxma's eyes followed the entire interaction.

"Hey, Rhax," Calix called, "Where is everybody?"

"We're missing only three," she said, sounding offended. "My brother has been busy for several days, and Jairus will be here soon. Eryx is in the fight. And don't hint that this gathering is lacking. His Majesty himself is coming."

"Oh, excellent. I didn't know. Who is Eryx up against?"

"Some field hand named Myron. I've heard that His Majesty has taken some special interest in him. Thinks he could rise up to become a Master someday."

Calix scoffed. "A Master? A Master of what?"

"Control. People are saying that my dear brother might not last long as the favored Master of Control, but I'd say there's no need to worry now that Tovi is here."

Calix responded cruelly, "There are plenty of treacherous backstabbers around here. He shouldn't get too comfortable."

A booming voice rose over the crowd. "Welcome, ladies and gentlemen, to today's fight. Please turn your attention eastward and show your respect to Their Majesties, King Damien, Prince Ajax, and Prince Jairus!"

There was an uproar as everyone in the courtyard below turned to face the very place where Tovi was sitting. The doors to Rhaxma's balcony flew open, and trumpets blared. A dozen terrifying guards emerged, each carrying two swords. When they were in position around the perimeter of the terrace, they planted their feet and crossed the swords in front of their chests.

Three royal men appeared. The younger of the princes, Jairus, looked as if he'd rather be anywhere but standing beside his grandfather. There was a dullness in his purple eyes and the straight line of his mouth, as if the world no longer held any pleasure for him. He was quite a bit taller than the king, and Tovi was stabbed with homesickness as she noticed he seemed to be nearly the same height and build as her brother.

Tovi's glance shifted to the old man at his side. Their eyes connected, and a cold, electric shiver surged through her. In contrast to Jairus, King Damien's face was intensely engaged. He was a man of average height and average build, and just like so many that Tovi had met, his eyes and hair were darkest black.

Prince Ajax was a cross between the two. He shared his father's colors, but he was as tall as his son. He also looked as bored as his son.

Jairus sat down with Xanthe, putting his arm around her shoulders. Tovi noted how their hair and eyes were the exact same hues. He even had a matching aqua patch in his short hair where Xanthe had her stripe.

"Are they related?" Tovi whispered to Calix.

He snorted. "I hope not."

King Damien sauntered toward Tovi, never taking his eyes off her as the others parted to give him plenty of room to pass. He moved with a confident precision that defied his age. She stood when he arrived in front of her, and he tenderly took hold of her hand between both of his own. "Tovi, my darling, we meet at last." He smiled with grandfatherly sweetness.

"It is nice to finally meet you, Your Majesty. I have heard a lot about you."

"Hearsay, all of it!" he exclaimed gleefully. "Don't you dare believe a word said against me. I'm really not such a grumpy old man as I'm sure they have told you." He looked her deeply in the eyes, and he seemed to lose himself for a moment, like he noticed something strange for the first time. His gaze flicked to her hair and back to her eyes.

Tovi smiled, but there was a strange tingling just beneath her skin that felt very close to fear. She had a hard time explaining it even to herself. She felt anxious in his presence.

The announcer's voice echoed through the streets again. "His Majesty's first contestant, Myron Xylander!" A large man with rippling pecs and biceps stepped up onto the platform as the crowd taunted him. He was bare-chested and wore loose gray shorts.

King Damien—with one last glance at Tovi—moved to his seat.

"And next, our champion, our Master of Power, Eryx Odessa!" The volume swelled to unbearable levels as fists shot into the air. An even larger man entered the ring. He was dressed the same as Myron, but he had a shaved head and his body had many white scars.

A whistle was blown, and the two men began hitting, kicking, kneeing, and pushing each other around the platform, clearly hurting one another. Tovi was horrified by the sight. What was even more repulsive was that the crowd seemed to be enjoying it.

Each thud of fist against flesh startled her, and her little jumps and spasms made Calix smirk. "You'll get used to it. Calm down."

It didn't take long for Myron to fall limp. Eryx raised a fist in the air, turning around to acknowledge the crowd. As the people responded and mirrored him with enthusiasm, something caught Tovi's eye. She looked back at the fighter lying on the platform. Myron, supposedly unconscious, was shifting his arm ever so slightly toward the edge of the ring where another man slid a long metal bar into his hand.

With one deft movement Myron leapt back to his feet and brought the rod crashing down on his opponent's head. A collective gasp followed by wild cheers erupted from the crowd. Eryx lay on the platform, black blood oozing from his temple. Myron continued to beat him with the metal bar, and the audience watched in pure, undisguised delight. Tovi had to close her eyes to ward off her nausea.

This time Myron raised his fist victoriously. He had won over the fickle crowd, which was cheering rambunctiously for their new hero.

Eventually everyone dispersed, most returning to their homes as they rehashed the entire fight and debated the legitimacy of using the metal bar. Wealthy citizens slipped into some of the large houses around the courtyard where sophisticated parties had already commenced. Music flowed into the street and the mood turned festive. No one bothered to remove Eryx from the platform.

Tovi went to the railing and looked down at his broken body. She couldn't understand the cruelty. "Why is no one helping him?" she asked, distressed.

King Damien approached and stood beside her, following her gaze. "Don't you worry about him, my dear one. He'll be fine. I bet you would like to learn more about us so there aren't any other little shocks and surprises like this one. Come and see me tomorrow morning for breakfast. I'll arrange some special lessons for you, and in no time, you will feel completely at home. Now, let's head inside. Rhaxma has quite the party planned."

King Damien wandered off to speak with someone else, and Tovi stood alone at the railing, unable to take her eyes from Eryx lying motionless in the deserted courtyard. After checking to be sure no one was looking, she slipped quietly down a side staircase. She hurried across the smooth cobblestones, climbed into the ring, and knelt by the crumpled body, pressing a discarded towel against his temple. She used her free hand to cradle the other side of his face. Soon the towel was drenched with a mix of crimson blood and a strange black sludge.

As she leaned over to get a closer look at another wound—this one along his jaw—Eryx began to stir. His eyes fluttered open and shut, and his breathing became uneven. His eyes opened just slightly, and he squinted into Tovi's face. Confusion wrinkled his forehead as he whispered something, and Tovi moved her ear closer to his lips so that she could understand.

"Tovi?" he breathed, barely audible. "Tovi . . . ?" Less than a second later he was unconscious again.

Tovi was stunned. How did this terrifying man know her name?

CHAPTER 22

There had to be another explanation.

King Damien stood at a window ignoring the sounds of Rhaxma's party. His eyes never strayed from the girl as she cared for his wounded weapon. So kind and gentle. But those colors . . . they were dangerous.

He watched as Tovi summoned nearby loiterers to carry Eryx home, but she stayed behind. She stood alone in the middle of the courtyard, looking so small, her gaze slowly swiveling from Rhaxma's party to Calix's home to Eryx being carted across the open expanse.

She took hesitant steps to follow after Eryx, but then she paused. After another moment and a few glances back toward the party, she seemed to make up her mind and walked briskly toward Calix's house.

As soon as she disappeared, Damien excused himself from the party and went home escorted by half of his guards. His son and grandson stayed behind with the rest.

"I was not expecting this," he muttered to himself, walking toward a certain place along the wall of his hidden corridor. Tovi had caught him completely off guard, and he hoped he had sufficiently masked his shock. The last thing he needed was for the Masters on that balcony to feel his mix of speculation and panic.

There had to be another explanation. He paced, searching for any plausible reason for those colors. Navy blue hair. Brown eyes with a little purple star.

It was a coincidence, he assured himself. It had to be. Tovi's colors were exactly the same as the young man in the mural, but that didn't mean anything. And those colors matched someone else from his past, someone he thought was gone.

Now as he looked at the mural, he knew that his denial couldn't keep up with the mounting evidence.

There had been too much recently. Too many pieces falling into place.

Just recently he had learned of the blue-haired man's name and location. Finally, one of his spies had spotted him going in and out of the caves in the foothills, dangerously close to the northern entrance to the mines. His name was Tali. Tali was from Adia. Tovi was from Adia. They must know one another. Unless there was another explanation . . .

Tali.

He stopped in front of the four painted faces and stared at him. So, his name was Tali. The face in the mural had plagued him for so long that it was hard to accept such a simple name.

Tali.

Tali. He said it out loud and hated the way it rolled off his tongue.

Tali was wandering in the forest, so close to this mountain. Too close. Then this young woman appears, the target of more than one of his weapons. And her hair and eyes happened to match Tali's. But there were no women in the mural with that coloring. Surely it couldn't be . . .

He shook his head and didn't allow himself to think about that night twenty years ago. There had to be another explanation. There *had* to.

He walked out of the corridor and into the bright throne room, blinking several times. One of his generals was waiting for him.

Damien did not sit down. Instead, he motioned for the middle-aged warrior to follow behind him. As they walked out of the throne room Damien asked, "How quickly could we mobilize the troops?"

"That would depend on our mission, Your Majesty. Will we be gone long? Lengthier trips require more preparation."

"Yes, that is true," he pondered. "I have a matter of urgency, and we will need everyone we can spare. They may need to camp below the clouds if they can't complete the task in one day. Prepare them with haste. I want an immediate report when you are ready."

"And what are the orders?"

They reached a large library. All four walls were hidden by leather-bound books in perfect rows. A large, ornate table stood in the center of the room and was covered in writing tools, ink, and ledgers. Damien pushed all this aside and unrolled a large map of the mountain and the lands surrounding it.

"Descend through the mines and exit through the northern gate. Once you are in the foothills, organize into small search parties. Leave no stone unturned," he said, gesturing with fluid motions. "You are looking for a young man with dark blue hair and brown eyes. There is a purple star on his left iris. He answers to the name Tali."

"Do you want him alive?"

"Preferably. But if not, his body will suffice."

The general gave a curt nod and left the room.

Damien stood over the map. His flattened kingdom was in the very middle. A novice map reader might not realize it was a mountain at all, as the markings for elevation were nothing more than irregular tick marks along the edges of the zones that spread out like the rings of a lopsided bull's-eye.

The mountain was surrounded by dense forest. Adia lay to the southwest, along with several winding valleys and rivers. The sea was southeast, and there were foothills and caves to the north. Beyond the foothills stretched prairie that faded into desert. But his people rarely travelled that far.

Damien's dream had always been to subdue the mountain, which he had accomplished quite successfully. He had always hoped that his heirs' ambitions would lead them to tame the wild lands beyond the blanket of cloud, that one day the entire known world would be under his legacy's command.

His fingers traced a river that wound from the western edge of the map through Adia. After several meandering curves and a large loop south of the mountain, it eventually came to the sea. There used to be streams on the mountain. Clear streams of clean water rushing down toward the valleys and pooling in bright blue lakes that reflected the sun and sky.

Damien lost himself in memories of his boyhood. He remembered the feel of grass under his bare feet, the sight of trees reaching up toward the sky with waving leaves greeting the birds of the air. An image of his mother came to mind, her perfect purple curls framing her laughing face. She was sitting under a blossoming cherry tree reading her favorite book, the binding well creased, and some of the gold lettering worn away from the cover. He could smell the fragrance of the flowers, feel the warmth of the sun.

He shook his head violently, willing the depths of his mind to recapture that wandering thought and hide it away. Those had been evil days of idleness. It was before his epiphanies. It was before he shared his ideas with the people, gaining support and power until he finally ruled the mountain. Through his dedication to his system, he had finally harnessed the masses.

He sighed deeply and sat in an overstuffed chair, still gazing at the map.

What to do about the girl? There *had* to be another explanation.

CHAPTER 23

"So good of you to come, Tovi. Welcome to my garden patio. This is my favorite spot in the whole city." King Damien sat at a table already laden with pastries, fruit, and bright juices. He was dressed exactly like the day before.

She gazed out at the garden. There was little color except the gray-green of hedges, perfectly shaped into a complicated labyrinth. The rest of it was paved with stone and ornamented with statues of soldiers aiming spears or wielding swords .

The previous evening, after returning to Calix's house after the fight, she had not known where she stood with Calix. Would he calm down? Or would he throw her out? She didn't want to stay, not after that outburst that showed his true colors. But, she had nowhere else to go.

She had climbed up to the room with the tall windows and canopied bed, where Cora had dressed her earlier in the day. She wondered if this was BiBi's room, and she sat in one of the windows to wait for BiBi to return.

But BiBi did not return to that room. Tovi heard her come up the stairs several hours later, singing a bit under her breath. The singing voice moved to the room next door, so Tovi peeked out.

"Tovi!" BiBi cried with a silly smile, stumbling just a bit as she moved toward her guest. "I had forgotten you are here. Is your room to your liking?" She hiccuped and giggled.

"It is fine. Are you sure this is not your room? Your closet is in here."

"No, no, no. Those are just a few of my old gowns. This is my room over here. You're in the guest room." BiBi hiccuped again. "Which is kind of perfect since you are my guest!" BiBi rested her face against her door frame and grinned, her eyes only half open. Then, they burst wide in an instant. "Oh no, Tovi! You probably don't have anything to wear to sleep. Hold on."

BiBi rummaged through some drawers, producing two night dresses. "Here. These will be a bit too big for you, but they will do."

Tovi had thanked her, went back to her room, donned the pajamas, and climbed into the giant bed.

She had woken in the morning and immediately began to cry. She had not dreamed about Tali for the first time in weeks, and she mourned this last connection to her family.

Tovi also hadn't seen any sign of Calix since the party.

She now had a hard time focusing on King Damien over breakfast. Her mind was consumed by her dreamless night, the events of the previous day, and the significant task of avoiding Calix while living in his home.

Tovi blinked and came back to the present as King Damien was saying, "I want to make sure we educate you properly. I have arranged a few special lessons, but first we must chat about what you already know."

Tovi gave a brief summary of the information BiBi had shared, including all that she knew about the marks of honor and how one becomes a Master. King Damien nodded occasionally to show he was listening.

"Excellent. Now, let me tell you more. You see, Tovi, the world is not such a complicated place. What I want is the very best for this mountain and the people on it. After many years of deepest thought, I know exactly what must be done in order for us to prosper and grow. That is why I hand out assignments. Each person is integral to the system of bettering our community. Some children are born with excellent brains. They must be put to the task of thinking and building and creating. Then there are those born with natural leadership and ambition who should be assigned to harness their desires and use them to better the world around them. There are those born with nothing but the ability to work hard. These skills are used so that the rest of us have food to eat, roofs over our head, and clothes to wear. So it is because of my great love for these people that I put them to work. Do you have any questions so far?"

"I don't think so."

"All right then. Take a look at this." He clapped his hands, and a teenage girl stepped forward. Like the servants in Calix's house, she wore a modest gray dress with a large hole cut out of the back. She turned so Tovi could examine her marks. "Each of these symbolizes a trait that people should pursue in order to be the very best version of themselves. All you need is to understand these seven ways of the world, and your life will far exceed anything you could ever dream.

"First, you earned your mark of Control," he said, pointing to the hissing snake near the base of the girl's spine. It was the same mark that adorned Tovi's shoulder. "Leeto taught you that it is good to take control of your life, to do whatever is necessary to fully realize your potential. When you chose to leave that letter for Ganya, you finally took control. Thus, you earned your first mark before ever stepping foot on this mountain. You are very bright, and I think there is excellent potential for you to earn more marks and maybe become a Master someday. Oh, yes, I have great tasks in mind for you."

Tovi had just taken her second bite of breakfast when Rhaxma joined them on the patio. King Damien smiled. "You will be spending the rest of the morning with Rhaxma learning about her specialty. Off you go!"

"Today we get to talk about the mark that looks like a set of scales," Rhaxma said as they walked out of the palace. "It's the mark of Perfection."

Tovi only half listened. Her attention was caught by Eryx who was standing outside one of the courtyard homes. There was a bandage over his jaw, but the rest of his wounds and their stitches were exposed. His eyes followed her as they crossed the expanse toward Rhaxma's house.

"In order for you to live life to its fullest, you should constantly strive for perfection. There are many aspects to consider, but the most important is how you look." They reached Rhaxma's home and went straight to a large parlor. The walls were covered in framed portraits of an entirely orange-haired, yellow-eyed family. "How you look changes everything. People will treat you with the amount of respect and honor that your appearance deserves. How you look has the power to make you a queen or ruin you. It is your choice."

A tall mirror stood in one corner. "All right, you stand right here," Rhaxma said, placing Tovi in front of it. She sat down on a puffy couch and rang a bell.

At this signal, a line of servants entered. "Ghita, go stand next to that mirror so Tovi can see you next to her reflection."

Tovi noticed the girl's face and how young yet tired she looked.

"Now, compare yourself to Ghita. In what ways are you prettier than Ghita, and in what ways is Ghita prettier than you?"

"I'm sorry?" Tovi faltered.

Rhaxma sighed and rose from her cushion. "You have so much to learn. First, look at her figure. See how it curves out right here and makes this pouch?" she asked, pointing to Ghita's midsection. "That is not right. To be perfect, you must have a very tiny waist. There shouldn't be any of this," she said, pinching Ghita's waist.

Tears were forming in Ghita's eyes, and she was biting her lip.

"That is horrible," Tovi said. "Ghita, you are lovely. Please don't cry."

Rhaxma looked at Tovi with fierce disapproval. "Do not give praise to this slumpy girl. If you condone this kind of treatment of your body, one day you will look just like her. Then, no one will ever love you, and you will be a complete failure." Beads of black sweat formed on Rhaxma's forehead and upper lip, and she quickly wiped them away. Collecting herself, she continued, "Now, take a look at Ghita's eyes. What do you notice about them?"

"They are a pretty color of brown," Tovi said, stubbornly picking out their best qualities. "They are very bright. And they do have a nice shape."

"Correct," Rhaxma retorted with one raised eyebrow. "They do have a pretty color and shape. However, look here," she said, indicating the space between them. "They are too close together. And, these eyelashes are very short. Yours are much longer."

Tovi took a moment to look at Ghita's eyes again, then looked in the mirror at her own.

"See how her nose is wider and dips down on the end? That is not nearly as pretty as your small nose and its nice little point. Her lips are too thin and cracked, and she needs to take better care of them. Her skin has these blemishes and pock marks, whereas yours is nice and smooth. Her hair is too frizzy, her ears are too low, and her teeth are too large.

"Ghita, you may leave. Cloris, please step forward."

They repeated the process several times through. Tovi refused to offend the servants, but she began to see herself differently when she looked in the mirror. For the first time in her life, she saw herself in bits and pieces. She was proud of some things, like her beautiful eyes and her nice little nose, but shame rose up within her as she surveyed her unruly hair and the straight lines of her body that looked nothing like Rhaxma's curves.

"Hello in there! Anybody home?" BiBi entered the room. "Can I speak with you for a moment, Rhaxma?" The two spoke quietly in the corner, occasionally looking over at Tovi.

While they spoke, Tovi continued to stare at herself. An image of Xanthe popped into her mind. The perfect face framed by lush hair. The perfect body barely hidden beneath silk. Tovi's cheeks grew pink and her eyes stung with the beginning of tears. Calix's voice rang in her ears: "You are worthless."

Would he have said that if she looked like Xanthe? Could he have overlooked the snake on her shoulder if she was more beautiful?

She rolled her shoulder, which was stinging worse than before. Her gaze moved down to her too-flat chest and her too-undefined waist. She had always been skinny, and Ganya had always wanted her to eat a little more. But for the first time, she realized how ugly her thinness made her. She wasn't womanly like Xanthe, Rhaxma, BiBi, or any of the other women in the upper circle. They all had hourglass shapes with swaying hips, overflowing busts, and tiny waists. She glanced at the two woman in the corner and then back at herself.

She took a deep breath. Fitting in mattered only until she concluded her search for Tali. Then she could leave this place that left her feeling so inadequate.

"Tovi! Turn around and look in the mirror. You've earned it!" Rhaxma squealed from the corner.

Sure enough, Tovi turned to find the scales branded just below the snake. It was hard to differentiate between the pain caused by each separate mark, so she hadn't noticed when it appeared.

"Well done, Tovi!" BiBi applauded.

Shyly, Tovi asked the question that had been forming in her mind. "What can I do to look . . . more like the two of you?"

They both burst into giggles. "You mean these, don't you?" BiBi asked, pointing at her chest. "And these?" She gave a wiggle of her hips.

Rhaxma laughed and rolled her eyes at her friend. "Some of us have them naturally," she said, poking herself in the chest and rear end. "Others of us . . . "

BiBi finished her sentence for her. "Others of us, like me, need a little boost." She reached into her dress and ripped a large pad from one of her breasts, offering it to Tovi to have a closer look. BiBi looked ridiculously lopsided without it. Then, she pulled up her dress to show Tovi similar padding tied around her waist that gave volume to her hips. "But at least I don't have to bind my waist like Rhaxma does."

Rhaxma smiled and lifted her dress too, revealing an undergarment that cinched in her waist. "I prefer it this way. When my clothes come off, men aren't as disappointed as when they realize none of that is really BiBi."

BiBi burst out in another round of belly laughter. Tovi flushed, a heat spreading across her face.

"I think tomorrow is our breakfast together, Tovi. I'm happy to take you to buy some for yourself," BiBi offered as she replaced her fake breast.

Soon BiBi left, and Rhaxma began to train Tovi on another matter of importance: comparing other people in order to surround herself with only the best. She brought two male servants into the room. They stood before Tovi, eyes staring straight ahead.

"All right. What do you think of these two, Tovi?"

She studied their faces, the shapes of their features, the width of their shoulders. She noticed differences, but she had no idea which was better. Should she say she liked the thin one with the bony face? Or should she approve of the thicker-set one who looked much stronger?

"Come on, Tovi. Which would you choose as better?"

"I don't know. I suppose I would choose him," she indicated the stronger but shorter of the two.

"Wrong. Trick question! Neither of them are good enough for you."

Tovi learned that day that tall was better than short. Muscles were better than being fat or skinny. The broader the shoulders, the better. Unless, of course, they were too broad. Skin should be smooth, teeth should be straight, and clothes should fit just right.

As the morning wore on, Rhaxma motioned for Tovi to join her on the couch. "We've covered almost everything. As you settle in, you will probably meet people on your own, not just our little group from our parties. There are certain things you must remember. First, never associate with any servant, unless they are actually serving you."

"Why?"

Rhaxma sighed, exasperated. "I was worried you wouldn't understand. That's why I made it rule number one. Why would you want to befriend someone who is so beneath you? They are servants for a reason: they are good for nothing else. Remember that, Tovi. It is very important.

"Moving on. The second thing to remember is you must watch out for those who are new to wealth and status. They are used to living near the Bottom Rung, and often they still act like it. They lack sophistication and hardly conform to our standards. Don't be seen out with them, or soon you will be laughing too loudly, using their terrible slang, and wearing clothes that are ostentatious rather than refined. It is better to stay with people who have been in this inner circle for a long time.

"Third, if you ever see someone with a heart mark on their palm, stay far away from them. They are common in the Bottom Rung, and they are illegal."

Surprised and taken aback, Tovi exclaimed, "But I have one!" She started to pull off her glove when Rhaxma nearly tackled her.

"Don't! Don't show it to me! You could be arrested for having it!"

"But why?"

"It's forbidden to have that heart. It's a sign of rebellion. When someone is caught with one, they are thrown in the prison below the palace and left there until it is gone. Don't show anyone, Tovi. Surely His Majesty would be forgiving since you are new here, but don't take any chances."

Hearing the chime of a nearby clock, Rhaxma led Tovi up several flights of stairs to the top floor of her home. They continued through a set of glass doors and onto a small terrace on the opposite side of the house from the balcony where they had watched the fight. A sea of gray rooftops stretched out before them. They were all nearly identical, with their small chimneys and angled walls. The closer they were to Rhaxma's home, the better they looked. But further out, Tovi could see crumbling stone, flaking paint, and cracked windows. Beyond that was the endless barrier of cloud.

"You have been lucky. You were brought here and right away live in the best home you could ever have on this mountain. You moved into the courtyard, the closest you can be to His Majesty. I was born here, so it's nearly the same thing. Everyone else—all those people—live out there, trying to get in. If they do well in their assignments, they might be able to get a few streets closer in their lifetime, but rarely does anyone make it to the center of the city. It just doesn't happen. They try, and I can't fault them for that. Everyone wants what we have, and that's why it's important to protect it. You must always be striving for perfection. If you don't, he will cast you out, and you will end up out there somewhere, lost in the crowd of forgettable failures." A black tear dropped from her eye and left a dark trail down her cheek.

"Just think what that would be like," she continued, full of sorrow. "To have nothing. To be seen as nothing. It is my deepest and greatest fear, being nothing. As long as we are perfect, as long as we spend every waking moment staying ahead of the others, everything will be fine." She stifled a soft sob, pressing her fingers against her lips, and blinking back more tears.

"This place could eat you alive, but if you trust me and BiBi and the others, you'll make it. You'll be perfect. You'll succeed. And isn't that what you want?"

Tovi wasn't sure.

CHAPTER 24

Late in the evening, Eryx entered the throne room where the Council of Masters was assembling, and he immediately sensed the aggravated tension emanating from some of his fellow Masters. Calix was completely silent, and Rhaxma paced. No one could account for Leeto, the only weapon not present.

King Damien tapped his fingers together. "I've heard that some of you are rather disgruntled by how our last challenge played out," he began. "I have summoned you here to tell you that my wishes have changed. Thus, the rules have changed as well." There was a sound of dissent from Rhaxma, but Damien silenced her with a raised hand.

"It is no longer enough that Tovi is here. I want her marked by all of you. The whole ring. I want her to lose the heart in her palm. When both of these tasks are complete, I plan to take her body back to Adia myself."

Eryx's heart pounded, but he willed himself not to show any reaction.

"You are going to kill her, Your Majesty?" BiBi asked, surprised.

"No, one of you will kill her, and that person will win this task. Yes, but only after she is completely marked. When the seven marks are engraved in her skin and her hand shows no sign of that heart, I will personally crown whichever of you takes her life." There was a dramatic pause before he smiled and turned toward Eryx. "What do you think about that, my boy?"

Eryx glared in response, refusing to display the terror that raced through his mind and coursed through his body. He left as soon as the weapons were dismissed and sat down on his own stone terrace, drinking from a large goblet and staring at Tovi across the courtyard. He was fairly certain that the distance and darkness concealed him and that he would go undetected by the Adian's eyes. She was only visible to him because she was foolish enough to leave her curtains open, and the interior light illuminated her patio.

What must she think of this place? He wondered if she realized how much danger she was in. She already had the snake and scales. Five more and she would die. Five.

He watched as BiBi joined her. The two women sat in chairs, and he could tell they were talking animatedly. He knew exactly what BiBi was doing, befriending her so she could teach her all about greed, while masking it with the title "Prosperity." If she succeeded, Tovi would get another mark, a diamond.

He hated watching BiBi work. He hated all of them and the way they didn't care how much damage they were inflicting. But he hated himself the most. He felt responsible. After all, he was the one who first spotted Tovi. He was the one who couldn't stop watching her each time she ran to the cliffs, who unknowingly led Leeto and Calix to her. Just thinking about it made his blood boil, and he heaved his goblet against the far wall of the balcony. He looked back across the courtyard. His outburst had drawn attention from the two women who were now looking directly at him across the expanse. Cursing himself, he stormed through his curtains and into the privacy of his home.

He stopped abruptly in his tracks. He was not alone.

That infuriating Silas from Adia was sitting at his table, with his dark brown hair—marred by one bright green spot on the side—and his speckled light green eyes.

"Shouldn't you be protecting her?" Eryx asked, his voice full of venom.

"I was hoping you'd help me with that."

"Do you think this is funny?" Eryx spat, his stance challenging. "You have no idea how much trouble she's in."

"I know better than you do. When you are ready to calm down and listen to me, I'd like to tell you my plan."

Eryx did not like being told what to do, and he made this clear by stomping to the table, jerking a chair from under it, and sitting down with as much violence as he could muster. Silas bit the inside of his cheek and seemed to struggle to keep from laughing.

When Eryx was settled, Silas said, "We have to keep Tovi from getting the rest of those marks. As you know, Damien said he wants her alive until she has all seven. To buy us some time, we are going to focus on saving her from the others. We have two days until her lesson with Xanthe."

Eryx knew what that meant, and it made his stomach contract violently.

Silas nodded; all trace of amusement was gone. "If Xanthe succeeds, Tovi will be left much more vulnerable to the remaining marks. Stopping Xanthe's lesson is a key to keeping Tovi safe."

"And how do you suggest we stop the lesson?"

"You know about the Hidden Heart, right?"

Eryx was surprised by Silas' knowledge of the concealed dealings in the Bottom Rung. "The HH? Yes, I know about them. What do they have to do with Xanthe's lesson?"

"I know you are trustworthy, so I'm going to give you some information that you must guard with your life. Understand?" After Eryx's curt nod, Silas continued. "Xanthe is a member of the HH."

Whatever Eryx had expected, it was not that. He scratched his head and allowed himself to relax a bit. "And how will that help Tovi?"

"Xanthe doesn't care about marking Tovi or winning the competition. She's sick of Damien, this mountain, and her life. Sound familiar?"

Eryx crossed his arms over his chest and waited for Silas to go on. It was one thing to break into his house. It was another to intrude on the personal thoughts he had never told anyone.

"I want you to persuade Xanthe to do two things. First, ditch her lesson plans about Pleasure. Second, invite Tovi along to an HH meeting."

"And how do you expect me to convince Xanthe? Tell her that you, a man she's never met, sent me to tell her this?"

Silas smiled. "I doubt she would believe that, but I think showing her that heart under your glove would go a long way."

Eryx closed his fists so tightly that he almost split the seams of his gray leather fighting gloves. They were his favorites, the ones with the cut-off fingers to allow him better grip—the ones that had always protected his most dangerous secret.

CHAPTER 25

BiBi woke pleasantly with the first rays of sunlight casting a golden glow in her room. She stretched her arms and legs before curling on her side. The silk of her sheets felt glorious on her pampered skin.

Her drowsy mind wandered through her schedule for the day. Breakfast with His Majesty and Tovi was first, followed by her lesson with Tovi. The thought of this tremendous responsibility and attempting to please His Majesty made her stomach twist unpleasantly, but she pushed that thought away. She had no plans for that evening, which likely meant a bubble bath, fabulous wine, and some peace and quiet. She smiled with anticipation.

As she swung her legs out of bed, her maid entered the room. "Good morning, Cora. Quite a bit of walking today, but I'm also visiting the Halo. Needs to be comfortable but make a statement, too." She yawned and stood. Cora got to work, undressing and dressing her, washing her face, fixing her hair, applying her makeup. "Is anyone attending to Tovi?"

"Yes, ma'am. One of the other girls is next door with her now."

"Good." Her mind wandered, contemplating Tovi's experience on the mountain thus far, and how different this must be for her. BiBi had been to Adia, and she was well aware of their rustic lives. The first time she visited the valley, she was so fascinated by the simplicity that she just sat in the upper branches of a tree watching the people all day. She was filled with a mix of envy and sadness and wistfulness which she didn't understand. She had everything she could ever want on Mount Damien. Why did something in her wish to stay among the trees? She didn't dare tell a soul.

She hadn't always been wealthy, and she remembered what it was like to have an empty belly as a child. But there was a difference between Adia and the Bottom Rung. In Adia, their lack of wealth wasn't the same as the poverty on the mountain. The valley was full of riches that she could feel even though she couldn't see. The Bottom Rung was just . . . How could she put it? It was just empty.

Her mission today was to teach Tovi the fullness that prosperity could bring, and she wondered if Tovi's Adian upbringing would make it a challenging lesson. Could there be a mental block toward gold when you have been lavished with the clear waters and orange rays of sunset in the beautiful valley?

When the servant was finished, BiBi looked in the mirror and smiled. "Thank you, Cora. I will be out most of the day. Please have a bubble bath ready for me after dinner. Draw a bubble bath in Tovi's room as well." Cora nodded. "Oh, and please go get her now. It is time to leave for our breakfast."

In her momentary solitude, BiBi frowned. She wasn't at all sure how today would go, but the pressure was on to mark Tovi. His Majesty had been extremely impressed by Rhaxma's quick work the day before, and BiBi knew he would expect her to deliver another mark today.

Tovi entered, and the two women shared the shy smiles of a new friendship. "Good morning, Tovi! Let's get going."

BiBi linked her arm through Tovi's as they crossed the cobblestoned courtyard. They small talked about the weather and yesterday's lesson with Rhaxma, and soon they were taking their seats with His Majesty.

As the newest council member, BiBi still felt some trepidation in his presence, but she was determined not to show it. "Good morning, Your Majesty," she said brightly, clasping her hands together to keep them from trembling.

"Good morning, my dears. Congratulations on your second mark, Tovi. What a quick learner you are! I am thrilled that you are acclimating so well. I think you will enjoy today's lesson even more than yesterday's. Today we are discussing Prosperity. You see, Tovi, it is really quite simple. Money and wealth are the solution to nearly every problem. And once you have no problems left, gold will fill you with security and joy beyond anything you can imagine.

"That is why, long ago, I set my workers to mining the mountain. The gold and stones found within have made me so prosperous that I am able to share my happiness and wealth with those closest to me. My prosperity starts here in the center of the city, and it flows outward in waves to those who have earned it. First to the families around the courtyard, and then some of it makes its way to the streets beyond.

"My people understand this concept, and they spend their lives working their way closer to me and my gold. They know that the closer they are to me, and the more money that they have, the more their lives will be filled with happy memories."

BiBi nodded with enthusiasm, trying to convey to Tovi how much she agreed with that statement.

Three of His Majesty's servants brought covered plates to the table, revealing a single egg stuffed with lobster and caviar. It would have cost His Majesty a fortune to send for the seafood, as the sea was so far away to the southeast. Tall crystal glasses came next, filled with champagne and pomegranate juice.

Tovi remarked how delicious it was, and His Majesty responded each time with something similar to: "Only the best for you, my dear. You want another, don't you?"

BiBi watched Tovi closely as a third and fourth round of eggs were requested, and she smiled to herself as she observed Tovi's clear enjoyment of the excellent cuisine. Perhaps the lesson today would be easier than she thought.

"Your Majesty, this has been absolutely delicious. May Tovi and I begin our lesson now? I don't want her to have a stomach ache as we travel all over the city today."

"Of course, of course! And what are the plans, BiBi?"

"First, we are going to visit the sorting tables at the mines so Tovi can learn a bit of a metaphor for what we keep and what we discard. After that, we will spend the rest of the day at the Halo."

"Excellent, excellent. Now, Tovi, I know you do not have money of your own yet, so here is a small gift to get you started." King Damien reached below the table and brought out a small blue velvet sack. BiBi could tell it held a fortune in gold coins. "I know it's a bit heavy, but it shouldn't be too much for you. There is a strap for wearing it on your shoulder if that is more comfortable."

The two women set out for the mines, and BiBi could hear the coins clinking together inside the bag. "Hold tight to that as we walk through the Bottom Rung. You never know what those people will do to get their hands on some gold."

When they reached the mines, they stayed at the top rather than riding a basket down to the floor thousands of feet below. BiBi showed Tovi the tables where the rubble was sorted.

"See here? This is a new pile, fresh from the bottom. See how the workers are sorting through it, bit by bit? Now look over here. This is where they place everything in new, smaller baskets based on type." She showed Tovi the piles of gold, iron, raw jewels, granite, plain old rocks, and debris. "The gold and jewels are sent away to be refined. Iron is made into weapons and building materials. The granite is used for buildings near the Courtyard."

The lesson continued as the two women touched the various stones. BiBi held up several raw diamonds and sapphires for Tovi to examine, and they both let gold nuggets pass through their fingers. As they explored, BiBi kept talking. "These lovely things will get even better when refined and shaped. A sign that you are prospering is that you desire these things, longing to touch them and make them yours. It is very similar to what Rhaxma taught you yesterday about Perfection. You should discard the junk," she said, gesturing to a pile of plain rock that was destined for repairing homes in the Bottom Rung. "And you should seek out the very best for yourself. Hold out your hands."

Tovi obeyed and held both gloved palms up. BiBi placed a sparkling ruby in one of Tovi's hands. She placed a crumbling, chalky piece of rock in the other. "See what I mean? Who would want that rock when you can have rubies?"

Tovi gave a noncommittal shrug of the shoulders, and BiBi's stomach twisted into a tighter knot. This wasn't sinking in. She was doing a terrible job, and she was less and less confident that today's lesson would be successful. Why had she brought Tovi here? She thought the gold and stones could turn her head, that the pretty things and glitter would be an easy sell.

Her mind whirled with thoughts of failure—and what that would mean for her future—as she watched Tovi set the ruby and ugly rock down. Tovi's hands grazed over the pile, and her eyes looked far away. She fingered the raw, unpolished rocks and then held one up close to her eyes for inspection. It was a fist-sized white stone with iridescent flecks of purple and teal.

"Interesting choice, Tovi. That's an opal," BiBi said. "It's very rare."

"Can it really make you happy?" she said in a strange, distant voice. "These rocks. They make people happy?"

Understanding dawned in BiBi like the pale yellow rays of morning that creep along and illuminate the world inch by inch. "Yes," she whispered. "I know what it's like to grow up unhappy. The answers are all right here. The fix . . . the solution . . . the way out . . . This is it. This will fill you in all of those empty spaces."

"We don't have money in Adia. We don't have gold and stones," Tovi said, still concentrating on the opal.

"Perhaps that is why you have been so unhappy, Tovi. Perhaps your life can completely change, just like mine. You just need the right things."

Tovi blinked several times and looked at BiBi. Louder than before, she said, "You're probably right. Maybe this is what I've been missing."

Sensing the serious moment was over, BiBi took the stone from Tovi, tossed some coins to a guard, and walked toward the arched exit. "Now, let's get up to the Halo for some real fun."

They walked back through the Bottom Rung and up through the neighborhoods toward the courtyard. But just as they were reaching the streets near the cobblestoned square, BiBi led Tovi down a road to the left. It was just on the other side of the large homes that sat near the palace.

"Stop and take this in for a moment," BiBi said, leading by example and taking a big breath as she glanced along the street. White buildings lined the road. They were the same height as those in the Bottom Rung, but they were clean and almost sparkled in the sunlight. Instead of sagging balconies, there were ornate iron railings. The ground floor of each building was made of mostly glass, showing off the dresses, jewelry, vases, and other wares. Everything was pristine, and so were the well-dressed citizens who walked along and popped in and out of the stores.

BiBi glanced at Tovi, whose eyes were wide and shining. She seemed to be enamored and maybe a bit overwhelmed. That was understandable. The girl had experienced so many new things in such a short amount of time.

"This is the Halo," she said, finally breaking the silence. "It is where we shop and eat and play. I think our first stop will be right over here."

They entered a shop to their right, and a small bell tinkled above the door. BiBi approached the counter where an elegant old man with a monocle greeted them. "How may I help you today, Miss BiBi?" he asked warmly.

"Good morning, Mr. Hector! I have a special project for you," she said, placing the raw opal in his hand. "It's for Tovi. What do you think?"

He looked the opal over carefully, and then he turned his attention to Tovi. His eyes flitted from her hair to her neck to her ears and back to her neck. "I know just the thing," he said.

"It's all yours," BiBi said. "We'll be back after lunch." She led Tovi back out of the store.

The next several hours were spent perusing shops, trying on clothes, and drinking fizzy wine handed to them by shopkeepers. Tovi seemed to be enjoying herself, and she had already spent about a quarter of King Damien's bag of gold on clothing and accessories like a set of diamond-encrusted hair combs and her own custom padding for her chest and hips.

BiBi discovered that Tovi wasn't gabby the way most of the women on the mountain were. Tovi was polite and responded to questions, but she didn't fall for any of BiBi's usual methods for drawing someone into friendship. She seemed to have no complaints about life in their courtyard home, and she couldn't be prodded into talking about men. What else was there to talk about other than Adia? And BiBi knew that talking about Adia was a terrible idea.

Despite the lack of gossip, BiBi felt hope bubbling up. Tovi's eyes shone brighter and brighter with each addition to her collection of belongings. They had already sent several boxes and bags to be delivered to the house, and Tovi remarked that she still had plenty of gold left in the bag. "I think I could buy anything I wanted with just this gold," she said in awe.

"I think you are right," BiBi laughed, linking arms with Tovi as they continued down the street. She stole a glance at Tovi's back, and her spirit sank a bit. Still no diamond below Rhaxma's scales.

As the afternoon grew hotter, BiBi led Tovi back to the first shop they had entered.

"Hello, girls!" Hector greeted. "I think you'll be very pleased. Come right this way." He led Tovi to a blue cushion, where she sat and faced a long oval mirror. Hector retrieved a black box approximately the length and width of her forearm. He pulled something from inside and draped it around Tovi's neck.

Even BiBi—so used to all things that sparkled—was in awe. What once was one large, raw opal had been cut and polished into more than a dozen teardrops. A delicate silver chain linked them together, with small round diamonds in between each droplet.

Tovi leaned forward to get a closer look in the mirror, her eyes bright and fixated. “It’s so lovely,” she said. Her face melted into the biggest smile BiBi had yet seen on her new friend, and suddenly Tovi looked relaxed and much younger. Her eyes swung up to meet BiBi’s in the mirror. “Is it really mine?”

BiBi sneaked a glance down. There it was: a diamond etched on Tovi’s skin. She had done it. She had taught the Adian. She sighed deeply. “Yes, Tovi. It is yours forever.”

CHAPTER 26

Meira stood at the wash basin in her room at the HH headquarters in the Bottom Rung, the only light coming from a feeble candle in the corner and a beam from the moon shining through the window. She wiped the grime from the mines off her skin with tired fingers. She spent every day the same: Mornings and afternoons deep in the mines, and evenings gathering information and plotting the safety and survival of all her brethren with hearts in their palms.

Every day was a challenge, but today had been exceptionally difficult. That morning, the mining crew had divided into their teams and headed to their assignments like normal. The vast majority mined the bottom of the pit, making the cavern inside the mountain ever deeper. A few, including Meira, were managers and inspectors, watching over the work, the pace, the methods, and the morale of those who spent so much time in this drudgery. Then, there was a small special team that Meira sent out each day.

To everyone else, this team was surveying the outside of the mountain, making sure all was safe, secure, and sturdy as the digging continued downward. Reality was very different. This special team was assigned to do something far more extraordinary, and only Meira knew that each of their hands was marked with a heart. Only she knew their real assignment. Her role as an inspector inside the mine was only a cover so that this team could continue to operate on Silas' orders.

Today, one of the regular, sweat-covered and dusty miners voiced his aggravation. "Why do they get to go outside everyday while we work in here?" he asked gruffly, slamming his pickaxe into the rock and leaving it there. "Why are they so special?"

"Yeah, why don't *we* get to rotate? I think it's our turn to go out there," said another. Discontent rolled through the crew rapidly.

Meira jumped up on a nearby ledge so she could be more easily seen and heard by the crowd. "Listen up!" she called. Only those closest to her quieted. "I said, listen up!" she shouted louder. Now she had about half of their attention. She glanced around, groping for ideas.

A basket only half full of debris sat on the ground near the mob. She jumped off the ledge, landing inside the metal container. She tugged on the chains once, rose in the air above the crowd several feet, and then tugged again. The basket stopped with a jerk and swung slightly. "Listen up!" she shouted again, but she really didn't need to. Her antics had won their attention.

"I hear you. It doesn't seem fair that we are inside while they get to be outside in the fresh air. Work hard for His Majesty today, and I will see what I can do to get us a holiday soon when we can all be outside and not work for a day. As to the task of that special crew, it is specialized and needs additional training. If you want to go through this rigorous training, talk to me after today. His Majesty may be displeased with you for wanting a new assignment, but I will do my best to present your concerns to him in a way that will not anger him. Now get back to work."

She could see her words had hit their mark. Their once-angry faces were now deep in contemplation, weighing whether fresh air was worth the potential of incurring King Damien's wrath. The day had gone by without further incident, but she could feel mutiny bubbling just below the surface.

Now, in the relative safety of headquarters, she was glad that she was so exhausted. She would sleep well, unlike the nights when she still had energy and her mind tossed from one thing to the next.

A throat cleared behind her, and she crashed backwards with a gasp, upsetting a basket of threadbare but clean towels. "Shhh . . . " the man said with a finger against his lips.

"Silas!" she whispered. "What are you doing here? I thought you didn't want them to see you yet." She jerked her head to the side, indicating the rooms nearby which were filled with members of the Hidden Heart.

"I had to come see you tonight. It's urgent. And none of them will know I'm here," he said with a sad smile. "Soon though. I'll meet with them soon."

Meira's pulse was finding a steady rhythm again, and she wrung out her wash rag and left it hanging on the side of the basin. "Why have you come?"

"There are three on the mountain."

"Three?" she gasped. "Three? Which twin is here?"

"The girl."

Meira nodded, taking in this information. "Does this mean it is almost time? You have said when the four are united—"

Silas interrupted her, "No, it is not time yet. That is why I have come, to give new instructions. The boy is in a cave to the north, a prisoner to Leeto. Soon Leeto will want to bring Tali to the mountain, and this must be stopped. It is not time for all four to be here."

Meira's heart started thudding again, but it was different than the quick bursts when she had been surprised and frightened. Now it was the heavy drum beat that warned of coming adventure. "What do you need me to do?"

"I'm sending you to rescue the boy. Take him to your mother."

A buzzing filled her ears. "I get to go see my mother?"

It had been years since she had left her mother, since she had left their little hut made of dried palm fronds and fallen sheets of palm bark. It had been years since she had walked in the sea and breathed salt air and stared into a purple and orange sunset while sitting on soft, warm sand.

She shook her head to release the images that tugged so painfully at her soul. "But I'm needed here. We are doing such great work. The mines are nearly ready, and we are discovering more hearts every day. They need me, Silas. The people in those rooms need me to lead them."

Silas put one rough hand on each side of her face and spoke with urgency. "Meira, this place has changed you, and I need you to remember exactly who you are. Your mother and the sea will remind you of that softer light that once shined in you. You have done great work here, and I am so pleased with how you have taken charge and turned my plans into reality, just as I asked. Now it is time for you to leave the rest up to me. Go, and be reminded of the girl who played and sang and twirled without the weight of the people's fate bearing down on her shoulders. That is the girl—now woman—I need for the next step. Your story is not over, but it must continue at the sea. It's time for you to go."

CHAPTER 27

For the third morning in a row, Tovi ate breakfast with King Damien, overlooking his garden of hedges and statues. This time blonde-haired, purple-eyed Xanthe was with them, silently pushing her fruit around her plate while Damien did most of the talking.

"Really, Tovi. This is precious. I can't even mention the love between a man and a woman without you turning such a darling shade of red. It's charming, really." King Damien laughed. "There's no reason to be embarrassed. It's part of your nature. But, don't worry. That's not all we're talking about today. Pleasure involves all sorts of things. Really, it's anything that gives you a thrill. It's anything that brings your life excitement. It's anything that you want more and more and more. You'll know it when the wanting keeps growing.

"Doesn't that make sense? A person should desire more of what makes them happy. It's logical. It's science. It's nature. Don't ever be content with a little when you could have much more. So, Tovi, what brings you pleasure? What gives you a thrill? What leaves you wanting more?"

She thought about it for a while, and her mind travelled back to Adia. "Exploring with my brother. Tea talks with Ganya. Building something with Avi . . . " her voice trailed off as her heart constricted, and she looked down at her plate.

In a softer, more comforting voice, King Damien replied, "Now, Tovi. You say that makes you happy but look how sad you are. You are not understanding what true pleasure is. What you mentioned are old memories. What do you have in your life right now that excites you? In the last few days, what has made your blood rush? The wine? The food? Anything?"

He paused, and he seemed to be waiting on her answer. Her mind was blank, and she looked into his eyes that were staring straight into hers.

After a while, he continued with his prodding. "What about Calix? Do you remember how you felt dancing with him behind that hedge?"

Tovi blushed even deeper. How could he know about that?

He continued, "If you want to feel like that again, you have to chase after it. Feel free to pursue even more of the pleasure that you desire. Now, before my next appointment gets here, why don't you two get started with your lesson? Xanthe is an excellent teacher, and she will help you with any questions you might have regarding this topic. But don't be long, girls. I have some surprises waiting for you when you return."

Tovi rose without a word and followed Xanthe into the garden. They walked in silence until they were deep in the ten-foot-tall hedges where they couldn't be seen or heard from the palace. Suddenly Xanthe turned and grabbed Tovi by the arms.

"Is it true? The stories of Adwin—is any of it true?" Those violet eyes that were normally so dull and lifeless were now shining with desperation. She let go of Tovi as if she had just realized she was holding onto her. "You have the heart in your hand, don't you?" Xanthe asked, her voice trembling.

Tovi didn't know what to do. Was this a trap? Should she lie? Why did Xanthe want to know, and what had come over her so quickly?

Seeing the hesitation in Tovi's face must have been enough of an answer for Xanthe. She was wearing short gloves with a single pearl button at the wrist, which she freed with shaking fingers. She pulled the glove off and turned her hand so Tovi could see her palm.

And there it was, the untidy brown heart so familiar to Tovi. "Xanthe!" she cried in dismay, grabbing hold of the girl's hand to cover the symbol. "You could be arrested for that. Why did you show me?"

"You have to tell me everything you know. You have to tell me if any of it is true. You lived in Adia, and they say Adwin does, too. Is it true?" Her voice was frenzied and fearful.

"I don't know him, but everyone else says they do," Tovi said.

Xanthe looked incredulous. "I have been waiting for so long to ask an Adian that question, and that's all you have to say? You don't know him?"

Tovi's anger flared. "How do you think it makes *me* feel? I don't know why I'm the only one who has never met him. I feel like everything I have ever known has been turned upside down in the last few days. Maybe he is real. Maybe he isn't. I have no idea what I should believe and what I shouldn't."

Xanthe began to pace. "I used to believe everything that His Majesty, my parents, and my teachers told me. I believed Adwin was evil. I believed that he was a tyrant who eventually abandoned us." She walked back toward Tovi, looking softer than she had before. "Then, about six months ago, there were some changes in my life. Damien ordered me and several others to go to Adia for one of his assignments. I . . . um . . . met some people who made me think about Adwin . . . in a different way . . . that maybe he was actually good. Then I started hearing whispers about people in the Bottom Rung who believed in him. I had to know more. So, I disguised myself and went to find them. It was difficult at first, but at last I was able to speak to people who know different stories about the old king. One of them even claimed to have met him."

"What did they tell you?" Tovi asked, entranced by this story. Adwin had always been a central part of her village's traditions. It was remarkable to hear of someone who would go to such measures just to learn about him.

"Why don't you come with me tonight? I'll tell Calix that I'm taking you out to teach you more about Pleasure and that you're sleeping it off at my house afterward. He'll believe me."

"All right," Tovi said, not sure what that meant or what she was getting into.

"And speaking of cover stories, you will have to pretend like this conversation never happened. I was supposed to teach you the power that your body has to manipulate men, so that you can get anything you want. You use their pleasure against them. I doubt they will ask too many questions, but if you feel caught, just say something like, 'I had no idea the world worked that way, but I see it now.' That will be enough to get you by."

Prince Jairus abruptly appeared in their small clearing. He furiously commanded, "Go back to the palace, Tovi. My grandfather is waiting for you." Tovi jumped up without hesitation, intimidated by his demeanor. She was only a few feet away when she heard him speak in a forced whisper. She stopped on the other side of the hedge to listen.

"What have you been telling her?"

"Jairus, she is from Adia! I had to find out . . . "

"Get your glove back on. Do you want him to throw you in jail? He will! He won't care how much I beg to get you out. Get back up to the palace and come up with some good story about what you were doing out here for so long. He noticed that you came into the maze and stopped. You could have at least gone all the way to your house where he wouldn't have seen you. It's like you want to be caught. You're just lucky he let me come get you. Just think if one of his servants had overheard you . . . "

CHAPTER 28

Leeto moved swiftly through the forest, due north from the north-facing exit of the mines. It was time for him to check on his prisoner. Time to convince him to share his secrets.

It had all gone as planned. Actually, it had been a bit too easy, and he congratulated himself frequently on the perfection of his scheme. He had been up in the tree watching the cave for about only four hours when Tali arrived. He had been prepared to be there for several days, but he did not complain that he would not have to spend a night out in the open.

Darkness fell, and Tali's fire crackled. Leeto longed to go near it to warm his freezing hands, but he had to wait. The night wore on, and the fire burned out. This was his cue.

As quietly as he could, he climbed down the tree and entered the cave. Tali was asleep on his pile of hay, turned on his stomach so that Leeto saw the side of his face and the back of his head. Leeto picked up the large, flat rock that Tali used as a cutting board. This next moment was critical. He must not kill Tali. He needed him for later.

He approached the sleeping man, raised the rock in the air, and let it fall just above Tali's ear. Tali did not stir, and for a moment Leeto panicked that he had hit him too hard. But, a quick check of his pulse and breathing told Leeto that Tali was still very much alive.

It was difficult work, but he was able to drag him to a nearby cave that he had previously scouted out. The cave had two chambers, and the innermost chamber could be blocked off with a round rock that rolled nicely in front of the entrance with little effort. When the chamber was closed in this way, someone unfamiliar with the cave could easily miss the back chamber.

He had dragged Tali into this back chamber, setting him upright against the back wall. His head rolled horribly to one side. Leeto tied his wrists and his ankles in knots that would be impossible to untie on his own. He left a pile of apples and a pouch of water next to him. He would be able to use his hands, still tied together, to move these items to his mouth, and they should last him for several days.

Just as Leeto was preparing to leave, the young man stirred. He looked with drowsy eyes at Leeto. "What happened?"

"What has Adwin instructed you to do?" Leeto asked, ignoring Tali's question.

This seemed to bring Tali out of his fog. His eyes cleared, and he looked Leeto over with a shrewd expression. "Why would I tell you?" he retorted. Then he grimaced. Leeto suspected a throbbing headache was setting in.

"Because I am the only soul who knows where you are. If you don't tell me everything you know, I might forget to come back and feed you."

"So be it. My loyalty is to Adwin, and I won't betray him, no matter what you offer or threaten."

"You are a fool, but that isn't surprising," Leeto snarled. "I'll just leave you here for a few days. You may be more talkative after some solitary confinement. And, in case you are curious, Tovi is loving her new life on the mountain. She will be one of us before long, and there is nothing you can do to save her from it. I hope you think deeply on that as you sit here alone, hoping to be found before you starve to death."

Leeto could see his own nasty smile reflected in Tali's angry eyes.

Now, a few days later, Leeto was on his way back. Perhaps Tali would be ready to talk.

Sunlight escaped through the canopy, turning everything in the woods to a paler, yellower version of itself. All was eerily silent. Even the birds and leaves were still. He did his best to not make a sound. Surely, he was alone. But one could never take too many precautions.

His schemes were still taking shape in his mind. What exactly was the best use for Tali Tivka? What if he couldn't get him to talk? Was he worth anything dead? If not, what form of torture could he use to pry Adwin's instructions from him? He could always make up a story about Tovi. Maybe he would divulge his secrets if it meant saving Tovi. How ridiculously gallant that would be. The boy would have to be a fool to fall for that, but Leeto wouldn't complain.

His ears twitched as he picked up the distant sound of voices. He stopped and listened intently. Next he heard the thud of feet against the earth. Dozens—maybe hundreds—of feet drew nearer. He climbed the closest tree and perched on a low leafy branch. Moments later, Leeto sharply inhaled. He recognized the uniforms of the men coming down the path. What was King Damien's army doing so far below the cloud?

"Company One, split to the right. Company Two, split to the left. All others, march on. When you have searched your area, return to base. If we are unsuccessful tonight, we will begin again tomorrow. Remember, he has dark blue hair and brown eyes. He goes by Tali."

Leeto grew very still. King Damien had decided to act much quicker than Leeto had expected. It must have been a stroke of pure luck that he already had captured Tali and confined him in a hiding place. If he had waited, he may have lost his chance.

After waiting for the army to leave the immediate area, Leeto scooted along the branch and shakily climbed down the tree while formulating an emergency plan. He would get Tali and smuggle him to the mountain. He could keep him locked somewhere safe while the armies continue looking in the woods below. He would feed King Damien false information, making him more and more desperate to find Tali. Then, when all seemed lost and the king was in a panic, Leeto could bring Tali out of hiding. That would surely earn him a reward. But how to get Tali through the mines and onto the mountain without being seen?

As the skies darkened, Leeto arrived at the cave. He looked left and right several times, making sure none of the soldiers had followed him. He slipped inside and rolled away the back stone. He let out a guttural moan and yanked at his hair.

The ropes were there, but Tali was gone.

CHAPTER 29

The "surprises" King Damien had promised Tovi earlier that day were now nothing but a memory, but she feared she would never get the images out of her head. They had been horrifying—a collection of sculptures and paintings he kept in a gallery in the palace. Each one depicted human bodies hideously contorted until they were almost unrecognizable. There had been so much anger in their eyes, pain and fear in their faces. Yet Damien described them as beautiful expressions of love and pleasure.

After dinner, Tovi and Xanthe made their way to the Bottom Rung clothed in less conspicuous dresses and covered in dark cloaks. They passed few people except near the pubs overflowing with night-time revelers.

They stopped outside of a building in sad need of repair. It was seven stories high with some of its windows broken out. A green wooden sign advertising tailoring swung back and forth in the slight breeze, causing an eerie scraping noise. There were sagging iron balconies stretching around the whole building on the second and fourth floors, and a man with green hair leaned against the upper railing, watching them in the street below. Xanthe lifted her gloved hand in a strange salute, like she was drawing half of a heart in the air. The man called something over his shoulder that Tovi couldn't hear.

A moment later a woman with hot pink hair and chubby cheeks answered the door. The woman's hands were bare, and when they were all inside, she held her palm face up. "Greetings in the name of Adwin," she said with a toothy smile.

Xanthe wasted no time. "Lyra, this is Tovi. She's from Adia."

Lyra's large teal eyes grew even bigger as she grasped Tovi's hands. "Adia?" she asked breathlessly. "Are you really?"

Tovi nodded, and Lyra threw her arms around her guest. "Wait 'til the others meet you!" Tovi followed Lyra through a maze of rooms and up several flights of stairs, and finally they came to a dark room lit by a few flickering candle stubs. Tovi could just make out a circle of nearly a dozen people sitting on the floor passing what looked to be a loaf of bread and a jar of honey.

"We have a special guest tonight," Lyra announced excitedly, one arm wrapped around Tovi's shoulders. "This is Tovi. She is from Adia!"

Even Xanthe couldn't help smiling at the uproar caused by this news. Tovi was hugged, kissed, and swung around the room as the clandestine rebels of the Hidden Heart laughed, exclaimed, and danced. When the hubbub finally died down, Tovi was invited to sit, and everyone returned to their place on the floor.

They all had unkempt hair of varying hues and patterns. The women had plain, kind faces, lacking makeup and smudged with the grime of their labor. The men had scraggly beards and rough looking hands. Their gray clothes were threadbare, but there was evidence of careful mending and patching. Even the disguises worn by Xanthe and Tovi were too extravagant to blend in with this group, but no one seemed to mind.

"Where is Meira?" Xanthe asked, glancing around the circle. The group's joy deflated into silence.

"We haven't seen her since last night," Lyra answered. "She told us goodbye and that she hoped to see us again soon. Said she was doing something for Adwin and couldn't tell us more. I think—"

"Tovi, you are very welcome here," the man with green hair greeted from the other side of the circle, cutting off Lyra's story with a kind but firm tone. He looked strangely familiar to Tovi. "We'll each introduce ourselves, and then we'd love to hear about you. My name is Hesper. I am a hunter, and Lyra is my wife."

"My name is Zephne," said the girl sitting next to Hesper. Tovi guessed that she couldn't be more than sixteen. If her hair had been clean, it would have been as red as an apple. She had eyes that reminded Tovi of a clear night sky. "I work in the kitchen in Calix and BiBi's home."

Startled, Tovi said, "But that's where I live."

"I know," Zephne responded kindly. "Most people don't notice us. Please don't feel bad." She smiled, and Tovi knew she meant what she said.

"Sorry I am late!" came a voice from the dim doorway, and goosebumps ran up Tovi's arms as she recognized bright orange hair and piercing yellow eyes. It was Leeto. How could he be a part of this group?

Then he stepped closer to the candlelight, and she realized it was not Leeto; it was someone who looked quite a bit like him but was much taller and broader. His nose wasn't quite as pointy, and there was kindness in his face.

"Who's this?" he asked, inclining his head toward Tovi.

"This is Tovi! She's from Adia!" Lyra squealed once more. "This is Thad. He's Leeto and Rhaxma's eldest brother. But don't worry . . . He's not one of them."

Around the circle they continued. Tovi learned that Stavros was a lumberjack who had the opportunity to travel down the mountain and get closer to Adia. Missa tended the bees that provided them with the honey they were eating. Lux and Galen were both former artists who had been moved to cleaning the streets when King Damien's interests changed from landscapes to portraits. Lyra was a seamstress, Illias was a hunter like Hesper, Magan and Rhea washed laundry in the palace by day and helped Lyra with her tailoring business in the evening, and Tovi recognized Ghita, one of Rhaxma's servants. She clasped Tovi's hands and ensured her that all was forgiven and that the horrible comparisons were not her fault.

"What's it like in Adia?" Ghita asked, her eyes shining with excitement.

Tovi closed her eyes, picturing home. Her audience leaned in, intent on drinking in each word. "Everything is perfect and green and covered in flowers. The sky is always blue, the sun always warm, and the river always cool. It's in a valley, surrounded by rolling hills and mountains in the distance—this mountain is one of them. Our homes are all built up in the tall trees, and there are bridges and ladders and rope swings. Sunrise and sunset are magnificent, and at night you can see the sparkling of a million stars."

The room had fallen completely silent. Lyra had tears in her eyes, which she unashamedly allowed to trickle down her cheeks.

In a hushed whisper, Stavros asked, "Is it true that he made it all?"

Magan interjected, "You know, Adwin. Did he really make the whole world like the legends say?"

"Our legends say that, too, but I don't know."

There was a strained silence as the group's hopes were dashed. Xanthe took this opportunity to cut in. "I know all of you are going to be a little disappointed. I was, too, at first. But I think that if we tell her the stories we have heard, we can compare them to what she has been taught. Maybe we can all learn something tonight. I do so wish Meira was here, though. She's the only one who says she's met him."

The others nodded in agreement, and Galen asked Hesper to share his story.

Hesper began, "When I was a boy, my mother taught me the importance of always wearing my gloves. She insisted that if I ever showed anyone the heart on my palm, I would be thrown in the dungeon for the rest of my life. She had the heart, too, and she warned me to hide it from my father who did not. Each day I put on my gloves and went to school, terrified of being found out.

"One day when I was outside, I overheard my parents fighting. I snuck to the window to see what was going on. I watched my father rip the glove from my mother's hand, and he roared in outrage. He dragged her straight to the palace. As promised, Damien threw my mother in prison.

"Scared that Father would come for me next, I ran away and hid in the alleyways of the Bottom Rung. Another little boy—about my age—lived in the alley, too. He looked so much like me we could have been brothers. I told him my story, and he showed me a secret door into the dungeon of the palace. He said he used it all the time, and that I could use it to check on my mother. Sure enough, there was a little trap door, hidden from view on the backside of the palace. It led directly down into the chamber, and the guards always sit at the top of the stairs on the other end. I went as often as I could, making sure not to be seen by anyone but Mother. It was really pretty easy.

"And that's when Mother told me about him. A man came every day to visit the prisoners. At the time I found it hard to believe, but she told me it was Adwin from the old tales. One day she looked at me sadly and told me goodbye. She said she was going to take his offer to be free from this mountain. I was still very young and didn't understand what she meant, and I didn't even know the right questions to ask. All I know now is that she was gone the next day. The other prisoners said that she left with the visitor."

"Wasn't she locked in a cell?" Tovi asked.

"Yes. Somehow, she got out. Nobody knows how they did it," Hesper answered.

"But what about when the guards realized she was gone?"

Lyra reached over and patted Tovi's hand as the candles around them flickered. "Strange things happen inside that jail. There have been many disappearances. Sometimes prisoners are beaten almost to death, and the next morning they have vanished from their cells. Others have grown old and sick, and they vanish as well. They were just gone. The guards must have thought that Hesper's mother simply disappeared like the others."

"But surely you know," Tovi said, looking around the circle of serious faces. "Don't you know what happens when you die?"

Hesper cocked his head to the side.

Tovi continued, "Haven't you ever seen someone fade and disappear?"

She could feel the pulse quicken in the room. "Tovi," Lyra said slowly, "When someone dies, they go into the eternal sleep. We bury their bodies outside of the city. No one just disappears."

CHAPTER 30

"Very foolish of you, my boy. Very foolish indeed," Damien said late in the night, sitting on his throne and surrounded by the candle-lit mural of the throne room. Calix stood before him, bravely taking the criticism. Despite Calix's stoic face, the king knew how deeply this would cut through the young man, how much it would make his insides writhe with torment. "You lost your grip on your power. You let your anger toward the girl rule you, and you stepped away from wisdom and control. I gave you several days to come back to your senses, and you have not. You hardly speak to the girl, this Adian you brought to my mountain. You are better than this."

"I'm sorry, Your Majesty," Calix said quietly, sounding like something was caught in his throat. "You are right."

"Now, it's not too late. She still lacks your crown and Xanthe's rose. Perhaps you could help her with both. This will be your greatest challenge yet, but I am confident you are up to the task. Woo her. Win back her affections. And do it soon. Understood?"

"Yes, Your Majesty," the boy responded with great relief.

"Good. She is with Xanthe tonight. She may earn her rose before you have a chance, but I have my doubts. Xanthe has not been her normal self recently. She seems to have lost her will to win, her appetite for power. My guess is that Tovi will return to you tomorrow, rose-less but knowledgeable enough to have something to work with. Use this, Calix. Do this for me."

"Yes, Your Majesty. Of course. Consider it done."

"Good. Now run along."

Calix prepared to leave just as Rhaxma entered. Their eyes met, and the king was fascinated by the energy exchanged. Nonchalant coldness from Calix. Burning hot desire from Rhaxma. One side of his lip curled up. Very few things were as entertaining as the imbalance of unrequited love, and it was this lopsided affection that had caused him to call both to his throne this evening. The idea for this little game had come to him earlier in the day as he observed Xanthe's distant and uninvested teaching methods. Today had been her chance, her opportunity, to mark the Adian. A few months ago, she would have been ravenous with her appetite for victory. What had happened? He tucked that question away to consider more thoroughly later.

When he was alone with Rhaxma, Damien smiled fully in her direction. He knew she was hurting. It was the prime opportunity to mold her pain into something constructive like Wisdom or Power. He put on his most fatherly and kindly demeanor. "Good evening, my dear girl. We have something very important to discuss."

"Of course, Your Majesty. How may I serve you?" He noticed an extra glitter in her eyes. Tears. Good, she was ripe for this type of assignment.

"Your lesson for Tovi was absolutely brilliant," he said tenderly. "Creative. Astounding. Unrivaled. I have not stopped thinking about your skill and potential. I think it is time that you step beyond your title of Master of Perfection. You could be great and so much more."

Rhaxma blinked several times. This was clearly not what she expected from being summoned here late in the evening. "Thank you, Your Majesty. But, what do you mean?"

"You will wear a crown someday, Rhaxma. You deserve it. Whether it is Adia or the Sea or the Desert to the North or somewhere yet undiscovered, you will be a queen, ruling side-by-side with my descendants. I want to mentor you, invest more time in you and our future. To prepare you for that day, you must hone the skills beyond Perfection." He let this sink in for a moment.

The tears were gone, replaced by shimmer and energy. It was as if he could see the visions sparking in her imagination.

"I want you to start with the rose. Xanthe failed to mark Tovi yesterday, and I'd like to see what you can do. This is a prime opportunity for you to teach her what her body can do, especially when there is something she wants to gain. I would start with identifying what she most desperately wants, and then pinpoint someone who could give it to her. Teach her what she must do to gain what she wants. Do you understand this new challenge?"

"Yes, Your Majesty. I think so."

"Good. Keep it just between us. I don't want the others knowing you are receiving special attention and instruction. However, I look forward to hearing about your success. Now, I must go to bed. Good night."

She nodded and left the chamber.

When he was alone, Damien stared at the muraled wall without really seeing it. His thoughts bounced from Calix to Rhaxma and back again. Who would succeed? Or would they unknowingly work together?

Yes, he wanted Tovi to have all the marks, but this game was really about something more. His own offspring may never show enough desire to be worthy of his crown. He needed a backup, and the winner of this new game would be the new focus of his attention.

A face popped into his head, quite uninvited. The slow uncurling of grief nearly took his breath away. Lena. She should have been queen someday. His little girl. Oh, what he would do to go back and keep her safe.

CHAPTER 31

Tovi gasped. "Bury bodies?" She was revolted by the thought.

Hesper asked urgently, "What happens when someone dies in Adia?"

"I was there when my grandfather died. I watched it happen. He grew very faint, like he was suspended between this world and another. Then suddenly he was completely gone. All those people in the dungeon, the ones who were old or had been beaten, they must have died. People in Adia say that we disappear and go on to a different world where we have an adventure with Adwin."

"Maybe our theory about the hearts is true then," Hesper said in wonder.

Zephne added, "We think that the hearts somehow mean we belong to Adwin. All of us have the heart, and we suspect many others do as well—even some of the Masters, like Xanthe. If the prisoners all have a heart, and having the heart means you belong to Adwin and his adventure, then it suddenly makes sense. Most of the people on this mountain who would disappear to this adventure would be the people in that prison."

"There's more to our theories, too," Hesper said. "Tell her about the mural, Thad."

Thad nodded. "My family is one of the oldest and richest on the mountain. My grandfather is Damien's closest friend. I practically grew up in the palace, and I still have to go frequently to keep my cover. I've been in the throne room a million times. It's this massive place—it is sometimes used as a ballroom—and all four walls are covered in one enormous mural. It's a story that you can follow as you walk around the perimeter. There is one man painted into almost every scene, and I figured out that he represents Adwin. As children we were taught that Adwin was evil and abandoned us, but I have seen the story. That's not what it looks like at all. It looks like the people here kicked him out."

"Yes." Tovi nodded. "That's close to what I have always been taught. I was told that the people here didn't want him, so he allowed them to have their freedom. He left the mountain only because they didn't want him here."

Thad smiled and clapped his hands one time. "That's exactly what it looks like."

"Do you know the end of the story? What do they tell you happens after that?" Zephne asked.

"He created Adia for his followers who left the mountain with him, he went into hiding, and now we have to search for him if we want to find him."

"No," Lyra said patiently. "After that. Do you know what's next?"

"Next? What do you mean? How could I know the future?" Tovi asked.

Thad continued, "There is a heavy red curtain covering something. There are guards stationed in front of it, so it's impossible to know what's behind it. We have made it our mission to find out what Damien is hiding behind that curtain, and we thought maybe you would know."

"No, I'm sorry. I don't know anything beyond what I have told you," Tovi responded, disappointed that she couldn't reward these kind people with the answers they so desperately sought. "If your family is so close to King Damien, why don't you just ask?"

Thad laughed. "Well, I pretend that I'm a drunk who is wasting away my life while living in my parents' house, even though I'm already twenty-eight and should be out on my own as a Master." He turned so Tovi could see his exposed back. There was no heart in the middle. "Everyone thinks I have no ambition and am happy just sitting around drinking my father's wine. If I suddenly asked questions about that curtain, it would raise questions and put my work with the HH in jeopardy."

They continued to share stories well into the night. When it came time to pull their cloaks on, Tovi was embraced by each member of the HH. They asked her to return as soon as she could without getting into trouble. The rest of the group divided loaves of bread, jars of honey, and a small stash of vegetables to take back to their families.

Xanthe and Tovi quietly made their way back to Xanthe's house. Her parents were already asleep, and Xanthe took Tovi straight to her own private wing. After donning soft pajamas, they lounged in her room and talked long into the night.

"Do you know why Calix brought you here?" Xanthe asked.

"I thought he cared about me, that he was offering me a different life. I know now that it was probably an assignment from King Damien."

"You're much smarter than they give you credit for, but it was more than just an assignment. It was a contest. About six months ago, King Damien gathered several of us younger Masters, one for each of his symbols. He named us the Council of Masters, and he told us that he had a great task for us with an unprecedented reward. It didn't go very well. None of us succeeded. Recently he added more incentive."

"Six months ago? But that's around the same time as Tali left. Do you think it is connected? What was the contest?"

"Mark an Adian. The first Master to have their symbol on an Adian and bring them to the mountain would win the prize."

Tovi gasped. "Do you think Tali was brought here after being marked?"

"No, I would have heard about it if someone marked him."

"Well, then, what happened?" Tovi asked, trying to hide her relief that Tali was not involved.

"Calix is too much of a perfectionist to jump right in, and Leeto is too much of a strategist. They both waited for quite some time and gathered information before even approaching Adia. On the other hand, Eryx charged right in. He has been spying on your village all this time, looking for the person he would try to mark. But something changed in him. None of us know what happened, but he became more subdued. He continued to travel to Adia, but he never spoke to anyone there, and he practically stopped speaking to people here. It's like he's in his own little preoccupied world. He doesn't allow people to get near him. His eyes changed color, and he shaved his head. That's when I started thinking about my color theory."

"What color theory?"

"Look at Jairus and me. His sister, Lena, was the one born with these colors. Jairus used to have two-toned hair, half brown and half maroon, split right down the middle. At some point when he was very young, he took on Lena's yellow hair and purple eyes. Even though she has been gone all these years, he still has her colors. I have had Lena's colors since I met Jairus. There has to be a connection between our loyalties and our colors. Something about Eryx's loyalty must have changed while he was in Adia."

"It makes sense. I love my brother more than anyone in the world, and we have the same colors. And look at Leeto and Rhaxma's family,"

Tovi said. Then after a pause, she changed the subject. "What brought you to the Hidden Heart?"

Xanthe played nervously with her own fingers and looked down at her lap. "I'm ashamed to say that I unleashed all of my wiles on someone in your village. I thought I had him, too. I can be very persuasive when I want to be. But I was wrong. Just when I thought he would act on his impulses, he turned away. I couldn't believe it. No man had ever walked away from me, and that's when I realized that this Adwin of yours—if he really existed—had to be more powerful than any of us realized. Just the thought of him gave that boy a strength that none of the men on this mountain have ever had. I came back, and that's when I went looking for the Hidden Heart. I had heard of people who believed in Adwin, and I was determined to find them."

Without thinking, Tovi rubbed her shoulder where her marks still prickled.

"They hurt, don't they?" Xanthe asked. "People who have the heart in their hand and the marks on their back, just like us, are the only ones who feel them. It's one of the things they taught us in school. The pain goes away if you can get rid of the heart, and you can get rid of the heart by believing their stories of evil Adwin. I don't know why, but I've just never been able to totally buy into what they told me. I've always held onto this tiny sliver of hope that there is something—someone—better out there.

"Listen, I know I hinted at this already, but I want to make sure you understand the importance of avoiding the rest of the marks. Damien has given us a new challenge. He wants you to have the full ring—all seven symbols. He also wants you to lose the heart on your palm. If that were to happen . . . " she trailed off, unable to find the right words to break the terrible news.

"What? What will happen?"

Xanthe sighed. "I really like you, Tovi. I'm going to do everything I can to protect you. But you *must* avoid those marks. If you don't, they're going to kill you and take your body back to Adia when the army goes to conquer it."

CHAPTER 32

Megara sat at the patio table, irritated that she had to waste her time on this pointless lesson task. Every few minutes she coughed, leaving black specks on her handkerchief. She barely listened to King Damien's speech aimed at the Adian brat.

"Today we have a very important lesson in store for you. It is all about Wisdom, the mark that looks like a sturdy chain. What would the world be like without wisdom? We would all be fools, Tovi. Fools about life and love and success. Wisdom is one of the keys to our perfect little world," King Damien began as they finished their breakfast. "I have brought Megara here today because she is the absolute finest example of someone who lives a life brimming with the fruit of wisdom. By the end of the day you will have a much better understanding of our world and your place in it. Now run along, you two. There is much to learn!"

Megara stood and began walking down the path toward the courtyard carrying a small sack. She wished Tovi would hurry up so they could get this lesson over with. There were much more important things on her mind.

The night before had proven to be most informative for Megara, and she was trying to decide what to do with her new information. Struggling to fall asleep because of her chronic cough, she had gone out to her balcony to get some fresh air. Movement in the courtyard below caught her by surprise. Looking closely, she realized it was Xanthe and Tovi arriving at Xanthe's house, just next door. Curiosity awakened within her, and she was consumed with the need to know what they had been up to. Staying in the shadows, she moved to the far edge of her balcony, only twenty feet from Xanthe's open window. She heard their entire conversation.

What would she do with this knowledge? What would King Damien think when he found out the future Queen Xanthe had the heart in her palm? Megara's insides purred with satisfaction. But for now, she must focus on her pupil.

Without any sort of introduction, Megara began to speak, looking straight forward and walking at a brisk pace. She could have been talking to herself for all the acknowledgment she gave Tovi.

"The key to understanding Wisdom is accepting that life will never be the way you want it. Others will always be better than you. They will have the things and people you want. There are not enough men, meals, drinks, or gold to make you happy. You must give up nonsensical dreams of happiness. Happiness is a mirage, something to forever chase and never reach. There will always be pain, heartache, misfortune, and loss. There will never be enough of anything for everyone."

They stopped on the corner of two dingy streets in the Bottom Rung. Children ran through the alleys wearing threadbare shoes. Bakers and merchants called out to passersby in coarse language. Megara watched Tovi closely. The Adian's eyes seemed to be caught by a group of men in gray uniforms who were sweeping and clearing trash from the gutters outside of a worn-down building with a swinging green sign.

"Look at them, Tovi. They are not worthy of any position in this entire kingdom except cleaning the muck off these streets. That is their role. It is their identity. They are worthless without their ability to work. Do you think they want that life? Of course not. But it's all they get."

Megara clapped her hands loudly. The commotion around her stilled, and all eyes turned in her direction. A woman with hot pink hair came out of the closest building, and a small girl peeked around her skirt.

"You, woman, come here!" she called. The mother, with her daughter still clinging to her, walked a few paces into the street, looking unsure and glancing several times at Tovi.

Megara opened the small sack in her hands and drew out several heavy gold coins. In a suspiciously sweet tone she asked, "What would you do with these if I gave them to you?"

"I—I don't know. Probably new clothes for my children. Some extra food for the pantry."

Megara turned toward the small girl and bent down so they were on eye level. "Do you want this, child?" She held her laden hand out.

The little girl pulled her fingers out of her mouth and tentatively reached toward the sparkling coins. As she was about to touch them, Megara pulled her hand back and straightened up. "Too late. I'll keep them." She put the coins back in the sack and turned to Tovi. "That is how life works. When something seems too good to be true, it is. When things look to be going your way, they aren't really. All we have in life is what we've earned and a tiny bit of luck."

She looked closely at her student. Tovi was very quiet, but her eyes were scrunched in anger. "Do you feel sorry for them?"

Tovi remained quiet, eyeing the people that had gathered along the street.

"Answer me!" Megara demanded.

Tovi waited a beat and then swung her glance up to Megara. "Of course, I do, but not as much as I despise you," she said quietly, grabbing the sack out of Megara's hand and tossing it at the feet of the pink-haired woman before Megara could register what was happening. "You're miserable and loathsome. I'd rather be a fool than die a little bit every day for the sake of your wisdom."

Megara brought her face so close to Tovi that she could see the details of the little purple star in her eye. Every nerve in her body prickled with a mix of sickly shame and enraged pride. But she refused to show it. Not to this wretched Adian. "I know things, Tovi. Things that will break you. You'll be sorry you didn't play along with this little lesson. I have other ways to teach you. Soon enough you will understand wisdom."

CHAPTER 33

As evening approached, Tovi sat on an elaborate cushioned chair in her bedroom, looking in a mirror as Cora pinned her hair. She wore her opal necklace, which was perfectly framed by the deep gray folds of satin that wrapped her body. As Tovi studied her reflection, her mind wandered to her life not so long ago, when the colors that sparkled from her necklace were the colors that appeared in the rivers and ponds at just the right time before dusk.

What a confusing place this was. The fullness promised by BiBi had not been enough. She still felt hollow, and the necklace felt heavy on her chest.

A quiet tap on the door made her jump out of her musings. Without permission, Calix entered and asked Cora to leave. The servant promptly obeyed, and Tovi watched her go with apprehension.

Tovi refused to turn around, so she eyed Calix through the mirror. He leaned against the wall, his hands in the pockets of his fancy gray trousers. The crisp white shirt was untucked and unbuttoned to mid-chest, his feet were bare, and he hadn't shaved that day. Tovi tried to ignore how handsome he looked in this less-severe, unkempt state.

He then spoke so softly that Tovi almost missed what he said. "I think it's time I told you something, Tovi. And then I have an apology to make."

She still did not turn, but she matched his gaze through the mirror.

"I am so ashamed by the way I have treated you. There is no excuse, and I have no right to even speak to you. But I beg you to hear me out." He paused, but when she still didn't turn, he resumed his speech. "Anger has been a part of me for as long as I can remember. I learned it from my father who used to beat my mother, my sister, and most of all me whenever he was unhappy. He died when I was young, and I was glad to see him go."

A black tear dripped down Calix's face, and Tovi watched it fall to his jawline. Her own anger was fading as this man opened up to her. As he continued, he walked slowly toward Tovi.

"I inherited his anger, Tovi. I hate it. His Majesty has worked for years, teaching me to harness it. And usually I can. But every once in a while, I fail completely."

He sank to one knee beside her and reached for her hand. She finally looked away from the mirror and into his face. More tears were building in his eyes.

"I raised my hand against you, and I will never forgive myself for it. I have shown my weakness in front of you multiple times, and it is fair if you think I hate you. But that is so far from the truth. Tovi, it is the opposite. You have taken hold of my heart, and you are all that I want. So, when I have been faced with disappointments that involve you, my love, I can't control myself. My rage is equal to my love for you. Can you see that?"

Without thinking, Tovi reached out her gloved hand and wiped the wetness from his cheek.

"Forgive me, Tovi. Please forgive me. I just want all of this to go back to what it felt like in that tree in Adia, or when we were dancing behind the hedge. Please, give me another chance to be worthy of your love."

Tovi's brow wrinkled as she concentrated, trying to think despite the way his words turned her mind to mush. Her heart twisted painfully at the thought of a scared little boy hiding from his father's wrath. She saw traces of that little boy still in front of her. "I forgive you, Calix," she said, leaning forward to kiss him softly. "But you must never strike me again."

"Never," he said, his eyes boldly staring into hers. "Never." He kissed her with hunger this time, and she could hardly catch her breath. It reminded her of their first kisses after the wedding, when she had been sorely disappointed. She sighed, coming to terms with the death of her romantic ideas about how love should feel.

"It's almost time to go. I'll ask Cora to come back and finish your hair," he said. "I love you, Tovi."

An hour later, on their way to the palace, Tovi looked down for the hundredth time, smoothing silver satin over her abdomen, feeling ridiculous with her padded chest and hips.

"You look beautiful," Calix said, leading her up a set of wide stairs. "Stop fidgeting."

The inside of the palace was extravagant. All she had seen on her mornings with the king had been the corridors leading to the patio. Tonight, she was escorted through plush parlors and chambers. There were thick purple carpets, life-size tapestries, and the gleam of precious metals and gems. Savory aromas swam through the air, coming from golden trays held high by male servants. A large woman with long black hair stood in a corner of the throne room singing a complicated melody.

There was general chatter all around coming from the well-dressed elite of Mount Damien. Golden chandeliers with hundreds of tiny candles bathed the space in rich light. The floor was a rich, caramel-colored marble, as were the majestic columns that supported the domed glass ceiling.

Just as Thad had described the night before, all four walls—from top to bottom—were covered in scenes painted directly onto the upright stone slabs. Part of the fourth wall was covered in a dark red curtain. Tovi noticed Xanthe standing near the wall, investigating parts of the mural. As soon as she could without being noticed, Tovi slipped away and joined her. Seeing the mural up close, she realized it had to be at least a hundred years old.

Xanthe pointed at one picture in particular and whispered to Tovi, "This one must be Adwin." She moved along, touching the same character in each scene. "Brown eyes, brown hair. Brown eyes, brown hair. Brown eyes, brown hair. It's the same person over and over again."

"Brown eyes?" Tovi responded, not sure what Xanthe meant. Bright blue eyes—not brown—sparkled from every inch of the mural. The hair was brown, but the eyes were definitely blue.

Their conversation was cut short as King Damien approached. He looped Tovi's hand under his elbow and led her out of the room. He called to his butler, "Please announce dinner."

There were several long tables set for the guests in the palace's formal banquet hall. King Damien sat in the center and placed Tovi in the seat of honor, directly to his left, with Calix on her other side. Eryx, seated directly across from her, stayed quiet and kept his eyes averted.

Tovi could not stop thinking about the mural. Brown eyes. Blue eyes. Had Xanthe been looking at a different person? But she had pointed very clearly at the blue-eyed man. And what about the face itself? It looked just like . . . But surely not. It must just be someone who looked a lot like S—

"Tovi, answer His Majesty when he speaks to you," Calix chastised, snapping Tovi to attention.

"I'm so sorry! I was thinking about . . . about all your beautiful artwork inside the palace. What did you ask?"

Damien chuckled. "It's quite all right, Tovi. I've only just realized that we've spent all this time together, but I haven't asked a thing about your family. I'd like to know more. Tell me about them."

"I don't know much about them really. I grew up with two guardians, not my parents. And my twin brother."

Damien's face went very white and his eyes flashed as if they reflected lightning. Recovering, he said, "Twins. How wonderful. What is his name?"

"Tali, Your Majesty."

Damien's smile was forced, and for once he was very quiet. There was a cold and exacting aura around him as he observed Tovi more closely throughout the final courses. He hardly ate.

CHAPTER 34

Ganya walked among the tall grasses that lined the bank of the river in Adia. The last light of the day sparkled on the water, which lapped with comforting rhythm against the moss-covered pebbles. Her dear friend Leora walked beside her, and both breathed in the fragrance of fresh water mixed with pine. They carried long, shallow baskets with handles looped around their bent elbows. Occasionally they would reach down to pull a plant up, roots and all, and sometimes they snapped off just the leaves or stems.

These had been long, difficult days for Ganya without her family. First Tali, then Avi, then Tovi, then Tali again—although this time she had been able to give him a long hug and grandmotherly farewell.

She looked into the distance, letting the breeze catch wisps of her white hair. She felt so much older, so much feebler, than she had just a few weeks before. She also felt a resigned peacefulness. She had been through challenges before. With Silas' help she'd make it through this one, too.

"I hope he knows what he's doing," Ganya said more to herself than to Leora.

Leora looped her free arm through Ganya's. "He always does, doesn't he? My suspicion is that all will be well. It just may be awhile before we know what 'well' looks like."

Ganya nodded and smiled at her friend. What a gift, to have a friend who was more like family. Leora had been like a sister for most of their adult lives. Nearly thirty years ago she had arrived in the early hours of the morning, soaking wet from the rising waters.

There were floods every few years, and that one was more intense than most. Once they got her to the tree house, it had been weeks before any of them stepped foot on solid ground again. Leora often laughed as she recalled her horror at being trapped up in the trees. "I thought I'd never get down. But perhaps that was Silas' way of getting me to stay put for a while."

She lived for a time with Ganya and Avi in the little room that would someday belong to Tovi and Tali. The Tivkas nursed her back to health, and Silas stopped in for daily visits, just as he had while she was imprisoned on the mountain. The dungeons in King Damien's palace had done great harm to poor Leora, and she didn't like to talk about it. However, Ganya knew her friend had been through unimaginable horrors. Leora often cried out in her nightmares, begging for her baby to be returned to her. When that would happen, Ganya would knock lightly on her door and enter the room without waiting for permission. She would hold her friend and let her weep as the candlelight chased away the demon memories.

For the last six or seven months, Leora had paid back all this kindness and more. She had walked the painful road with Ganya. Tali's disappearance, Avi's death . . . and then Tovi. A runaway. Ganya looked up toward the cloud-shrouded mountain and shuddered. Her life was unrecognizable from what it had been just a year ago.

They walked at a slow pace, and both were quiet until one of Leora's feet made a loud squish. She poked at the wet ground with a toe. "Do you think it is rising? How long has it been since the last flood?"

"It's about time for another if my memory serves me well," Ganya said. "And the ground always knows before we do." She ran her own feet over a watery patch of grass. "I noticed it several days ago, but I hoped I was wrong. Now I know the waters are coming."

"We'll need to tell the others," Leora said. "We can send them out tomorrow to start storing up some rations. The last few have been mild. This one could be the same, or it may be a real doozy."

They turned their backs to the river in unison, walking slowly toward the village in the treetops. "I am afraid of only one thing," Ganya said, her voice quiet, barely heard over the breeze.

"What is it?" Leora asked.

"When the waters rise, there is no going out or coming in. What if Tali and Tovi can't get home?"

Leora squeezed Ganya's arm. "Silas will get them home, my friend. He always does."

CHAPTER 35

When the grand feast was finished, the party adjourned to the patio. It was lit by several thick candles that were taller than Tovi. They were placed directly on the ground at regular intervals along the edge of the space. Their flames reached high above their heads and cast orb-like glows.

Tovi stood alone and was grateful for a few seconds of peace. As she looked around, her eyes caught those of Eryx, the fighter who had somehow known her name. He was walking toward her but stopped several feet away. They stood and stared at one another for a moment before he turned and escaped into the palace.

Checking to see that Calix and Damien were still engaged in lively conversation, she quietly followed Eryx through the wide open doors. She tiptoed through the banquet hall and down a lushly carpeted corridor, but there was no sign of Eryx anymore.

She wandered for several minutes, studying paintings and tapestries, before winding up in the throne room. She walked directly to the mural, starting her investigation to the right of the door. The first few inches were a solid, pale blue, and then rough outlines of trees and slopes began to form. Within feet, the walls were covered in an incredible landscape complete with rolling hills, vibrant plains, and a bright morning sky. She scanned the rest of the room and saw that the story ended abruptly behind the thick red curtain.

She went back to the beginning and started looking at the details. She found the face that was in almost every scene on the wall, and she frowned in concentration. Definitely blue eyes. How could Xanthe think they were brown? The man in the mural reminded her of Silas, with similar shaggy brown hair and a tall, lean frame. Her heart ached with homesickness.

She was nearly halfway around the room when the images began to change. Darker colors crept into the palette, and somehow the story was familiar. She saw a young boy sitting against a tree, contempt pouring from his eyes. Words and images flowed back to her from a distant memory, a time when Ganya had first told her the story of Adwin. "Once there was a young boy who lived on a mountain. He sat beneath a tree while the other children played."

She was puzzled. This mural seemed ancient, but the events it portrayed happened only fifty-some years ago. Ganya and Avi had been part of the story, following Adwin off the mountain and into their new valley home. The cracks and chips in the faded paint didn't make sense.

The next several portions of the mural showed the two together, the pouty young boy and the blue-eyed man. It showed them fishing, building a treehouse, playing a guitar and fiddle. The boy no longer looked angry. His face radiated with a joy that mirrored the man beside him. She heard Ganya's voice again. "Adwin loved the boy and took him as an apprentice, even though he knew who the boy might become . . ."

"We were very close in those days," a soft voice said from across the room, making Tovi shiver. "But that was before he left me."

She turned to see King Damien sauntering toward her, his metal-tipped boots clicking against the marble tiles. "See there? That's me," he said, pointing to the boy.

"That's impossible."

"Why would you say that?" he asked, now standing close beside her, staring at the mural.

"Look at the way it's fading, and some of the paint is cracked. It must be at least a hundred years old."

"You underestimate the durability of sacred prophecy, Tovi. These stone slabs have been here for much longer than that. The palace was merely built around them."

She looked at it again, trying to understand.

"This is not a history book quite yet, dear girl, although many of these scenes have come to pass since the artist put paint to stone. See, there I am with Adwin when he taught me how to fiddle." He pointed to one of the scenes Tovi had already examined. "I believe he goes by a different name now."

"No, we still call him Adwin."

Damien laughed, cruel and hollow. "So, you haven't figured it out yet, have you?" He gazed at the painting and laughed again before turning toward Tovi. "Really, I think you have. You have just been denying it. Just as I have been denying what the color of your hair and that little star in your eye must mean."

Tovi looked at him quietly, waiting for him to continue. Her pulse beat loudly in her ears.

Damien looked at the mural, running a pale finger over one of the scenes that depicted him as a young boy. "Adwin took a new name when he left the mountain. He is the man you call Silas."

Tovi lost all sense of stability, her world dropping out from under her and the walls tipping and swaying. A loud buzzing filled her mind, and she reached out to steady herself against the stone. Her mind flashed to the ridge, his painting studio, the dance floor at a wedding, his sparkling blue eyes.

"Yes, yes, my dear. The one who stole you from your parents? The one who took your brother? The one who allowed Avi to die? He and Silas are one and the same."

Details collided in ways she had never processed before, and she felt like she might get sick. On top of the buzzing in her mind and the heartbeat in her ears, the edge of her vision was going black.

Silas had taken her from her parents and never told her the truth? Silas took her brother and never told her where he went? Silas listened to her constant questions and never gave her the answers that were right there? He could have saved her from months—years!—of torment, and he didn't. He had actually *caused* the pain and agony.

The love she had for Silas was thrown under a shroud of darkness and hatred like nothing she had known before. She wanted him to hurt. She wanted him to be as broken as she was.

She felt another slice across her back. She took a ragged inhale, still holding the wall for support. Damien chuckled softly.

"There are many secrets that you don't know, Tovi. Secrets so deep that few understand. These walls don't just tell our history. They also tell our present and future. We will get to that with time. Right now, I want to tell you the true story of Adwin. I'm afraid it diverges dramatically from the tales you have been told. By the end, you will see that Silas is not a friend to be trusted.

"You see," he said, pointing to the scene of the pouting boy under the tree, "this is where your people changed the story. I'm sure you've been told that I was an evil child, a greedy little boy who wanted attention. That is partially true. I didn't understand the ways of the world yet, and I must admit I was jealous of the adoration poured onto Adwin. All I wanted was to know what it was like to be loved. My parents had always despised me, and I had no siblings. I was very alone.

"That was when I first started dreaming of a new way. I had ideas, grandiose goals and inspired vision. I could see that our mountain needed to change if it was going to thrive. But Adwin didn't want me to steal any of his power. I see that now. He began teaching me all sorts of things and taking me along on extraordinary quests. I thought we were becoming the greatest of friends, the most powerful of allies. It wasn't until later that I realized he was only manipulating my young heart.

"He thought he could squelch my desires and aspirations by distracting me from them, and he was successful for several years. But in the end, I was not to be deterred. I began teaching others about the possibilities for a brighter future, a future based on Pleasure, Adoration, Perfection, Prosperity, Wisdom, Power and Control. Before long I had most of the city behind me. I went to Adwin and shared my philosophy with him. I so desperately wanted his partnership. Above all else, I wanted him beside me as I ruled this mountain," he said, walking Tovi past several scenes of growing torch-bearing mobs.

"Soon enough, I had so much support that there was no use fighting it. Adwin fled from the mountain, swearing he would one day retaliate and win the mountain back."

Tovi and Damien walked along the wall, watching as the mural illustrated parts of his story. When they reached the place that showed Silas heading for the valley, they stopped. "My heart has never completely healed from that moment when he walked away. It all could have been such a happy ending. Instead, he chose to leave me, and I will never forgive him for that."

He wandered through his own musings for just a moment and then apologized. "Forgive me for rambling. It is hard to be concise when telling a story so close to my heart. I just can't stand to see you being misled the way I was. That man who claims to be a good king spends more time making you those silly flowers than fixing all the hurt in the world."

The sound of several voices drew near, and party guests swarmed through the door. Calix approached Tovi and Damien and said, "It got a bit chilly outside. We didn't interrupt anything, did we?"

"Of course not. Just a little history lesson," Damien answered as a servant refilled his glass with blood-red wine. Speaking directly to Tovi, he said, "We will continue our lessons in the morning. See you at breakfast."

He vanished into the crowd, leaving Tovi confused, heartbroken, and bitterly furious. The buzzing had subsided, but it was replaced by a throbbing headache and a feeling like she was in the room but not fully present.

It was quite late when the guests finally dispersed. Xanthe accompanied Tovi and Calix back to the house and up to the terrace. She asked if she could speak to Tovi privately, and Calix reluctantly agreed.

As soon as they were alone, Xanthe whispered excitedly, "So, what do you think? Why do we see the mural differently? I mean, it has to mean something that I see his eyes as brown and you see them as blue. It's got to be something important. Don't you think?"

"I have so much to tell you," Tovi said weakly, massaging her temples. She recounted her conversation with Damien as quickly and quietly as she could.

"So, you *do* know him? You just didn't *know* that you know him? This is unbelievable, Tovi! It's all true, then! He's real . . . Tell me *everything* about him."

The excitement in Xanthe's voice grated on Tovi's nerves. "You don't understand. You don't know what he's done to me."

Calix stepped through the door and looked at Xanthe with annoyance. "It's late. Shouldn't you be leaving?"

Her face fell back into its lifeless mask. "Haven't you noticed that Tovi hasn't earned her rose yet? His Majesty asked me to give her some extra tutoring since she's proving to be slow with this one. And apparently *you* haven't been any help since she's been here."

His eyes narrowed, and Tovi was fairly certain that he didn't buy it. But either way, he went back into the house.

"Tomorrow night," Tovi said. "Tomorrow I'll meet you at the HH, and I'll tell all of you everything."

Xanthe nodded and rushed home. Finally, Tovi was alone with her confused and tortured thoughts. She stood at the railing of her balcony, eyes searching the skyline punctuated with lit windows. He was out there. She didn't want to miss him, but she did. She wanted to hate him, and it was easy. How could she love and despise the same person so thoroughly? How could Silas, her dear friend, have done those things? How could he be responsible for kidnapping her from her parents? How could he be the one who stole her brother? What kind of monster would do this to her, all the while pretending to love her?

His face swam before her eyes, and another wave of hatred coursed through her veins. The marks on her back were on fire, and she could hardly bear it. She wanted desperately to go home, but she didn't know where that would be.

Calix came out to the terrace and stood just behind her. He wrapped his arms around her waist and kissed the back of her neck.

He gently tugged her toward the door, and she let him lead her back inside. Any distraction was welcome. She hoped that giving into his desires would dull the hate and pain in her heart.

CHAPTER 36

King Damien sat on his throne, thrilled to see the last few lingering guests leave. There was too much circling his mind. Tovi and Tali. Twins. Dark blue. Brown with a purple star. A boy and a girl.

His thoughts flipped to a night twenty years ago. How different his life was then. His adoring wife still alive. His son married to the graceful and kind Thomae. Two young grandchildren, a boy and a girl, bringing light and life and joy to the palace. And then it all changed so suddenly. He rarely thought about that night and the horrors it held.

Everything had been completely fine. Thomae's pregnancy had been healthy and just like the other two. But, the birth of the third child did not go as planned.

A strong baby boy with brown eyes and a purple star in his left iris. The wispy fuzz on his head was dark blue. The moment Damien laid eyes on him, he knew he was the third conqueror in the prophecy.

And then the unthinkable. Princess Thomae began to moan. The midwives pressed on her abdomen and looked stricken. "What is it?" the King demanded.

Twins.

Within a few minutes another baby arrived. A little girl with bright blue eyes.

Terrifying colors. He had feared it would one day happen, but he had been prepared to stop them from having a fourth someday in the future. He thought he had time. He thought he could find a way to keep his family together while ensuring there would never be a fourth. But she was here. The fourth.

Within the hour he had sent them to be executed. The mother and the babies. He had adored five-year-old Helena with her violet eyes and blonde curly pigtails, but she had sneaked in the room to get a peek at the new baby. She had seen there were two. No one could know. She had to be killed as well, but it had nearly been the end of him to give that order.

He could still hear Thomae's screams as the babies were whisked out of the room. She never even held the second one.

Worse than those screams, he could still hear little Lena's whimpers and cries of "Grandpapa!" as he turned his back and the guards took her away. He could still taste the vomit in his mouth as he was violently sick all that night.

Lena. Such a bright and shining star in his dark sky. When he allowed himself to think about her, one particular memory always surfaced.

She was four years old, and she sat on his lap wearing a pink dress. The mountain hadn't turned away from colorful clothing yet. Her blonde curls bounced around her cherub face as she giggled. "No, Grandpapa! It goes like this!" she cried gleefully, straightening Damien's crown, which he had purposely set on his head at an angle.

"What do you mean, young lady? Do you think this looks silly?" he asked, pushing the crown off one ear again.

She was beside herself, scrunching her eyes and nose and shrieking the way only a small child can. "Yes, Grandpapa! You *are* silly."

He helped her straighten the crown once more. "Would you like to wear this crown someday when you are old enough?" he asked tenderly. She shook her head and frowned. "Why not, my dear girl? You can have my crown and my throne."

She looked lovingly at her grandfather as if contemplating something very serious. He had a hard time remembering she was only four and not a very, very wise old soul. "Grandpapa, your chair is too big for me, and it is a very heavy crown."

He shook himself and blinked away the black tears that had collected in his eyes. He must not think of sweet Lena now.

How had the babies survived? And did anyone else know their true identity? It was clear Tovi was completely ignorant of her rightful place in this very palace. What about the boy? Did he know? Is that why he was wandering somewhere in the hills?

A subtle cough roused his attention. "Excuse me, Your Majesty," Megara said from the doorway. "May I interrupt your thoughts?"

"Come in, dear girl. What is it?"

She approached his throne swiftly, and he could tell by the shine in her normally dull eyes that she had something delicious to tell him. "I must report a heart. It's Xanthe. I'm sorry, Your Majesty. I know she is almost family."

Damien froze, staring intently at his weapon. "Xanthe? Have you seen it?"

"No. I heard her speak of it. She and Tovi have attended some sort of secret meeting for rebels with hearts in their hands. It's disgusting, Your Majesty."

"Thank you, you may go," he declared.

"But, Your—"

"You may go," he said more forcefully. Megara's face crumpled in disappointment, but she turned around and exited the room.

Damien closed his eyes for a moment and sighed. He had never felt so tired.

CHAPTER 37

Lyra and Hesper stood on the upper balcony of the HH headquarters keeping watch for approaching members—or worse. It was a calm, cool evening, and Hesper's arm rested across Lyra's shoulders. Their children were tucked in bed, and being alone reminded Lyra of the years of their courtship. She smiled up at her husband, who leaned down and kissed the tip of her nose with a laugh. Then, a movement below caught their attention.

A figure appeared in the distance wearing a cloak with a hood. He, or at least Lyra guessed it was a he, stood in the middle of the road as if he was waiting on someone or something. Just a moment later, Xanthe turned a corner very close to him. The man put out his hands in a gesture of trying to stop her.

A few words drifted to them in the quiet of the night. "Don't" and "Further" were clearly heard. Xanthe attempted to struggle past, but he blocked her path.

"I should go help her," Hesper said.

"No! We can't be caught out there together. No one would understand why you would protect a Master who was suspiciously found in the Bottom Rung."

Before Hesper could argue, two palace guards appeared, taking hold of Xanthe. The women in black body suits looked fierce and lethal, even from such a distance. They dragged Xanthe out of sight.

"Oh no!" Lyra whimpered. "What does this mean? Where are they taking her?"

Hesper continued to stare at the mysterious, cloaked man who still stood in the street. He had not done anything to stop the guards, but he didn't appear to be one of them. And then, the cloaked man turned and looked directly at the spot where the couple stood.

As Hesper and Lyra watched, the stranger raised his right hand to shoulder height and made the secret salute, drawing half a heart in the air.

Lyra gasped. Surely this was no friend of theirs. But how then would he know . . . ?

The man was walking toward the HH. "Come with me," Hesper commanded. "I will go outside to meet him. You lock the door behind me, and then tell everyone to hide. It may be time."

"But Meira has not returned! It can't be time."

"We may have to go without her."

"I can't lock you outside, darling. What if something happens to you?" she wailed, holding Hesper tight.

"I will be fine. After I have determined if he is friend or foe, I will give you a sign. Come back to the window after telling the others to hide. If I give the HH signal, you must leave me and go to the mines with the others. If I knock three times, you may open the door for us. Understood?"

Lyra trembled, hating her husband's bravery but determined to match it. She nodded and followed him down to the entrance. She closed and locked the door behind him, whispering, "Oh Adwin, if you are out there, protect him!" and she hustled back up the stairs.

"Quickly, friends! Into hiding. Something is amiss outside. Hesper has gone to investigate. Quickly, quickly! Help the children into the closets, that's right. Everyone else, you know where to go. Be ready. If I come back and say we must go to the mines, then do not hesitate to obey me. I will be right back."

After seeing everyone safely into their hiding places, she ran back down the stairs. She pulled back a curtain and looked through the glass.

Hesper was weeping in the embrace of the strange man. The stranger's cloak had fallen back, revealing messy hot pink hair.

Still clutching the man's shoulder with one hand, Hesper wiped his eyes with the other. He led the stranger to the door and knocked three times.

Baffled, Lyra opened it. She looked into the stranger's big teal eyes, and somehow, she knew every second of waiting had been worth it. Every doubt, sleepless night, and moment of danger paled, and she would do it all a hundred times more for this man.

"Adwin," she said, and his broad smile confirmed it. "Please, come inside." She couldn't stop staring at his face as he entered and removed his cloak.

"Is there somewhere we can speak privately?" he asked.

"Of course. Right in here," she answered, still staring in shock. "Let me tell the others that they may get out of their hiding place."

"Good idea, but please don't tell them I am here. I need to speak with both of you first, before I meet them."

Lyra nodded and once more made her rounds of the building, asking the members of the HH to wait upstairs while she and Hesper met with their guest. When she returned to the downstairs sitting room, Adwin said, "Your husband asked about Xanthe, and I wanted to wait until you returned so I could tell you both. She is being taken to the palace, where she will be put in prison for her heart."

Lyra gasped. "Why did you let that happen?"

"I know this will be hard to understand," he said with great pain and sadness evident in the creases around his eyes. "But I had to stop her for many reasons. One of those reasons is for her good and just between her and me. The other is much broader and far-reaching. If I had allowed her to pass, the guards would have caught up to her right in front of this building. All of you would have been in grave danger, and there wouldn't have been time to go into the mines. Everything you have worked for, in my name, would be wasted."

"You know about that?" Hesper asked.

Adwin tried to answer, but Lyra hastily interrupted, "My dear, who do you think commanded Meira to prepare the mines? Of course, Adwin knows about the mines."

"It would be better if you called me Silas. That way if you are ever overheard, you may be protected. Very few people on the mountain know my new name. And you are correct, I gave the orders for Meira to create tunnels and hideaways in the mines. But it is not time to utilize those yet. I have come for a different reason."

"What is it, Silas?" Lyra asked, trying out the new name and liking it.

"Two reasons, actually. First, I must ask a dangerous favor of you and the HH. Second, and more importantly, I have come to break bread with my bravest, most loyal friends. Someday you will understand why I waited so long, but that wait is now over. I am so pleased and so proud of both of you," he said, taking both Hesper and Lyra into his arms as if they were children. They let him surround them and both wept. Their long wait was indeed over, and their hope had been turned to reality.

CHAPTER 38

Lying in the dark of Calix's room, Tovi stared toward the ceiling and listened to the deep, even breaths that told her he was asleep. Her back was on fire, and she couldn't get comfortable. She quietly rose from the bed and tiptoed down the hall, making her way to her own room and her now-familiar terrace.

Sitting under the stars in the cool of night, Tovi tried to accept the truth about Silas. Her best friend. The king who stole everyone she had loved. How could they be one and the same? Her head pounded and her heart ached. She wanted to scream that nothing made sense, but she knew deep inside that everything *did* make sense.

A commotion in the courtyard made Tovi stand and approach the railing. Two guards pulled Xanthe by the arm, dragging her toward the palace. "Let go of me!" Xanthe protested, her voice echoing against the stone buildings. The women ignored her.

Forgetting everything else, Tovi ran barefoot down the stairs and out the door, staying in the shadows but following as closely as she could. She sneaked into the palace, staying just a few paces behind the guards and Master causing such a big scene. When Xanthe was led into the throne room, Tovi stayed at the door, peering in and listening.

"Do you know why you are here?" King Damien asked calmly.

By now Xanthe was disheveled but still beautiful. Her hair was in disarray, and her dress had slipped off one shoulder. "No, I do not know why I was dragged here so roughly in the middle of the night."

"Take off your gloves."

Xanthe opened her mouth to say something but stopped as soon as she heard the command.

"I said, take off your gloves."

They were the same gloves she had been wearing when she spoke to Tovi in the garden, the ones with the pearls at the wrists.

"Your Majesty, I—"

"Take off your gloves!" Damien bellowed, the veins in his eyes momentarily expanding so they looked webbed.

"I don't underst—"

Damien rose from his throne and descended to the girl, grabbing her wrist, and unceremoniously tearing the glove away. When the brown heart in her palm became visible, he closed his eyes and took a deep breath. Through clenched teeth he said, "She is not fit to be a Master. She is not fit to be the wife of a future king. She is not fit to stay alive. But in my mercy, she may live. Take her to the dungeon."

Tovi could not bear to watch as Xanthe struggled against the guards and pleaded with King Damien. She covered her ears and spun around, ready to leave, but her path was blocked. Jairus stood just behind her, his expression pained. How long had he been there?

"Can't you do something?" Tovi whispered. Jairus turned his gaze to Tovi, and there was such a pleading fear in his face that for the first time Tovi felt sorry for the young prince.

"Not while he is this angry. It would do her more harm than good. But I'll do everything I can once he's calmed down," he answered quietly.

At that moment Prince Ajax entered the throne room from the opposite side. Jairus motioned for Tovi to be quiet, and they both watched intently through the opening.

Damien paced while Ajax stood still. They were now alone in the throne room. "What is it, Father?"

"My son, I fear for our future."

"What happened?"

"For all these years, we were under the impression that Jairus was your only surviving child. We did everything in our power to make sure the others were killed. After tonight, I am confident that three of your offspring are alive, and I am more concerned than ever that all four may be out there."

"How could this be?"

"Your daughter was in the palace tonight."

"Lena?" Ajax asked, and Tovi was certain there was a hint of hopefulness in his tone.

"No, the baby girl."

"The baby girl? The twin? How can you be certain?"

"She has taken on the boy's colors, but it is her. I have no doubt that Tovi is your fourth child."

The conversation continued, but Tovi heard nothing of it. She turned to face Jairus, and she could feel the blood rushing out of her head and pooling in her toes. Her brown eyes met his violet, and they stared at one another. Several truths crashed through her mind.

She was looking at a brother she never knew she had.

She was a royal descendant of King Damien, a princess of this mountain.

Her grandfather had wanted her dead. Her father had let him try.

Both men were standing in the adjacent room.

Her long-held dream of loving parents shattered. Everything about her identity was thrown off kilter. In all her time of wanting to know who she was, she never dreamed it would be something like this.

Suddenly and unexpectedly, Silas' face came to mind. A deep longing to speak to him, to talk things through with him, and to just be with him came over her, but her very next thought reminded her of her rage. He must have known, and he kept it from her. How dare he? And why? The hatred she felt earlier in the evening overwhelmed her once more. He knew she had a family. He had kept her from them. How many times had she told him she wanted to know her parents? All along he had known. He could have told her. And he didn't. How could he? How evil must he be to do this to her?

Having nowhere else to go and not knowing what else to do, she ran out of the palace and across the cobblestones, not caring if she was seen. She pushed away the voice in her mind that called to her.

Next time, don't do it alone. Next time, run toward me.

She ran straight inside Calix's home and up the stairs to her room. She closed herself in the bathroom, surrounded by her unrecognizable reflections, wondering how she had become the woman looking back at her.

The pain in her back increased, searing the skin along the base of her spine. She began to weep again and desperately tried to imagine that she was at the ridge. She conjured images of the mountains, the sky, the flowers, his face. No! Not his face! Anything but his face!

Silas. Responsible for taking her from her family. Responsible for stealing her brother. Responsible for keeping unfathomable secrets. Despite all these thoughts, his kind face in her memory held firm. She longed more than anything to talk with him, ask him her questions, and get answers that could soothe her pain. But she hated him! And she missed him . . . She hated him and missed him and hated him. It was all too much.

She turned her back to one of the mirrors and craned her neck so she could look at the new symbols, and her sobbing grew heavier and louder. Five terrible marks: snake, scales, diamond, flames, rose. Five marks that showed her unworthiness, her dirtiness, and her failure. Silas would never forgive her if he saw them. He would never accept her, now that the truth was out. He would look at her as the despicable, weak offspring of King Damien, someone unworthy of his time and attention.

As she thought these things, she watched in the mirror as a coil of chains was sliced into her skin. It was her sixth mark. Wisdom. Only one to go. The ring was almost complete, and then she would die at the hands of one of the Masters.

Her eyes darted from reflection to reflection, her mind absorbed in the darkest of thoughts. She had to find a way—any way!—to get the marks off her skin. She ran to the sink, filling it with hot water and soap. Doing her best to wind her arms around behind her, she frantically scrubbed with a small towel.

Her skin was red and raw, and the back of her dress was soaked. But the marks were as dark as ever. Wave after wave of grief and pain washed over her, engulfing her in panic. She fumbled around inside a cabinet looking for something that would help her. She found a porous stone that the servants used to grate away dead skin. Grabbing it with shaking hands, she went back to the large walls of mirror and knelt, once again turning her back. She looked over her shoulder as she attempted to scrape away the ugliness. She used every ounce of strength that she could muster, but all she accomplished was making herself bleed.

She collapsed, lying on the cold floor, her body heaving with hopeless sobs. She reached behind her and dug into her back with her sharp fingernails. She pulled at her flesh, tearing it apart until something thicker than blood oozed out.

As she teetered between unconsciousness and reality, she heard Silas' voice.

I know it hurts. You can't make it go away on your own. Just remember that I love you. No matter what happens out there, I'm always here for you.

At first, she thought he was there, calling to her. Then she realized it was only bits of memory, words he had once spoken in a different place and time.

She cried herself into oblivion.

CHAPTER 39

"She needs help. I want you to go to her," Silas explained for the third time.

"If she's in so much trouble, why don't you just go yourself?" Eryx asked, irritated that this man kept finding a way into his house.

"I will if you refuse, but it would be better for all involved if it was you."

It took all of Eryx's strength to feign nonchalance and hide his terror and rage. Every instinct was screaming for vengeance, and he wanted nothing more than to find Calix and . . .

"You are not to lay a finger on him," Silas said.

"Then don't send me into his house."

"He is not responsible for her current state."

"He's responsible for bringing her here, and that's enough for me."

"Listen to me, Eryx," Silas commanded firmly. "One of us needs to go to her, care for her, and give her a reason to hope. As I've told you before, it would be better if it was you."

"Why?" he yelled, slamming his fist on the table. "You keep going around in circles saying the same things, but you won't tell me why. Why should it be me?"

"Because you need this just as much as she does."

Eryx hated that answer. He glared at Silas for a few more moments before silently rising from the table and stomping out the door. As Silas had told him to do, he climbed the balconies of Calix's home until he came to Tovi's terrace. He slipped inside her bedroom and made his way to her bathroom.

What he saw made him stop in his tracks and stare through burning eyes.

Her fragile body was contorted on the floor, the torn flesh around her marks bleeding red and black. If it weren't for the slight rise and fall of her breath, he would think she was dead.

Six. Six of the seven marks. The ring was almost complete. His heart broke at the sight of his own mark staring back at him. When had she earned the twisted flames? Who had marked her? When had she begun to experience the slow decay of true hatred in her heart? It was something he felt every day, and ever since he first saw her, he had hoped it would never touch her.

And the rose. Not the rose. He rubbed his temples and willed his stomach to stop churning.

It took him several moments to compose himself, but then he went to work. He found towels that would serve as bandages and did his best to care for her ravaged skin. Tovi stirred. She tried to twist her neck to see her helper, but she cried out in pain instead.

"Lie still," he commanded quietly.

She obeyed. After a few more bandages, he lifted her off the ground and carried her into the adjoining room. He placed her on her bed as gently as he could, but she winced when he slid his arms out from under her.

Outside, it was still the deepest dark of night. The room was feebly lit by a few candles. In the trembling, flickering glow, she caught her first glimpse of her rescuer.

"Eryx, what are you doing here?" she asked quietly.

He stood completely still a few feet away from her, his arms across his chest. He weighed his options. Tell her the truth? Make up a story? After they stared at one another for several seconds, he responded, "I couldn't sleep."

"Why did you help me?" she asked, peering into the darkness to better observe his face.

In a dangerously low and strained voice, he rebutted, "Why did you help me after the fight?"

She didn't answer, and the two glared at one another. A dark crimson pool seeped into the pillow behind her, and she lurched forward severely with a groan.

Eryx moved quickly and methodically, kneeling by the bed and firmly pressing a towel over her deepest wound.

"Thank you," she said weakly, suspicion in her voice. "Are you trying to mark me? I know all about it."

Instead of responding right away, Eryx finished re-bandaging her torn back and pulled a chair up beside the bed. "No, you already have my mark. But I didn't give it to you. I don't know who did."

Tovi observed his face. He watched her gaze move sleepily from scar to scar, to his chin, his mouth, his nose. Then she gasped.

"Eryx," she whispered. "Your eyes."

He looked away, ashamed of his weakness for the girl. He pulled off his gloves and turned his palm for Tovi to see the shape of a heart, identical to her own. Maybe that would distract her from his eyes that matched hers.

Her mouth dropped open. "Eryx, I never would have thought . . . " She traced the heart with her finger, and Eryx swallowed hard.

"Why did you help me?" he asked gruffly. "After that fight. My servants said it was you."

"I couldn't just leave you there. And then . . . "

"And then what?"

"And then, when I came out to the platform, you woke up for a moment. And . . . And you recognized me. You said my name."

Eryx stood so quickly that the chair fell backwards behind him. "Did I say anything else?"

"No, just my name," she explained. "Had Calix told you about me?"

"Calix?" he spat. "It's the other way around. I saw you first. It wasn't you I was after. It was your brother. I thought for sure I would be able to get him to fight me. I was confident that eventually I could get under his skin. But then things changed."

His face contorted with the memories he had conjured. "One day you were with him. I wasn't close enough to hear you, but I could see you. You were laughing at something he said." He closed his eyes, feeling the full torture of the last six months.

Eryx set his chair upright and sat down. Abruptly changing the subject to something safer than his emotions, he asked coarsely, "What made you tear your back to shreds?"

"I learned some things tonight," she began, halting over her carefully-chosen words. Eryx could tell she did not fully trust him. "I was overwhelmed, out of my mind. I think I was just desperate to get the marks off me."

"That's not how it works. Those marks are permanent," he said, not realizing until too late how gruff his words were. Tovi began to cry, and the sight of her tears made him feel clumsy and awkward.

"I didn't mean to—I'm sorry," he faltered.

"It's all right," she said and sniffled. "It's not your fault. It's just that I found out all in one day that my entire life has been a lie. I didn't know that all my years of searching for Adwin were completely pointless because it was Silas all along. I don't know why he never told me. Was it because I would be so angry with him for taking me from my parents? Was it because he knew all along that he would steal my brother? Was he hiding all these things from me? And then, tonight, I eavesdropped on a conversation between King Damien and Prince Ajax, and I learned who I really am." Her tone escalated throughout the speech, and now she was crying out in desperation. "Prince Ajax is my father. I was the fourth child, and Tali was the third."

Eryx stared at the miserable girl, struggling to comprehend all that she was telling him. Could it possibly be true?

"Earlier tonight, Xanthe was arrested," Tovi continued through her weeping. "Now she's in the dungeon because of the heart in her palm. She is the only person on this mountain who cares about me."

"No, she's not," Eryx blurted without thinking.

"Eryx, I—" Tovi said, but he shook his head to stop her. He was too afraid of the things she might say.

"Tovi, you have to listen to me," he implored. "You need to get out of here. Go back to Silas. He loves you, even if that's hard for you to believe right now. I'm sure he can explain everything. Go back to Adia. Damien will kill you if you stay. Promise me you'll think about it. As soon as you feel better, run. Go back to Silas. Got it?"

"You don't understand. He won't take me back the way I am now."

"Yes, he will. Just leave here, Tovi. Promise me."

She nodded, and that's all he needed.

"All right. It will be a few days before you are well enough to travel down the mountain. You won't be able to use the mines without being seen, so you'll have to hike down."

"But the cloud! Won't it make things worse?" she protested.

"Don't listen to all of that garbage. Blindness, death . . . none of that is true. I've been through it before, and nothing happened. I'll go with you to protect you . . . if you want me to."

There was an awkward silence before he continued.

"You have your lesson about Power in just a few hours. Don't miss it, or Damien will wonder what's wrong. Don't say anything about knowing your identity. Don't say anything about Xanthe. Don't say anything about this conversation. Got it?" Tovi nodded once more, and he left without saying goodbye.

Soon enough he stood on the palace patio, listening to King Damien greet Tovi for her morning lesson.

"Good morning, dear girl," Damien said with his usual merry voice and frosty eyes. He didn't remark on the bandages or Tovi's brutalized skin, but his eye lingered on them. "Today we are in for a treat as you learn about Power. I see you recently earned the mark, but there is a beautiful art to this discipline that you must refine in order to really taste its benefits. Now I thought we'd do something a little bit different. As we eat, we will have a demonstration of sorts."

Eryx and one of his old mentors stepped forward into the sunlight. Tovi kept her eyes averted.

"This is Orestes, and I believe you are acquainted with Eryx," Damien said, smiling with malicious anticipation. "Orestes trained Eryx when he was a boy, and now the they are the most powerful men on this mountain, except for me of course. They understand that it is sometimes necessary to use brute strength to accomplish your goals. And when you are up against a foe that is stronger than you, it is important to harness anything that might give you an edge over your opponent.

"Now, these two are going to begin fighting in a very literal sense, but we are going to use it as a teaching tool. Watch for the metaphors. You are surely bright enough to catch on."

Eryx let his instincts take over, just like in every fight. He didn't let himself think about how he was inflicting pain on his old friend and was being hurt by him in return. He pushed thoughts of Tovi's watchful eyes out of his mind. Fists pummeled flesh, and blood and sludge seeped through reopened wounds. The two men were well matched, and it lasted much longer than most fights.

With each hit and kick, King Damien narrated, "Say someone makes you angry. They deserve pain. Or, what if they take something that was yours? They deserve to be punished. Is someone blocking your path to success? You must get them out of the way."

With a horrible crunching noise, Eryx's open palm connected with the underside of Orestes' chin, throwing him backwards into a stone column. Two servants stepped forward to drag him off the patio. Eryx turned to Damien. "Do you wish me to stay, Your Majesty, or may I go?"

King Damien observed the fighter for a moment before declaring, "I want you to stay."

Eryx gave a curt nod and stood still. King Damien had always suspected his attachment to Tovi. Eryx knew the king was asking him to stay just so he would have to witness her training. He clenched his jaw and willed himself not to care.

Tovi had barely touched any of her food as the fight had progressed, and now she sat stirring the cold leftovers around her plate.

King Damien asked, "Didn't you like your breakfast? Or was it the entertainment you found distasteful?"

"It is hard for me to watch fighting, Your Majesty," Tovi admitted, staring at her plate.

"Look at me as you speak," he demanded too calmly. "I have been lenient with you on many matters, but you must start behaving as one of my servants, which is what you are if you live on this mountain." Tovi looked up to meet his gaze. "There, that's better, isn't it? You know, Tovi, I think it is time we had an important talk."

The hairs on Eryx's neck rose.

"It's very important for you to know the truth, Tovi, and if I am not mistaken, you have been told many lies since coming here. Lies about me, lies about your people, lies about Adwin, whom you call Silas. Hear me clearly, Tovi. Xanthe is in prison because of these lies. She will stay there until she is willing to admit the truth. That is how far I have gone to protect you, Tovi. Now, answer me honestly. Who else has spoken to you about Silas since you have come here?"

This was it. Tovi would divulge the truth about the heart hidden beneath his fighter's gloves.

"No one, Your Majesty," Tovi said calmly. King Damien's unblinking, calculating stare bored into her, but she held her ground.

"Well, well, well," he said as he sat back in his chair, a smile barely turning up one side of his mouth. "You have progressed further than I thought."

CHAPTER 40

The sun was setting around the side of Mount Damien, but instead of the colors Tovi would have seen in Adia, there was only a brief, red semicircle in the sky before everything turned to gray. Still, Tovi stared at the place on the cloudy horizon where the sun had just vanished, wishing she was home.

She was seated on Rhaxma's balcony. A golden candelabra with at least fifty candles spanned the entire length of a long table. A single diamond floated in each candle's melted wax, casting glittering reflections around the terrace. Strands of pearls were looped in asymmetric heaps around the entire tabletop with its golden plates and sparkling crystal.

She noticed how Rhaxma glared in her direction with fury in her eyes, which darted from Calix's face to his hand that rested possessively on Tovi's waist.

It was a small group. Leeto had been gone for several days now. Xanthe had been arrested, and Jairus was absent. The group consisted of hostess Rhaxma, Tovi, Calix, BiBi, Eryx, and Megara.

As everyone settled into the meal, the patio doors opened unexpectedly. Rhaxma stood and squealed, throwing herself into the arms of her brother. "Leeto! Where have you been!" she cried with unashamed joy.

Calix had just been lifting his cup to his lips, but on sight of Leeto, the crystal shattered and sent the deep red wine spraying onto the white tablecloth. Shaking the wetness from his hand, Calix stood, staring formidably at the man with orange hair and burning yellow eyes. His neck veins looked ready to burst.

"Calix," Leeto greeted smoothly. "How are you, old friend?"

Calix reached across the table, grabbed Leeto's shirt in his fists, and dragged him to the other side, knocking over the candelabra and engulfing the entire table in flames. Everyone jumped from their seats to avoid the spreading fire, watching the two who were eye-to-eye.

Calix's snarling face was illuminated by the inferno. "Let me be the first to congratulate you on your pointless victory."

"I don't know what you're talking about, Calix. It must be an honest mistake," Leeto said a little too coolly, darkness creeping into his eyes.

"You know exactly what you've done," Calix roared, still holding onto Leeto's shirt and tugging him toward the balcony railing. "Don't lie to me, Leeto. I know you! You've been gone for days, hoping that my anger would subside."

Losing the innocent pretense, Leeto hissed back, "I've been gone for many more reasons than that. It won't be long now before I rule Adia and this mountain, and there is nothing you can do to stop me."

A growl escaped from the back of Calix's throat. He lifted Leeto off the ground, bending him over the railing and looking him full in the face before heaving him off the terrace. There was a brief, horrifying moment when Leeto's hands clawed at the air, as if trying to catch a lifesaving hold. One awful thud later, Leeto's body lay on the cobblestone below, his limbs splayed at unnatural angles.

Rhaxma nearly threw herself over the railing as she screamed and reached for her brother. It was Eryx who grabbed her around the waist just in time. There was another shriek as their mother ran into the street, falling on her son and crying for help.

Calix, taking one last look at the crumpled body below, spit once on the ground and sauntered through the door, leaving Tovi behind. She stood in shock, her eyes darting between the dead body and the table that was in flames. She had never seen death and destruction like this before.

As the others helped Rhaxma inside, Eryx took hold of Tovi and whispered urgently in her ear, "You have to get out of here. It's not safe. Silas can protect you. You *must* leave. Don't wait until you are stronger. Get out now."

As he let go, she saw the look of panic in his eyes. She stumbled backward and made her way through the doors, down the stairs, and out into the warm night. Teresia Pyralis still clutched at her son, blood from his cracked head making black rivers between the cobblestones.

Not bothering to stay hidden, Tovi ran straight through the middle of the courtyard in plain sight of all the Masters and the palace itself. All she knew was that she wanted to get as far away as possible—off the vile mountain and back to the safety of Adia and Silas. She headed in the direction of the mines, but she had no idea if she would be able to operate the baskets without help. If that failed, she supposed she could descend the outside of the mountain on foot. It would be extremely difficult, and she had no food or shelter or even decent clothes for climbing. How could she make this journey in just a silk dress? She shook her head to clear it. She couldn't worry about that now. She needed to focus on getting as far away as possible. She hadn't run this fast since her morning sprints to the ridge. Her lungs burned worse than her throbbing back.

She was still within the confines of the square when an angry hand grabbed her and swung her around. Calix looked as if he was willing to murder again. "Where do you think you are going?"

His fingers digging into her arm, he dragged her to the palace, up the stairs, and in through the front doors. Her fighting and clawing didn't seem to faze him. He didn't stop as he took long strides through the hallways, finally reaching the throne room.

CHAPTER 41

"Well, my dear, this is not how I wanted things to end for you." Damien said, looking down at his granddaughter. He could sense her weakness and fear. "Where were you going just now?" he asked with ice in his foul voice.

"Nowhere. I just panicked," the girl faltered.

He cackled. "You are becoming such a natural at Control. It is a pity you want to leave here in such a hurry. No matter. I am a gracious king, forgiving and merciful, even to the likes of you. Everything will go right back to normal if you look me in the eye and tell me that you know the truth: that Adwin is nothing compared to me, that he could never be as powerful as me, that he could never be worthy of your love and loyalty like me."

Tovi looked away from him and seemed to be searching the mural for something. Damien watched her closely, wondering what had captivated her so completely. Her eyebrows drew together, and her head tilted to the side. Her gaze focused on something in the design, and there was a sudden intensity in her stance. Something was coming over her so strongly that it was visible. She began to transform, and he began to panic. Her hair faded from navy blue to light brown with thick golden streaks. Her eyes lightened to a sparkling baby blue, and the purple star disappeared. She looked up toward him, a dangerous energy emanating from her.

The girl in the mural. One of the four. Adrenaline pumped through his veins as he took in her new colors that confirmed his fear. She was not only his heir; she was also one of the conquerors in the mural. Helena. Jairus. Tali. Tovi. If Lena had survived her execution all those years ago, the four could very possibly be reunited. The prophecy could come to pass. They could conquer the mountain and vanquish his legacy.

"You are nothing compared to Silas," Tovi stated, her gaze now locked on her captor. He looked back at her. So lost in his thoughts of the prophecy, he had momentarily forgotten she was there.

He stood from his throne and marched toward her, grasping her arm just where there were fresh bruises. He pulled her to the wall and forced her to look at certain scenes. "Look at him, Tovi! He left us. He hated us. And he hates *you,* too. Do not be deceived by his lies. He hates you, Tovi. He *hates* you!" He was now in a frenzy, nearly jumping up and down with each emphasis. Black sweat was dripping into his eyes, clouding his vision. He swiped at the thick sludge, and he noticed his hands were webbed with dark veins. He was losing control.

"Don't you see what a mess he left us in? Don't you see what he has done? Look at this! Do you see the squalor? Do you see the suffering?" He pushed her toward the darker bits of the mural, the part after Silas had left. "Look at what happened when he abandoned me!"

Tovi pulled her arm from his grip and matched his glare.

Damien grabbed Tovi's hand and yanked her glove away, exposing the brown heart. The sight of it made him want to kill her right then, regardless of his blood in her veins. The only thing stopping him was that he couldn't risk her disappearance in front of Calix and so many guards. Better to let her rot in the dungeon without ever knowing her true identity.

"Get her out of my sight!" he roared.

As the guards held her by the elbows and started yanking her toward the door, she aimed one fiercer look at him. "Good night, Grandfather," she said.

He seethed and watched her go. How did she know? How long had she known? Had she played him like a fool this entire time? Was this a part of the prophecy?

His frantic thoughts ricocheted in all directions. The prophecy. His offspring. How had she survived? How did she make her way back to this palace? Was it all a plot? A plan? A scheme that was somehow better than his own? Who had planned this? Who was responsible? Surely the girl didn't do this on her own.

He gritted his teeth and glared at the mural.

Silas.

CHAPTER 42

The prison beneath the palace was made up of one long, dark corridor. Cells lining each side were separated by rusted metal bars. Water dripped down the stone perimeter, leaving furry green paths of mold and decay. There were no windows, leaving the space dank and dark, save for the dim light from a few mounted torches.

Guards led Tovi past cells inhabited by prisoners who looked less than half alive. Each of them stared through blank eyes as they sat on the cold stone floor. Coming to a halt near an empty stall, one of the guards twisted an ancient key, which screeched and scraped before the lock popped.

"In you go," he said gruffly.

As the door swung shut behind her, the voice began. At first, she thought someone was speaking to her, and she looked around for the source. It didn't take long to realize that the torturous words were in her own mind.

You are worthless Tovi Tivka . . . Completely worthless . . . You abandoned all the people who loved you in Adia, and now you have failed the few friends you had on this mountain . . . You are despicable . . . The pain you put Ganya through has nearly killed her . . . Xanthe will surely die in this place . . . And all of this you have done for yourself . . . You are selfish, Tovi . . . You are worthless . . .

The words and guilt brought her to her knees, and she knelt near the door of her cell, clutching the bars with cold, white hands.

Her mind travelled back to just a few moments before, as she stood in the throne room looking at the mural. Everything had suddenly made so much sense. All the stories she had learned as a child and since coming to the mountain dropped into place in their correct order. She was the child of Prince Ajax, and King Damien feared she and her siblings would one day rebel. He had sent them to die. Silas hadn't stolen her from her family. He had saved her life, and Tali's.

She had too many questions to count, but in that instant, while King Damien spewed his hate and lies, she had known without a doubt that Silas—Adwin—was good. He was good, and he loved her. Questions still spun around and around in her mind, but somehow clinging to that truth made everything else a little more bearable.

In the far corner of the cell to her right, a man lay curled on his side. His back was completely blank, void of any marks. Every few minutes he let out a moan of pain and shivered.

To Tovi's left was an old woman sitting against the back wall picking black crust from under her fingernails. Her pale lavender hair was stringy and dirty, and she had to frequently brush it out of her face. She wore frayed and patched clothing, and she seemed to be talking to herself in a low whisper.

Looking across the narrow corridor to the cells on the other side, Tovi saw a gleam of silver.

"Xanthe . . . " Tovi whispered.

Xanthe, who had been sitting against the side of her enclosure, looked at Tovi with unspoken disgust. Tovi began to drown in the voice again.

Look what you've done to Xanthe . . . She will never forgive you . . . She will die here, and it's all because of you . . . And your marks? Those marks will never come off . . . You are ruined . . . No one can fix this . . . If Silas sees them, he will hate you for what you have done . . . For what you have become . . . There is no turning back . . . You are worthless . . .

"She won't talk to you, you know," came a raspy voice. Turning, Tovi saw the old lady had moved closer, gripping the bars that separated them with gnarled, wrinkled fingers. Large, dull eyes looked through the metal rods, darting between Xanthe and Tovi. "I've tried and tried, but she don't respond to nobody. 'Cept the visitor man."

"Who is the visitor man?" Tovi asked, the question echoing through the chamber.

Hesper's story of his mother's time in prison flowed back through her memory. Was this the same visitor that had taken his mother away? Tovi's heart beat fast as she thought of Silas' face, hoping with every last bit of strength that the visitor was him.

"Shhhh, the guards sit up top of the stairs, but you still don't wanna be too loud about these things. The visitor man isn't allowed, you see," she whispered. "Come, sit down." She gestured as if she was in her own living room. They took seats in the corner, each resting their backs against the stone wall. Even with the metal bars between them, they were only inches apart.

Tovi whispered this time. "I'm Tovi."

"My name's Ismene."

"How long have you been here?"

"Longer than I care to guess. If it weren't for the visitor man, I wouldn't even know how long a day lasts. As it just so happens, he visits every day, near enough the same time, so we are kinda aware of the passing time. But if it helps you to understand, I was just a mite older than you when I came down those stairs."

"That's awful!" Tovi cried, trying her best to hold down her volume.

"Oh, you get used to it, lovey. It's not so bad. You'll get used to the voice . . . and sleeping on the rocks. You'll forget what food tastes like out there, too."

"You hear the voice?"

"Indeed, I do. That is part of the prison, you see. While you are here, in this here dark and terrible pit, you will hear all the things that old Damien has tried to teach you. The problem is, you are here because of that heart in your hand. The two don't go together too good, if you know what I mean, and that's why you hear the voice and feel the pain.

"For the first few years of my time down here, I tried to get rid of it. Damien promised me that if the heart was gone from my hand, I could go back to my family, that life would be perfect again. It's hazy to me now, but I don't really think it was ever that perfect to begin with. It's just another one of his tricks. Anyhow, I tried every which way to get rid of the blasted thing," she said, holding up her hand for Tovi to see. It was crisscrossed with jagged white scars. "Several times I tried to scratch it away, sometimes with my own nails, sometimes with my teeth, even once by rubbing it over the rusted part of these bars. It never worked."

Tovi was reminded of her own irrational attempts at scraping the marks off her back.

"Tell me about the visitor. Who is he?"

The ragged lady brought her face close to the bars, and Tovi could feel her warm breath on her skin. "I don't know his name, but he comes and sits with me every day. Comes and visits with each one of us, without fail. Comes in a secret door so he doesn't have to pass them guards. He's as old as me, I reckon, with wrinkles as droopy as mine. And each and every time he comes, he offers to take us away, take us to a better place out yonder. A place more beautiful than we can imagine."

Tovi's heart sank. Wrinkles? It couldn't be Silas. "Why don't you go with him?" she asked, trying to hide her deep disappointment.

Ismene's eyes grew sad and she started picking at her fingers again. "I don't s'pose I know why. He says it'll be hard, and I just don't know if I've got it in me. I wanna go, just don't know if I can. Strange things happen in this place. Strange things indeed. See that young feller over on the other side of them bars? One day, he took the visitor man up on his offer. Told him he was ready to leave and get out of here. I heard him with mine own ears. Then, the visitor man says to him, 'It's gonna be hard. And it's gonna be worse before it gets better. But it'll be worth it.'

"They left, and I thought he was gone for good. He wasn't the first one to leave with him. But a few minutes later, he was back. Two guards had hold of him, lookin' confused, tryin' to figure out how he got out from behind them bars. They was still locked, you see.

"Next day, the visitor man took a 'specially long time with him, telling him it was okay, and they'd try again. But that boy won't even look at him no more. Won't talk to nobody. Guess he's shamed it didn't work out the first time.

"So then, when he offers that same freedom to me, I just think about how hard it's gonna be. I think about how I just don't think I can make it, and how I'll feel if I get throwed back in here. And I decide that it's probably best for me to just stay put."

After a short silence, Ismene's head dropped to her chest and she began to snore. Without the distraction of chatter, the voice came back to Tovi.

You are stuck here forever, Tovi . . . There is no chance of escaping from what you have done, all the people you have hurt . . . And even if you could escape, where would you go? . . . Everyone hates you . . . You are alone in this world, and it's all your fault . . . You failed everyone . . . You failed Ganya . . . You failed Avi . . . You failed Tali . . . You failed Silas . . . And he thinks you are worthless . . .

All Tovi had to keep track of the time were the rhythmic drops of water punctuated by Ismene's snores and the young man's painful moans. After what seemed like eternity, she heard footsteps coming down the corridor. Was this the visitor? Was it King Damien? A guard? Who was coming in the middle of the night?

She peered through the darkness and saw a man drawing closer. It was too dark to make out his face, but she recognized his voice immediately.

"Xanthe, are you awake?" came his hushed whispers.

Xanthe's dress rustled as she moved closer to the bars. "Jairus," she cried, letting out a sob that echoed against the walls.

"Please don't cry, sweetheart. I'm going to get you out of here." They grasped hands through the bars.

"I don't want you to end up here, too," Xanthe despaired, releasing one hand to cup the side of his face.

He placed his hand over hers. "I don't want this life without you, Xanthe. I will find a way. I promise you. We'll go live somewhere out in the forest. We'll start over away from this horrible place, away from Grandfather and all that has happened. Don't give up, Xanthe. Please don't give up," he begged.

They kissed softly, allowing their pain and tears to mingle. "I'll come back when I can. Stay strong, my love." He turned toward his newfound sister for one agonized second before walking briskly up the aisle, not looking back at the now-sobbing Xanthe.

Tovi's guilt engulfed her again.

If you had held your temper with Megara, Xanthe wouldn't be in prison . . . She wouldn't be in terrible danger . . . She and Jairus wouldn't be separated . . . They wouldn't be experiencing this misery . . . How could you do this to your friend? Your brother . . . You are a failure, Tovi Tivka . . . You have ruined their lives . . . Nobody wants you . . . Nobody loves you . . . You are worthless . . .

Tovi didn't sleep. She lay awake, listening to the voice and Xanthe's weeping. The longer she lay there, the weaker she felt, as if the voice was draining every last bit of strength and resilience she had left.

Just when she thought she could bear it no more, there was a strange trembling, like the rocks below her were crumbling. She stared into the far corner of her cell where ruffled green leaves and an indigo flower flecked with orange pollen poked up through the floor and bloomed like an umbrella. She crawled over and lay her head beside it, running her fingers over the petals. Warm tears trickled down her cheeks, and she whispered, "Silas . . ."

CHAPTER 43

Eryx stood hunched over his bathroom sink, his fingers threatening to crush the marble edge of the countertop. How had he let this happen to her? How had he just stood there and watched Calix drag her to the palace? He should have taken her and run as fast as he could, straight to Adia. Now he was left to wonder if that was to be the last time he would ever see her alive.

He splashed his face with water and looked up into the mirror, his tormented gaze freezing as he took in the changes. He leaned forward, looking closely at his eyes; they were bright blue, as blue as the sky over Adia. The short hairs that had appeared on his scalp, the ones that he shaved away every morning, were much lighter than usual. He ran his hand over them in disbelief.

What happened? The last time his colors had changed, it was because his heart had betrayed him and fallen for Tovi Tivka. He had worn her colors like a disgraceful badge hoping no one would notice. But these colors? Where did they come from? His love for her was as strong as ever. Had Tovi's allegiance changed? To whom? He knew no one with these colors, had never seen anyone in Adia or on the mountain with these eyes.

He could feel the frustration building as he frantically searched his memory. His heart thudded loudly in his ears as he told himself that Tovi could never love him. She already loved someone else. Weren't these new colors proof enough? He felt like such a fool.

Eryx rarely displayed self-pity, but these thoughts were especially potent, triggering the rage that was always so close to the surface. His oldest scar, which marred the skin just below the left side of his collar bone, ripped open, allowing blackness to ooze out through his shirt. He glared at his reflection, wondering whose eyes were looking back at him. Not knowing what to do with his grief and wrath, he slammed his fist into the mirror.

Shards scattered everywhere, and black blood seeped from a deep cut between two of his knuckles. He let it flow, knowing that bleeding to death would be better than the fate Tovi faced.

Eventually he moved to his kitchen table and wound bandages around his hand, trying to think of anything other than Tovi.

"I'd say the mirror got the worst of it," Silas said from the doorway. "May I come in?"

"I'm not used to you asking," Eryx said without looking up. He wasn't surprised that he had shown up. He realized with annoyance that something in him had been waiting for Silas.

"Want me to take a look at that?"

"No."

"I can fix it."

"I don't care." He continued to wrap his wounds, never showing any emotion. Not even anger.

"What happened?"

Finally, Eryx looked up, but only for a brief second. Then he went back to work.

Silas wasn't deterred. "I already know what's upsetting you. Why won't you talk to me about it?"

"If you already know, then why ask?"

"Because I care about you," Silas said, exasperation evident in his tone. "You are the strongest person on this mountain, and I don't mean just your muscles. You have been through horrific tragedy, and yet you still have the capacity to love. I want to be your friend, Eryx. I want to help you find a better way."

This time Eryx looked up and stared at Silas, but he wasn't really seeing the Adian. Images of his family and a better time raced across his mind, speeding past so quickly that he could grasp none of them.

The men looked at each other, one with frustrated respect and the other with the pain of unspeakable memories. "Horrific tragedy? It was my fault. I killed them."

"It wasn't your fault."

Eryx had just finished binding his hand. "It was my hatred that bred dissension within my family."

"It was their choices that destroyed them. You are not blameless, Eryx, but you have taken far too much of the guilt. But that's not why I'm here."

"What do you want?" Eryx yelled, banging his newly-bandaged fist on the table and releasing the tension that had been building since Silas entered. "Another favor? I did everything you asked. I got Xanthe to avoid her lesson and take Tovi to the HH. I went and took care of her when she was bleeding to death. But then, when she really needed me, I just stood there and watched them take her to the palace."

"Again, you are shouldering blame that isn't yours. You did everything right."

"I should have taken her straight to Adia. I could have, you know. I could have just taken her and run away. There was that moment . . . That moment when I was telling her to run. I was too much of a coward to run with her."

Eryx buried his head in his hands and completely lost control. He didn't care that Silas was there to see it. He screamed. He cursed. He let wave after wave of grief pour out as his massive shoulders heaved.

When Eryx finally looked up, Silas was sitting calmly on the other side of the table, his speckled yellow-green eyes shining with shared pain.

"If it's not to remind me of my failures, why are you here?" Eryx asked.

"To see if you're ready to start over."

Start over? It would be impossible to undo the evil he had committed. "What do you mean?"

"I want you to leave this mountain. Come to Adia with me and begin a new life. You don't have to live with the marks on your back that cause you so much pain."

"I won't leave Tovi here."

"Fine. You don't have to live with the marks here either. We can start the process anywhere and at any time."

"What process?" Eryx asked suspiciously.

"There is a way to get rid of the marks immediately, and I offer this to you whenever you are ready. However, the dark sludge that burdens your veins has seeped throughout your body. You see it when you spit or cough or bleed. It has taken over your stomach, your lungs, your heart. I will take away the marks, but we must do the work of ridding your body of this darkness together."

"How?"

"I'll tell you as we go."

"Will it hurt?"

"Yes."

"Then why would I do it?"

"Because when your blood is clean and rich and your tears and sweat run clear, you will experience a kind of freedom you could never achieve with the power of your own might. The difficult task of ridding your body of this disease is worth it, Eryx. I want this for you."

Eryx's heart thumped loudly, and he was more aware than ever of the sluggish blood in his veins. Then Tovi's face came to mind, and his murderous hatred of King Damien, Calix, Leeto, and all the others surfaced, calling him to action.

He clenched his teeth and looked at Silas. "If I can't find this freedom on my own, then I don't want it." He pushed back his chair and stormed out of the room.

CHAPTER 44

"Everybody up! Time for your breakfast. Everybody up!"

A guard walked down the line offering porridge and water to prisoners who recited, "I am grateful to His Majesty, King Damien, the true king of the mountain." This guard was nothing like the sleek guards that kept watch over the royal family. He and his fellow officers were pudgy, oily, and unwashed. They looked strong but not very smart.

When the breakfast distributer reached Tovi, he looked at her expectantly. "You heard what they said. You say it, too, and I'll give you your breakfast."

"No."

"Excuse me?"

"I won't say what the others said."

"You have to, or I can't give you your breakfast."

"Then I won't eat."

"I've been ordered to give you your breakfast."

"Fine, give me my breakfast."

"No, you have to say it first."

"I won't say it."

The guard looked flustered. "Hey, Cyd," he called. "What do I do with one who refuses?"

"Tell her she has to say it," Cyd yelled back.

"I did!"

"Tell her she won't get her breakfast."

"I did!"

"Okay, then take her to His Majesty. That's what we had to do with the last one."

When the guard was finished doling out food, he came back and took Tovi from her cell. Holding her by the arm, he pulled her down the aisle and up the stairs. They reached the patio where King Damien was breakfasting with Prince Ajax and Jairus.

"Excuse me, Your Majesty, this one refused her breakfast."

"I see," King Damien said calmly and evenly.

Tovi stood uncomfortably before her brother, father, and grandfather, affected by her exhaustion, hunger, and sore muscles.

Damien rose from his seat, circled the table, and grabbed her hand, looking at the palm. "You stupid girl. I see that one night in prison was not enough for you. You have held onto that heart," he growled. He clamped his hand into a fist, crushing her fingers as if he could squeeze Silas out of her. "Remember this: all of your pain is because of him. All of it!" He continued to spew hateful lies, but she couldn't hear him over her own screams. There were several loud cracks as the bones in her hand gave way. Damien opened his fist to find her fingers hanging limply. Turning them over as Tovi groaned he saw that the symbol was still there, and it hadn't faded at all. He grabbed a knife from the table.

She tried to run, but she was weak, and he had an iron grip on her wrist. The guards moved several feet closer. Her father watched passively, as if he was bored. Her brother turned his face away.

As her grandfather savagely cut into her flesh, trying to dig deep enough to carve away the heart, he cried out, "He doesn't love you, Tovi! Where is he? Why isn't he stopping me? He's not who you think he is! If he really loved you, he'd be here, saving you from all this pain. Right? Am I right? He doesn't love you! He hates you! He left you! He doesn't care! You should hate him! He deserves it! He left you just like he left me!"

All at once, Damien seemed to come back to himself, his wrath only apparent in the pulsing vein in his neck and the webs of black in his eyes. Tovi crouched on the ground, cradling her mangled and bloody hand.

"Look at me, Tovi," Damien ordered, standing before her. "I said look at me! Look me in the eye and tell me that you still love him."

This dare seemed to strengthen her, and Tovi bravely stared back. With trembling lips, she declared, "I still love him," drawing out each word, savoring their meaning.

Damien threw the knife to the ground so that its bloody blade clattered across the stone patio. "Leave me. We will continue this lesson tomorrow."

One of the guards took her back to the dungeon. On top of everything else, Tovi had suffered a good deal of blood loss. She dozed in and out of consciousness, unsure where reality began among her tormented thoughts. Ismene's voice floated to her from the next cell, but it sounded much further away. "Listen for the other words, Tovi. The other voice. It's there, I swear it."

And there it was. She could hear it, quiet at first and then overpowering the other. It spoke to her from her memories, but it sounded like the words had always been meant for this specific moment.

What would your precious Silas think of you now? Pathetic, selfish, ruined . . . I love you. No matter what happens . . . *You have become a vapid, greedy, bitter liar* . . . You can talk to me about it. All of it . . . *He will hate you for it* . . . I won't get mad . . . *Where is he right now? He has abandoned you! You are alone* . . . I've been with you the whole time . . .

Tovi scooted toward the flower that stood bravely in the darkest corner of her cell, the stone cracked around its stem. She lovingly traced the tip of each petal with her fingers, just as she had when she was at the ridge with Silas. She had so many questions that she longed to ask him. So many things she didn't understand.

One thing plagued her mind the most. If Silas could make a flower bloom out of this dismal rock bottom, she knew he could also find a way to save her life a second time. She knew he could, but after all she had done, she didn't know if he would.

"Psst, Tovi," Ismene whispered. "Do you hear that? Here he comes. The visitor man!"

Tovi sat up straight. She couldn't see him, but she could hear muffled voices from the far end of the corridor. Occasionally she heard soft footsteps as he moved down the line. She adjusted her angle so she could get a glimpse of him, but to no avail. She would have to wait until he was closer to get a good look.

Her heart was hammering. This old man would offer her freedom. Could he really get her out? Where would he take her? Could she trust him?

She still couldn't see his face, but he had moved close enough that she could just barely make out his stature. He looked too upright and strong to be the elderly man that Ismene had described. "Are you sure, Ismene? Are you sure it's him?"

"As sure as can be, Tovi. Can't you see him through them bars?"

He had moved another cell closer and was crouched right beneath one of the few torches. Messy light brown hair with golden streaks.

Smooth skin and soft tunic flecked with indigo, orange, and green paint. She put her hand to her mouth to stifle a loud whimper.

Hot tears flooded her cheeks during the agonizing wait while he inched closer. She watched through her bars as he spoke softly to each prisoner. She didn't know why Ismene saw him as an old man, but she didn't care. He was moving down the corridor, visiting each cell, side to side across the aisle. When he got to her neighboring cell, he sat right down on the floor and whispered, "Dion, I'm back, just like I promised. Are you ready to talk to me?"

Dion, the boy lying in his cell with no marks on his back, stopped moving and took a shuddering breath. Silas continued, "Are you ready to leave this place?"

The young man moaned in agony, but still there was no response.

"I was there, Dion. I know what happened. I will be here when you decide it is time to leave. And I will keep reminding you that we can do it. It will be hard, but we can do it. Together. You're worth it to me."

Tovi could hardly bear the sound of his voice. She longed to reach out to him, and at the same time she feared the look of anger and disappointment that was sure to be on his face when he found her there. What would he think of this mess she had become?

Silas stood and crossed the corridor to Xanthe's cell. It seemed to Tovi that he purposely didn't look her direction as he turned. He must hate her. He must be so disappointed . . .

The beautiful Master, with her lemon yellow hair in disarray, was standing at her door, her fingers through the bars. "You came back," she said in disbelief.

"Just like I promised."

"Even though I was so awful to you yesterday."

"Nothing you do could keep me away. Do you think I'll be able to persuade you to leave with me today?"

"No."

"Why?" Silas asked, unfazed.

"You could be lying to me. You might even be working for His Majesty. If you were really Adwin, you wouldn't want me in Adia. I've done terrible things."

"That voice in your head is telling you lies. When you are ready to let me in, we will start answering all of those lies with the truth."

Xanthe bit her lip.

"May I come in?" Silas asked.

Her eyes looked hopeful for just a moment before she closed them. She shook her head and walked to the far corner of her cell, lying down and curling into a ball. "I will be here, Xanthe. Every day for as long as it takes. You are worth it." She didn't respond.

Tovi's heart pounded. She knew it was her turn, and she clutched at the bars to help her stand on her shaking legs. After all she had been through, this took every last ounce of effort.

She expected his anger. His hatred. His disapproval of everything she had done and everything she had become. Still, she longed for her turn to look into his eyes, to see him again. She wanted to go back in time, back to the ridge and their mornings together. She wanted to see all of it more clearly. She wanted to hear him say that she was worth it. But would he?

Silas finally turned his gaze on Tovi. The grin she knew so well appeared as he crossed the small expanse between cells. Her ugly, heart-rending sobs doubled in intensity, and she reached through the bars, needing him near. Instead of staying on the outside of the cell like he had for the other prisoners, he walked straight inside—through the solid barrier—and took her in his arms, holding her tightly to his chest. Instantly, the voice in her mind quieted and her bloodied hand mended.

"I have missed you, Tovi," he said into her hair.

"Silas," she wept, trying to catch her breath. Her fingers gripped the back of his shirt.

"Are you ready to go home?"

She nodded, unable to speak.

"I need to explain some things to you first," he said, pulling away just enough so he could look at her. "This is going to be the hardest thing you have ever done. The pain you feel because you are in this prison is nothing compared to what will happen as you try to leave it. It is dark, ugly magic, the last project that Damien completed before I revoked his powers. It is one of the final weapons against you, but you must remember that none of it is real. Damien knows that it feels better in the dungeon than it does trying to make your way out, and he thinks that will keep people inside. Many times, it has worked.

"As long as you are with me, you will make it. Focus completely on me. If you feel like you are about to break, ask for help. Got it?" Tovi nodded before he continued. "Here's what's going to happen. We are going to run right out of here, through the hidden door. The guards at the top of the stairs won't know, but we will be seen by others once we're outside. They will come after us. There is no way around it. We will have to keep running as fast as you can. Once we are on the other side of the cloud and in the forest, it will be harder for them to find us. But while we are out in the open on these city streets, we will be vulnerable.

"If all does not go as planned, and believe me, it rarely does, you must listen to me very closely. I will give you instructions as you need them, and you must obey them immediately. Understand?"

"Yes," she answered with a sniffle.

"All right." He smiled. "Let's go."

He began to walk back through the bars, holding one of Tovi's hands. "How am I supposed to get out?" she spluttered.

He surprised her by smiling. "Nothing about this prison is real. These bars only exist to those still imprisoned by them. The minute you decided to leave, they became nothing but a bad memory. Come on, you'll see."

Still unsure, she stepped her foot forward. The bars looked very solid and very real. Ismene was still staring. Xanthe watched from the corner of her cell.

Tovi took another step, not knowing what to expect. Then, just where the bars met the ground, she moved her foot forward. Looking up at Silas, she smiled.

Boldly she walked into the corridor, and searing pain coursed through her. Her back felt like it was lit on fire. She gasped and let go of Silas' hand. As soon as their touch expired, the voice flooded back, more merciless than ever.

No one loves you! You are deceptive, spiteful, ruined! Run away from this man! Hide in your cell! You don't have what it takes to leave here!

Silas caught her before she hit the ground, and the thoughts were silenced. The pain still raged.

Even more serious than before, Silas lifted Tovi's chin with one finger. "I love you. You are honest, thoughtful, and good. No one has what it takes to leave by herself, but with me you'll make it."

She nodded, beginning to understand the perils of their mission.

Down the corridor and out the secret door, they ran as quickly as Tovi could manage. They made it out of the palace safely, but within moments they were seen. Tovi clung to Silas' hand as they sprinted across the courtyard, the formidable royal guards emerging from the palace at top speed, their long swords sheathed but ready at their backs.

Tovi and Silas passed through arched tunnels and wound through the streets, pushing through crowds and passing the HH as Tovi was reaching the limit of her exhaustion. Every muscle ached and her head was buzzing from the combination of hunger and high adrenaline.

She despaired as she looked over her shoulder and saw the guards gaining ground. "I'm not strong enough, Silas!"

"They are following much closer than they ever have before. If I keep running with you, they will follow us all the way to Adia. Everyone will be in danger. You have to keep running. No matter how tired you are, no matter what the voice says, no matter what you see, keep running. You *are* strong enough, Tovi. Go straight to the mines. Hesper is waiting for you there. Then, when you get to the bottom, run for Adia. You know the paths. I've had you practicing this kind of forest running every day for six months."

"No! Silas, don't leave me! I can't do it!"

"We won't be separated for long," he promised. "It's time, Tovi. Run straight for the mines. You will make it. Be strong!" He stopped and turned toward the guards. She stumbled forward as the voice shrieked in her head, accompanied by the one calmer, stronger voice.

Run . . . *Stop where you are! Not one step further!* . . . Keep running as fast as you can. You know the paths . . . *You will never make it! You are too weak!* . . . You are strong enough . . . *The guards will find you. They will catch you. Turn back now, and I will give you mercy . . .* It's time, Tovi. Run straight for the mines. You will make it! Be strong! . . . *Turn around and see what happens to your beloved Silas . . .*

The last, cruel words stopped her in her tracks. Full of fear, she turned back. For one split second she saw Silas standing and facing the oncoming guards. She tried to shout to him, to tell him to run, but she didn't have time.

He flung his arms out just as they reached him, as if he was trying to gather them into an embrace. The tips of several blades emerged through his body at different angles, crimson stains spreading in blotchy patterns and soaking his tunic. He hit the cobblestones, arms still outstretched, and began to fade. Iridescent waves of light rose from the ground, starting at his body and stretching along and beyond his arms. Within seconds, these curtains of shimmering color extended so far that Tovi could not see the end. And then, to her horror, he had faded completely. He was gone. All that was left were the waves of light.

"Silas!" she wailed. "Silas!"

The guards turned their attention to Tovi and charged in her direction. When they reached the shimmering curtain, they rammed into it as if it was a solid wall. Piling up one behind the other, they could not push past it. They frantically ran along the waves, looking for a gap in the protection, but they found none.

Unable to ward it off any longer, Tovi succumbed to the blackness of shock, exhaustion, and pain.

CHAPTER 45

Rhaxma stared at her brother's lifeless body encased in glass. The parlor in the family home was brightly lit with candles, even at this hour of the night. They couldn't leave their beloved Leeto in the dark.

She hardly registered the tears that fell, one after another, dark streams rolling over her cheeks and past her mouth that hung slightly open.

He was dead. He was dead. He was dead.

He was gone. How could he be gone?

Her mind flashed violently to that scene, to a table engulfed in flames, and Leeto's body broken on the cobblestones. Her mother beat her to him and was already cradling his head and screaming for help. She could see it all in slow, vivid motion. She was right back in that moment, clutching his bloodied shirt, begging him to be alive.

She closed her eyes and reopened them, focusing on his face through the glass. His skin so white, his hair so orange. His yellow eyes open, staring at the ceiling. He looked like himself, except for the paleness of his lips and the vacant dullness in his unmoving eyes.

It was not normal to keep a body in the home for so long. Usually the dead were buried on the third day in a cemetery on the north side of the mountain. But, with the magical wall encircling the city, they could not reach the burial ground. Many friends offered solutions like burying Leeto in their gardens, but the Pyralis family was not satisfied. Leeto must rest with his ancestors in the cemetery. They would wait until they found a way through the wall.

He was dead. He was gone. Forever.

It had been several days, and until this night, Rhaxma had stayed away from the parlor. She couldn't look upon her dead brother. She couldn't see his lifeless form.

But tonight, as she lay awake in her large canopied bed, reliving his death repeatedly, she had a sudden urge to be near him. She wrapped herself in a silk robe and quietly descended multiple flights of stairs. No one else was awake, and she felt the vastness of the family estate. It made her feel empty and alone.

Now, as she stood over his coffin, her grief pouring from her eyes, she began to whisper.

"How could you leave me like this? I need you. I need you to be here with me." Her voice broke, and she pressed her hands against the glass, wishing she could touch his face. "I've always looked to you for direction, always leaned on you for strength. I don't think I can do it without you. Why did you leave me?"

Her crying escalated, and her shoulders heaved with each sobbing inhale. A face she had once loved flashed before her eyes, and a wrathful loathing ripped through her so ferociously that she let out a scream that felt more like a roar. She laid her forehead on the cool glass.

Calix. He had done this. He had caused this. The marks on her back pulsed with burning pain. Her mind focused on one thing: She didn't just want Calix to hurt. She wanted to ruin him.

"Rhax? You okay?"

She jumped and turned. "Oh, Thad, it's you," she said, the animal inside her retreating into its hole in her heart. Thad was the oldest of her four brothers. Three brothers now, she corrected herself.

Like the rest of the family, Thad had thick orange hair and piercing yellow eyes. Despite turning twenty-eight earlier that year, he still lived in the Pyralis mansion along the Courtyard. So did Simeon and Andi, their other brothers. Most children left the house by twenty five, but not in this family. Their love was too deep, and their anxieties of what could happen were deeper. The death of Leeto confirmed their fear that being out of each other's sight for too long could only lead to tragedy.

Thad was a drunk with no aspirations, but she still loved him so. It was nothing like her closeness with Leeto, but she was glad that it had been Thad to come join her tonight. He was simple and sweet and kind.

Thad put his arm around Rhaxma and looked down at his cold brother. "I still can't believe this is real," he said.

Rhaxma rested her cheek against his shoulder. She didn't say anything, but her mind raced with thoughts of Calix. Her breathing became ragged again as her hatred mingled with her deep, aching grief.

She kept returning to the word *ruin*. She must ruin him. She would get no satisfaction from killing him. She must find something worse.

CHAPTER 46

Light played against Tovi's closed eyelids in strange, rounded patterns, as if dancing through swaying leaves. The first conscious thought Tovi had was: But that's impossible. There aren't any trees here on the top of the mountain.

Images came back to her of her past days. The look on Calix's face when he saw Leeto's mark. Eryx being brutally attacked at the first fight. Starving families in the Bottom Rung. Leeto's body lying contorted on the ground. Dion curled into a ball in the corner of his cell. The evil that reflected in King Damien's eyes as he cut into her hand. The swords piercing through Silas right before he faded away forever.

Then, still with eyes shut against the world that had caused so much heartache, she noted the softness she was lying on, the coziness of the material she was wearing, so unlike the silk she had become accustomed to.

She cracked her eyes open and tried to decipher her whereabouts. Flowers everywhere. Vines in the window. Waving willow leaves in the distance. *Home.*

Bittersweet tears began to flow, and when she wiped them away, she noticed they were tinged with black. She was safe and at home, but she couldn't erase the image of Silas with the swords through him. Strong, loving, perfect Silas. How could she live without him? It had taken her so long to understand, and now he was gone. She tried not to think about the ridge. She tried to force her mind away from her perfect memory of his eyes. She could still hear him, sitting on a fallen tree, telling her how much he loved her.

She tried to steady herself by taking deep breaths as another surge of guilt rolled over her. How long had she been gone? She ticked through the days in her head. Could Ganya ever forgive her? Who had brought her home? How long had she been here?

Careful of her aching muscles, she turned her head and prepared to call for Ganya. But the sound was caught in her throat as her eyes expanded to twice their normal size.

She was speechless. She had watched him die. She had seen the swords push through his body, the blood pooling around him when he fell. The horrible translucence before he was completely gone. This was impossible. How could he be sitting beside her?

"You forget who I am," Silas said tenderly, answering her unspoken question and leaning down to kiss her forehead.

She thought about this for a minute. He was right. There was much more to this man than she had ever known. "What happened?"

"Damien's guards have changed their tactics. They are getting smarter. It used to be much easier to get someone away from them. It was time for me to leave a barrier between them and you."

"A barrier?"

"Yes, a barrier. My life stands between you and our enemies, and they can't get past it."

"But what about everyone else? There are people on the mountain who want to know you, Silas. We can't just leave them there."

"Are you referring to Hesper, Lyra, and the rest of the HH?"

"You know them?" she asked.

"Of course, I do," he said, smiling at her underestimation. "They already know that the heart in their palms allows them to pass through the barrier. As for Xanthe, Jairus, and many others, they belong on this side, but it might take some time to help them understand. As it so happens, another Master has already figured it out."

There was so much to think about, so many questions to ask.

Knowing her thoughts, Silas asked, "Where should we start?"

"Tali. Where is he? Is he safe?"

"Yes, he is safe. At this very moment he is arriving where I have sent him."

"Will I see him again?"

"Yes, most likely you will."

"My family."

"What would you like to know about them?"

"Is it true? Is Damien my grandfather and Ajax my father? Is Jairus my brother?"

"Yes, to all of that. Next?"

She thought through all that she had learned and decided to start from the beginning. "What really happened with Damien on the mountain? Why did you leave?"

"The story you heard as a child is the truth, although told from a limited perspective. I was very close with Damien when he was just a boy. I knew the potential he had, leadership and innovation that could be used in great or terrible ways. I tried to teach him as much as possible so that he could make wise decisions when it came time."

"Why didn't you stop him?"

"For the same reason I let you leave," he answered, amused at the shocked look that came over Tovi's face.

"But, I'm nothing like him. It's not the same thing."

"You are both deep thinkers. You both question the way the world works and seek answers to why I have made things certain ways. You dealt with it by listening to Calix and Leeto and running away when they offered answers that seemed to make sense. Damien dealt with it by pushing me out of his life and trying to push me out of everyone else's life, too."

Tovi thought about this with deep frown lines creasing her forehead. "I don't want to be like Damien."

"Actually, some of the traits you share with him are the very best things about him and you. I enjoy the hard conversations, even when they move to difficult territory," he said.

"Really?"

"Yes, the hard questions are always worth it."

"What about Ismene and Dion and everyone else still in the prison? How does all of that work? And why do some people have the heart in their palms, and some don't? And why do you just walk into some cells and stay outside of others? And why do you let it all happen? Why don't you just help everyone escape? Or destroy the dungeon?" Now that she had started, she couldn't stop the flow of questions. She began to yell, angrily swiping the tears off her face with the back of her hands. "Why do you let people hurt like that? Why do you let Damien ruin their lives? Why don't you take care of them? Why don't you show yourself to them? Why don't you take them all away? Why do you make me flowers while there is suffering and hunger and pain?"

Silas did not interrupt, and his solemn gaze stayed locked on Tovi. When she finally paused, he took a deep breath before responding. "Those are very good questions. It's going to take the rest of your life to answer all of them, and I know that will frustrate you. I could tell you the answers right now, but that won't help you understand. We have years and years ahead of us, and we will walk through it all. Every question that you have. For now, we will start with this: if I used my power to make you trust me, against your will, it wouldn't really be trust. Does that make sense?"

"Not at all."

"Think about it this way. Would it prove that you love Ganya if I chained you to her and never allowed you to leave her side?"

"No."

"Does it prove that you love Ganya when you choose to spend time with her, delighting in your conversations and listening to her wisdom? I don't use force to try to win anyone's heart. It wouldn't work. I spend my time building our trust so that you will be prepared to make decisions when the time comes. What was the first tactic that Calix used in his attempt to win you away from here?"

Tovi thought back. "He told me he didn't believe the stories about Adwin."

"Exactly. He knew that if he began to dismantle everything you had been taught about me, he would be able to convince you to leave."

Eyes squinting in concentration, she asked, "Is that why he always met me at the ridge? He knew that was my special place with you, and that I was getting closer to understanding who you really are."

He nodded. "That's exactly why he used the ridge for those meetings. He wanted to make you think of him instead of me when you were in the place that is closest to your heart."

"That's horrible!"

"And it worked, didn't it?"

She nodded. "You said that a Master already came through the barrier. How did they know they could?"

"I don't think it was a matter of *knowing* he could get through," Silas said, his mouth curving up into another amused grin. "I think he was determined to force his way through with his own power. He was pretty surprised by how easy it was. Do you feel strong enough to get up and look out your window?"

She nodded, unsure why this was important. Silas helped her sit up and scoot closer to the window. Sitting on the floor of the porch, leaning against the railings, Eryx was fast asleep. His chin rested on his chest, and she couldn't see his face. There was a plate of untouched muffins next to him, along with a mug of tea that looked like it had gone cold long ago.

Silas chuckled. "Ganya has been trying to get him to come inside, but he is being a little stubborn."

CHAPTER 47

Many miles from Adia and the mountain, Tali followed Meira through the thickening underbrush. With every mile, the heat had risen. Even with a torn sleeve from his tunic wrapped around his forehead, sweat dripped into his eyes.

He hadn't known what to think of this girl when she showed up at the cave to liberate him from Leeto's ropes. She was dirty, and her hair was wrapped in filthy cloth, yet she carried herself like someone who was in charge.

Then, she had explained who she was. More importantly, she explained who he was. "Tali, I need you to believe me, even though I know that will be hard," she had said, offering him bread and water.

Famished, he tucked into the refreshments before looking up. "Okay, tell me what you have to say. I'll let you know if I believe you or not."

She told him all she knew about his identity, and he couldn't get used to the idea. A royal prince? Offspring of an evil king? Why hadn't Silas told him? And what would Tovi say when she found out? He smirked at the thought. His sister would not like this news.

"Silas sent me to get you out of here, and we need to get going," Meira said, not giving him time to let it sink in. "It won't be long before Leeto comes to check on you. Also, the army from the mountain is coming. Let's go."

He looked into her eyes and saw excitement—not fear—in them. He recognized the same anticipation that he felt when heading off to a new adventure. He hopped up and followed her out of the cave.

Instead of leading him back to Adia, she took him around the north side of the mountain. They circled to the east and then veered south. They didn't talk much, but it was an easy, companionable silence. When they did speak, they found they had many similarities. A thirst for adventure. A natural positivity and hopefulness. A trust in Silas. A willingness to go wherever he sent them.

The journey continued through untouched wilderness. There was no shortage of steep ravines and high passes. If Tali's estimates were accurate, they were gaining only about ten miles a day due to the difficult terrain. Meira did not seem to tire, and this spurred him on.

When most would grow exhausted and want to give up, Meira seemed to grow lighter with each day. She was preoccupied most of the time, with smiles playing at her lips on more than one occasion. It was clear: She couldn't wait to see her mother and the sea. Tali had to admit he felt the same.

Finally, after several days, they had reached their destination.

"Here we are," Meira said, her eyes alight with excitement. She pulled back several thick ferns that were the same height and width as a fully grown man. Through the foliage, Tali took in his first glimpse of the vast ocean.

His feet discovered soft sand, and he breathed in the salty air. Bright turquoise water rimmed with foam lapped at the beach, and he had never heard anything like the rhythmic roar of the waves. Palm trees towered, their trunks covered in vines with bright pink flowers, and noisy white and yellow birds soared through the air.

Two huts stood on the beach, less than ten feet apart. One was weather-worn and bleached from the sun. The other looked brand new, the palm fronds making up the roof still green.

Meira gently pushed Tali out of the way and ran toward the huts calling, "Mom! Mom! I'm home."

Tali stood back, not wanting to interrupt the reunion but longing to run to her as well. A woman who looked just like Meira came out of the hut. The only differences between the women were the slight wrinkles on the older woman's face and her pure white curly hair with a hint of sea green at the very ends.

"Lena!" she cried, running to embrace her daughter. Tali smiled. Of course, he thought. Lena was her real name. He would have to get used to calling her Lena instead of Meira.

It was beautiful to witness the reunion, and he watched with a deep hunger and pain that he didn't want to show. But try as he might, he couldn't shove it away like he usually could.

The two women were talking animatedly, but the crashing of the ocean waves drowned them out. He watched their faces, unable to look away, yet feeling like he was spying on something sacred, a place where he did not belong.

Lena gestured to the spot where Tali stood. Thomae's face suddenly lost its smile, and her eyes widened in a look of horror or shock. She lifted her hands and clutched her cheeks. Both women turned to look at Tali. Thomae's knees gave way, and she would have collapsed if Lena hadn't caught her.

Tali stepped from the shadows. It had been a long journey, and he had enjoyed getting to know his newly-discovered sister. But this was bigger and so much more. He had never known about Lena, so he hadn't had the opportunity to miss her. He *had* always known he had a mother somewhere, and he had always longed to find her, even if his longings hadn't been as vocal or demanding as Tovi's.

And there she was. His mother. She was just feet away. And she was far more wonderful than he had dared to imagine.

They walked toward one another, and when they were close enough, she reached out to touch his hair with trembling fingers.

Not knowing where the word came from, and having never said it before, he sobbed, "Mama," as his face crumbled.

Through her weeping, Thomae's smile returned broader and more glorious than anything he had ever seen before. She wrapped him in her arms and kissed every inch of his face, laughing and crying and whooping.

"My baby! I never thought I would see you again!" She kept laughing, and Lena joined in. "I'm going to kill Silas when I see him. He told me to build another hut. He didn't tell me it was for you!"

The three cried and laughed and talked into the night, never tiring enough to sleep.

CHAPTER 48

"What is he doing here?" Tovi asked, eyeing Eryx.

Silas took a long time, apparently trying to decide how much Tovi should know. Then he said, "Eryx followed us from the palace to the edge of the city. He saw everything. He saw the swords go through me, he saw the barrier go up, and he saw you collapse on the other side. He ran at the barrier at full speed, scooped you up, and brought you all the way here. The guards were irate. Knowing that Eryx was a Master, they didn't try to stop him. They probably thought that he was trying to stop you and that he would be caught by the barrier."

"Wait, Eryx brought me here? I thought you did."

"I would have," Silas said. "He just beat me to it. And Hesper helped." Tovi looked out the window again. She didn't know what to make of that man.

Tovi sat back against her pillows. Changing the subject, she asked, "Why does Ismene see you as an old man?"

"How old am I to you?"

"My age. You grew up with me."

"And, how old is Ismene?"

"Ancient. Do we each see you as our own age?"

"Yes, but it's more accurate to say that the only way you are able to understand me is through your own experiences. When you are a child, with simple wants and simple needs, you see me as a child. A friend and playmate. As you grow up, you get more complicated. Because you get more complicated, your understanding of me gets more complicated, too. But, there's more to my appearance than that. Do you remember how Xanthe saw me in the mural?"

"Yes. Brown eyes, brown hair."

"Here's a hint: When Xanthe was born, her eyes and hair were brown. And someday, when she is loyal to me, they will return to that color."

Tovi thought long and hard about this.

"Okay, let me give you some more clues. To Tali, whose deep-down allegiance has always been to me, even when he didn't fully understand, I have blue hair and a purple star in my brown eyes."

"Seriously? But how does it work? Does everyone see you differently?"

"Yes. When you were born, you were completely unique. You might have the same color eyes as someone, or a similar look to your hair. But, no one out there is exactly like you. I know that you and Xanthe theorized about how your colors work, and you were mostly right. When your deepest loyalties shift to someone other than me, you take on their colors. Jairus is still loyal to his sister, so he looks like her. In turn, Xanthe's allegiance is to Jairus, and she looks like him. That's how it works most of the time. But with me, it's different. You see, when I sit in my studio and paint people into existence, I give them a piece of me. I know this will be hard to understand, but when you are in your true, intended colors, you reflect that part of me that I gave only to you. This shows up in your strengths, your passions, and even in how you look. It's when you give your heart away to someone else that you lose that resemblance."

"And I was always most loyal to my brother."

"Yes."

"And, that means Eryx was loyal to me?"

"For the past few months, yes."

"But I want my allegiance to be to you. It took me a long time, but I'm sure of it now. When will my colors change to show that?"

"Take a look," he said, handing her a small hand mirror from the top of her night stand.

She was astonished by what she saw. The thick make-up had been washed away, and astonishingly blue eyes blinked back at her. "When did it happen?" she asked in awe, combing her fingers through her light brown hair with thick golden streaks.

"When you were in the throne room with Damien."

"Does Eryx have his true colors now, or does he have my new ones?"

Silas looked at Eryx as he spoke. "He still has yours. Be kind to him, Tovi. He doesn't understand his own feelings or how to handle them. I hope he chooses to stay in Adia, and if he does, he will need some space. His pride is very wounded by his changing colors, which he sees as a sign of weakness. Be his friend if he allows you close enough. Otherwise, give him room to heal."

Now that Silas was explaining everything to her, Tovi was hungry for every last bit of knowledge. "What about all the pale-skinned black-haired people on the mountain? Is it because they love Damien the most?"

"Sometimes. But those aren't his real colors. Damien loves himself more than anything or anyone. He has lost his coloring because he has no one to reflect, not me or anyone else. So, when you see someone with those murky black eyes and matching hair with sickly white skin, they either love themselves most of all, or they are loyal to someone else who feels that way."

"Okay, I have another question," she said. "Why did you let Damien break my hand and cut into it? Couldn't you have stopped him?"

"There was a lot going on right at that moment, things that I'm not going to share with you right now."

"You were too busy with something else? You just decided not to help me?" she spat, getting back some of her old surliness.

"Tovi, I am not a one-thing-at-a-time type of guy. I'm always with you, whether you see me or not. What I meant was there were many dynamics right there on that patio. I always do what is best for you, even when that means I have to allow you to experience something painful."

"You were trying to teach me some sort of lesson?"

Appalled, he shook his head. "No, that's not how it works. I don't sacrifice you to wicked lessons. I know countless creative ways to teach you, ways that don't bring you harm. Like I said, there is a lot I'm choosing not to tell you, and I want you to trust me that keeping those things from you is truly best. But hear me say this: I knew that if I intervened in that room, it would have sent Damien into a frenzy. It would have set certain things in motion, and it just wasn't time yet. It would have been much harder to get you to safety. And, it would have closed the opportunity to cast that barrier exactly where I did, which is exactly where it needs to be."

They sat silent for a while as Tovi tried to decide which question to ask next. Finally, she went for the one that had been on her mind all morning, but she had been too scared to ask. "Silas," she said tentatively. "The ugly marks on my back . . . how do I get rid of them?"

"They are already gone."

She shook her head. "No, I can feel them. They still burn a little."

Silas reached for her hand and held it between both of his. "Tovi, listen to me. They are gone. Remember how I told you Damien uses tricks to keep you from me? This is one of them. Your marks are not there anymore. They have not disappeared from the world, but they left you the same moment you decided to leave that prison with me. If we had a big enough mirror in here, I would show you. But for now, you'll have to trust me until you're a little stronger and can get a good look for yourself. Your back burns because Damien likes to remind you of your marks. He wants you to think that you carry them with you."

"Where did they go?"

Silas released her hand and turned his back to her. He reached over his shoulder to grasp his tunic and tugged it up as far as it would go. Water welled in Tovi's eyes as she looked at the circle of black designs imprinted deep in his skin. It didn't look like hers or anyone's that she had seen. Instead of the crisp, detailed pictures that had engraved so many backs, this looked like layers and layers of designs, all garbled together to make one big mess. If she didn't know what she was looking at—this pattern of overlapping snakes, diamonds, crowns, and so on—she would have thought it was just a ring of jagged lines, like a wreath made of bramble or a crown made of thorns.

"Silas . . . " she said, bringing her hand to her mouth in horror. "I'm so sorry . . . Does it hurt?"

He let go of the tunic and turned back to her. "Yes, and you are worth it."

CHAPTER 49

King Damien sat on his cold throne, fingers tapping together in front of him. He looked as calm and shrewd as always, but this was just a facade for the frantic thoughts racing through his mind. He could not let Adwin win.

He had gone out to examine the shimmering curtain of light that had sprung up when his guards so foolishly tried to kill Adwin. He knew very well that his old enemy wasn't really gone. So what was this wall of magic? Returning scouts informed him that it encircled the entire mountain. They said it felt like glass when they pushed, but it would not break no matter what they tried. There was no getting out.

He hated feeling trapped. He looked up and down the translucent waves. Citizens of the mountain were gathering outside, whispering behind hands and eyeing their king. He didn't dare touch the wall, lest they see his inability to break through the barrier. Not wanting witnesses to his helplessness, he strolled with calculated casualness up the streets toward home.

When he arrived back at the palace, internally fuming, he went straight to the throne room and burst through the red curtain. He looked at each of the four faces. His grandchildren. His heirs. His enemies.

Adwin had Tovi, and Damien guessed that Tali was with them as well. Was it possible that Lena survived just like the twins? Did Adwin have her in his clutches, too? Three of the conquerors gathered by

Adwin was a dangerous thought. Three of his grandchildren. What a shocking turn of events.

That left only Jairus under Damien's control. He weighed his options. If only he could trust the lad, this would be so much easier. With his careless disregard for power and control, Jairus was too likely to be won over by manipulative Adwin. It would be better to take all necessary precautions.

Prison or death for the boy? Memories of Jairus as a little one came to his mind. A sweet face, a childish giggle. His little feet padding down the hallway, chasing his sister Lena. He pushed those thoughts aside and refused to let himself be hindered by emotion.

He looked intently at the faces in the mural. Unfortunately, Tovi had proven that his prison was not nearly secure enough. If Adwin could get her out, he surely could take Jairus as well. Then Adwin might have the full set. This could not be.

He left the secret corridor and summoned a butler. "Bring Jairus to me. And keep Ajax away from here. I don't care what you tell him, just make sure he is nowhere close to this room while I speak to my grandson."

He returned to his throne and brought his fingers together in front of his face, tapping them together one at a time. It would hurt his muddied heart to do away with the boy, but it must be done. He must do it himself to avoid another mistake. And the quicker the better.

Jairus' death would ensure that the prophecy could not come to fruition. With one of the usurpers dead, it could not be.

Nearly an hour ticked by. Finally, someone entered, but it was not the butler who had left to find Jairus. It was a guard from the prison.

"Excuse me, Your Majesty," he said, his face pale and sweaty. "I bring news from the dungeon."

"Go on."

"Another prisoner has escaped, Your Majesty. We don't know when it happened. We have not left our post."

Fury sped through his body. How many times must they search that prison for the way out? How many times must he replace his guards?

"Who was the prisoner?" he asked, not bothering to hide his anger.

"Master Xanthe," the man replied, unable to maintain eye contact with the king. He looked at the floor, and his hands shook.

Damien stared at the guard while his mind raced. Before he could recover himself, his butler returned. "Where have you been, and where is Jairus?" Damien bellowed, the veins in his eyes dark and pulsing.

"I'm sorry, Your Majesty. We have searched throughout the palace. Prince Jairus is not here."

Just then another guard entered the room. "Your Majesty, I'm sorry to interrupt you. There is something you must know."

Damien's head was already spinning. Xanthe gone. Jairus gone. He looked at the guard. What else could there be?

"The house in the Bottom Rung, the one with the green sign. No one was there. It was empty, Your Majesty."

"Everyone out!" he screamed, his jaw quivering and his chest throbbing with pain. "Out! Get out!" They ran for the door to save themselves from his fury.

He ripped the red curtain off the wall and threw it to the ground. He walked with fast heavy strides to the scene he hated. The conquerors. What if the blonde in the mural was really Xanthe? He had always counted on them being his grandchildren, including Lena. But now Tovi, Jairus, and Xanthe disappear on the same day. And the rebels who thought their existence was hidden disappear as well.

The army. The army following the conquerors. It all clicked in his mind. Adwin had the four conquerors and an army. The end was coming. He must stop it.

He found Adwin's face and stared at it.

Like a maniac who didn't know he was speaking to paint and not a real man, Damien shouted, "So, you have them, do you? You have the conquerors gathered all together, ready to lead the army. You cleared them out of that rat hole in the Bottom Rung." Black spit sprayed on the mural as he became more and more agitated. "Where are you hiding them, Adwin? You can't hide them forever! They can't get through your glass curtain, so it is only a matter of time before I find them and kill every last one of them.

"It is no longer a game, old friend. This is war."

COMING NEXT IN

TALES FROM ADIA . . .

Water rushed below the treehouses, and Adians gathered on porches and along bridges. There was always a sense of wonder on the first day of the flood.

Ganya stood beside her friend Leora and watched as a little boy shrieked and clapped his hands. "Look at the water, Mama! Look at it!" Several teenagers were gathered on one of the bridges, their legs dangling over as they watched and pointed.

The water was far enough below that only an occasional spray reached the village. It was moving very fast, and the water had turned brown from all of the dirt and silt. It looked like frothy, bubbling mud.

"The water came quicker than we expected," Leora observed.

"Yes, but we're ready," Ganya said, her usual cheer dimmed. Tovi had not come home the night before, and she feared what this could mean. Was she out there somewhere in the flood?

Silas raced through the crowd, running full speed along a branch, upsetting the festive mood. "Ganya! Leora!" he called. "Grab some blankets!"

It took a moment to take in the shift of the atmosphere. Something was wrong. And when Silas told her to do something, Ganya did it, no questions asked. She rushed inside, Leora at her heels. She threw open a trunk and tossed a blanket to Leora. She grabbed another, and they hustled back outside.

Silas was perched precariously above the water, one arm anchored in a rope ladder, the other reaching for what looked to be a bundle of dark cloth that had washed against the tree trunk. "What is he doing?"

Leora asked. Silas' mouth was moving, as if he was talking to the dark mass, but they couldn't hear his voice over the roar of the water.

Then, the bundle moved. First a hand shot out, and then a round, pale face looked up. The girl squinted as water sprayed in her face. She nodded at Silas and took hold of his hand. They climbed ever so slowly up the rope ladder. She slipped several times, sagging against the rope and clutching Silas' hand.

The gathering above held their collective breath. The youngsters had moved closer to the action, intrigued by the stranger. What had happened to this poor girl? Where did she come from? How had she survived the surging water?

Silas and the girl reached the landing at the top of the ladder. They were soaked through, and the girl was trembling. Leora wrapped her in one of the blankets while Ganya offered hers to Silas.

"No, I'm fine," he said. "She could use that one, too."

Ganya draped the second blanket around the girl and gently combed the dark hair out of her face. "Can you stand up, dear? We'll get you dry and warm up by my fire."

The girl looked at Silas, her eyes big in her pale face.

Silas smiled. "It's safe, BiBi. Ganya will take good care of you. I will come see you when you're settled in."

She nodded.

The poor dear. What a story she must have to tell, being swept up in the flood and finding herself clinging to that tree for her life. She definitely wasn't from Adia, but Ganya knew of no settlements upriver. She ticked through the villages and towns she knew. The city on the mountain, a cluster of resistance fighters in the northern desert, the cave people in the far east, the marshes directly south. But northwest? She was very interested to hear this young one's tale.

"Come, come. Let's get you dry," Ganya said, leading the girl to the house in the willow.

The girl suddenly stopped just outside. "This . . . this is Tovi's house."

Ganya's heart skipped a beat, and she peered closely at the girl. "Yes, this is our home. How do you know my Tovi?"

The girl opened her mouth a few times like she was trying to say something but couldn't quite find the words.

"We'll get to that later," Ganya said, trying her best to comfort the girl with a smile and a grandmotherly arm around the shoulders. "Come inside. We'll find some dry clothes and get you warmed up by the fire."

The girl fit well enough into one of Tovi's soft dresses. She kept running her hands over the blue-green fabric as she sat in one of the big comfy chairs while Ganya warmed some brothy soup. "What is your name, child?"

"Bibianna. Most people call me BiBi."

"And how did you end up in your predicament today?"

Silas appeared in the doorway. "That story will have to wait for now," he said, taking the other big chair near the fire. "BiBi, I know why you are here, and I know who sent you."

Ganya did her best to keep stirring the soup as if nothing was amiss. Were her ears lying, or was this sweet girl a villain of some sort?

She took a peek at the girl, who was staring at Silas, her hands trembling in her lap and her bottom lip quivering.

"You don't need to be afraid of me," Silas continued. "Do you remember what I told you the last time we were here together?"

The girl barely nodded. "You said that soon the mountain wouldn't be safe for me, and that you hoped I would come back here when that time came."

Silas nodded. "No matter your reasons, I am glad you are back. This is where you belong. There are many people trying to control you on the mountain. None of them are here. They cannot get to you, and you cannot get to them. You are trapped here until the flood is over. I hope you will use this time to rest, take some deep breaths, and learn a thing or two before the water recedes. You will stay here with Ganya. She could use the company."

"Where is Tovi?" the girl asked shyly.

Silas glanced up and locked eyes with Ganya, and she did not like the look on his face.

For more information about

Maggie Platt

&

Kingdom Above the Cloud

please visit:

www.maggieplatt.com
www.facebook.com/AuthorMaggiePlatt
@_maggie_platt_
www.instagram.com/_maggie_platt_

More from Ambassador International

Dreaming of attending art school in London, gifted artist Beth Wilson paints masterpieces in the studio-attic of her home—but she's stuck in a rut. She paints the same theme over and over. If she doesn't come up with something new her art teacher will drop her. Solution: work for her Mimi and help her research the life of her fourth great-grandfather, Allen Hamilton.

Once Upon an Irish Summer
by Wendy Wilson Spooner

What happens when Grace Summer becomes torn between the boy of her dreams and the boy almost next door? *Loving Grace* is a refreshingly sweet story with a focus on friendship, God, and being true to yourself.

Loving Grace

by April Smith

Barely out of their teens and training as assassins, Rigel members are taught that the Kalideyes are evil. Maru and her team fight against all odds during their training. Facing horrors, nightmares, depression, and injuries not many will survive long enough to kill the Kalideyes. But it isn't long before Maru learns of the truth behind the enemy, so when she is forced to fight for her life, who will be her savior?

Made for Mercy

by Lauren Smyth

Made in the USA
Monee, IL
23 May 2020

31732641R00164